Sarah Mlynowski was born in Montreal, Canada, and studied English Literature at McGill University, where she wrote a newspaper column. After graduation she worked in the marketing department of various publishing companies in Toronto, before moving to New York City (where she still lives) to become a full-time writer. This is her first book for teenagers. When she's not writing, she's trying to kick-start her magical powers. If she succeeds, she promises to cast spells for world peace, twelve months of sunshine a year and more *Star Wars* movies.

Coming Soon

All About Rachel: Frogs and French Kisses

ALL ABOUT RACHEL

Bras
&
Broomsticks

Sarah Mlynowski

MACMILLAN

First published 2005 by Delacorte Press, USA

This edition published 2005 by Macmillan Children's Books
a division of Macmillan Publishers Limited
20 New Wharf Road, London N1 9RR
Basingstoke and Oxford
www.panmacmillan.com

Associated companies throughout the world

ISBN 0 330 43280 X

1 3 5 7 9 8 6 4 2

A CIP catalogue record for this book is available from
the British Library.

Typeset by Intype Libra Ltd
Printed and bound in Great Britain by Mackays of Chatham plc, Kent

For Aviva, my baby sister.

*And yes, she'll always be my baby sister, even when
she's seventy-two and I'm seventy-nine.
(Fine, Aviva, seventy-eight-and-a-half.)*

Thanks to the power of a billion to:
Laura Dail, my extraordinary agent, who loves Rachel
and Miri as much as I do; Wendy Loggia, for her superb
guidance and never-ending enthusiasm; Beverly
Horowitz, Isabel Warren-Lynch, Tamar Schwartz,
Gayley Carillo, Emily Jacobs, Jennifer Black and
everyone else at Delacorte who worked their butts off
for my book as well as Sarah Davies, Lauren Buckland,
Laura Burr and everyone else at Macmillan whose butts
went into overtime on this side of the pond; my mom,
Elissa Ambrose, for adding many of the jokes and most
of the punctuation; Lynda Curnyn, for always answering
my emails re: IS THIS LINE FUNNY? / DOES THIS
MAKE ANY SENSE? within half a second; Jess Braun,
for reading everything I've ever written since we were
nine, and because she would never in a million years try
out for the fashion show; Robin Glube, for all her help;
for their love and support, Bonnie, Ronit, Jessica D.,
Vickie, John, Dad and Louisa (my SM – in this case
stepmom, not stepmonster); and Todd, my VOH (Very
Own Husband), for making every day magical.

1

Better Than Ruby Slippers

I've wished for lots of things in my fourteen years . . . a boyfriend, world peace, cleavage. But none of my wishes have come true.

Until now.

I'm standing by my locker, zipping up my black puffy coat, when I notice the sneakers.

They're the green suede designer ones I admired at Bloomie's last week. My mom said I couldn't have them because they cost more than our TV.

And they're on my feet.

'But how—' I mumble, blinking in confusion. Where are the beaten-up black boots I always have on? 'I mean, when . . .?'

Did I accidentally swap shoes with someone after gym? Am I a thief?

Impossible. The only time I ever took anything that wasn't mine was when I inadvertently wore Jewel's retainer. Gross, yes. But criminal? No.

My heart starts beating erratically. This is so weird. How did these shoes get on my feet?

Wait a millisecond. Maybe my mom bought them to

1

surprise me? Not that she normally does stuff like that, but I have been on my best behaviour lately (after being grounded for something completely ridiculous, don't even ask) and she's big on rewarding good deeds.

I guess I must have laced them up this morning without even noticing. Lame. But I went to bed really late last night, and I'm always zoned out when I'm tired.

That still doesn't explain why I didn't notice I was wearing them until now though. I glance back down. The shoes are a luminous green. Sparkling, even. They're practically *screaming* at me to notice them.

Whatever. New shoes! The ideal accessory for my awesome after-school plans. I smile like someone who just got her braces off.

'Can I borrow your phone?' I ask Tammy. She's busy rummaging through her satchel. The least I can do is thank my mom – maybe she'll cave on a cellphone for me next.

'Cool shoes,' Tammy says, glancing down. 'When did you change?'

'I . . . didn't. I've, uh, been wearing them all day.' Haven't I? Now I'm totally unsure again.

Tammy gives me a thumbs-up sign with her right hand and passes the phone with her left. She uses finger signals to indicate her thoughts. She learned to scuba dive with her family last year in Aruba and now frequently communicates by underwater mime. Thumbs-up means 'Let's get out of the water', which means she wants to hightail it out of here.

My mother answers on the first ring.

'Mom, thanks for the sneakers. They're perfect! Sorry I didn't notice them this morning.'

Pause. Then muffled static.

'You still there?' I ask, tapping my heels together. Who knew green suede could look so glam? 'I can't hear you.'

There's furious whispering in the background, and then a loud '*Shhh!*'

'You need to come home,' my mom tells me.

'What? Why?' I ask. My stomach free-falls.

Another pause. More furious whispering. 'I have something to talk to you about,' my mom says. Her voice sounds uneven. 'Something extremely important.'

'But I have extremely important after-school plans!' My destiny is waiting for me at Stromboli's Pizzeria! This is a complete and utter disaster. 'And when I called you an hour ago you said I could go!'

'Things have changed,' my mother says, her clipped words ruining my life. 'I want you back at the apartment.'

My down-filled coat starts to feel like a furnace. 'Can't we talk about whatever is so earth-shattering later?'

My mother heaves one of her why-must-I-carry-the-weight-of-the-world-on-my-thin-shoulders sighs. 'Rachel, enough.'

'Fine.' I sigh right back. I have a sigh of my own, and it's just as martyrish. In a small triumph, I press the pink End button before she can say goodbye.

'I can't come,' I tell Tammy, handing her the phone. My cheeks feel all blotchy. Why couldn't I have just thanked my mom when I got home?

Tammy adjusts her light brown ponytail and makes a fist in front of her chest, her 'low on air' sign, meaning she feels bad for me. Tammy is an excellent sympathizer, as well as smart and reliable. She's always there when I need someone to talk to and, more important, when I unintentionally sport poopy bagel seeds between my teeth, she immediately and covertly lets me know by tapping her lips. She's a great friend. It's just that – OK, I hate to play favourites – I like Jewel more. But the way Jewel has been treating me, I might as well be walking around with an *I-just-got-dumped* sash across my non-existent chest.

Sigh.

Over the past four months, since she strutted her stuff for the JFK fashion show tryouts and got in, Juliana Sanchez (Jewel for short, Bee-Bee for shorter/longer) has morphed from my sidekick and best friend into a card-carrying member of the inner circle. Yes, she made the A-list. Except for a few minutes in maths class, I hardly ever get to talk to her any more. I miss her.

Going to Stromboli's would have been a step towards reclaiming our Bee-Bee status. (Sorry for the cheddary Best Buds acronym, but Jewel and I have been using it forever.) The entire cool crowd will be there. I was lucky even to have been asked. Mick Lloyd invited Jeffrey Stars, who invited Aaron Jacobs, who invited Tammy, who invited me. And you don't go if you don't get an invite. You can't. You wouldn't know what pizza place/coffee shop/parentless apartment the A-list selected, so you wouldn't know where to show up. If only they would just choose the same place every time, like they did on *Friends*. Monica never showed up at a new coffee spot, The *Not-So-Central Perk*, wondering where everyone was.

Down the hall I see Raf Kosravi at his locker, pulling out his coat. A strand of his midnight black hair falls into his matching dark eyes, and he brushes it away with the back of his hand.

Heart. Beating. Erratically. Not. Because. Of. Shoes.

Sigh. Because of my mother, I will potentially be missing out on precious flirting time with Raf, the boy I'm in love with.

I am also in love with Mick Lloyd. Yes, I know it seems strange to love two boys at the same time, but since I've never spoken more than two words to either of them ('Happy Holidays!' to Raf and 'Excuse me' to Mick), I'm not concerned about my divided heart. Mick Lloyd is the cute, blond, all-American type that's cast on every dating show. Big smile, dimple in each cheek, great hair. Raf is more mysterious-slash-sexy. He's not too tall, only around five foot six (which is still much, much taller than me at five foot one – I'd *better* still be growing), and has a lean, fit body like a champion tennis player or an Olympic swimmer (not that I've ever watched professional tennis or swimming). Raf is also in the fashion show with Jewel.

Ah, the fashion show. It's *really* a dance show with a catwalk and designer outfits. Or so I hear. Since I'm only a freshman, and the show is in April, I've never seen it. And since a former JFK student who's now an It Guy Hollywood director launched the idea ten years ago, it's always been a cool thing for guys to do. Like football or baseball. There is an overlap of boys who play football with those who are in the show. Unfortunately for the school trophy case, the quarterback is a better dancer than he is an athlete.

Mick isn't in the show, but he does play on the JV baseball team, the only sports team at our school that doesn't always lose. And – impressive residence alert! – he lives in a massive brownstone. Since his mom and dad are frequently out of town, he throws a lot of wild parties (not that I've ever been). Raf and Mick are both very, very A-list. But that isn't the reason I like them.

Raf buttons up his coat and slaps one of his friends on the back.

Sigh.

I am such a liar. *Of course* that's why I like them. I don't even *know* them, so why else would I like them? They're hot and cool – as in sexy and popular – and if either of them were interested in me, I would actually have a real kiss to brag about. (I claim my first was with a Texan named Stu whom I met on a cruise. This is a total lie. Although there was a boy named Stu from Texas, he was seven.) Plus, I would instantly be promoted from the B-list (B+ on an excellent hair day) to the A-list.

I really want to be A-list. Yes, I know I'm being colossally pathetic, and I've seen enough movies to know that popular people always get their comeuppance. And being A-list in high school doesn't guarantee you'll be cool in college. But . . . like blondes, the A-list always seems to have more fun.

I ask you: is it so wrong to want to be happy? Is it so wrong to want to be liked? Is it wrong to want my life to be like a soda ad, with lots of laughing, jumping and high-fiving?

Aaron, otherwise known as Tammy's connection to the A-list, waves to her from across the hallway.

Tammy doesn't believe it, but Aaron has a thing for her. Aaron isn't quite A-list, but he went to junior high with Mick and is friends with Mick's best friend, Jeffrey, so sometimes he gets invited through a few degrees of separation. Tammy says that if Aaron liked her, he would have asked her out by now. Instead they've become 'friends'. They IM every night. Tammy claims she doesn't like Aaron, but I don't buy it. She giggles around him *and* her hand signals go into overdrive.

'Ready?' he asks, bundling his scarf like a helmet around his neck and over his ears. He looks like one of the evil sandmen in *Star Wars* who tries to kill Luke.

Yikes. Only a freak would allude to *Star Wars*. How am I ever going to achieve cool status when I'm such a loser?

I need to start laughing and jumping. Maybe if I raise my hand, Tammy will give me a high five?

Not.

Instead, Tammy gives Aaron the scuba OK, which conveniently happens to be the universal OK sign, an *O* with the thumb and index finger. This has always mystified me. Where's the *K*? What if you just want to say *Oh*, as in *Oh, Raf, why don't you notice me*? Or, *Oh, at least I have cool new shoes*.

'See you tomorrow,' she tells me.

Oh why oh why do I have to go home?

I turn the corner on to Tenth Street and run the last bit to my apartment building – I hate to do this to my virgin-new shoe soles, but I have no choice. My earlobes have frozen into blocks of ice, and now the doctor will probably have to amputate. Seriously. That's what they do with frostbite. Just call me Van Gogh.

I press the Up button to call the elevator. To pass the time – what's taking it so long? – I make a mental list.

<u>Possible Extremely Important Topics Mom Insists on</u>
<u>Discussing Today of All Days</u>

1. Maybe her travel agency, HoneySun (they specialize in honeymoons, wink, wink), has folded. Maybe she's going to tell us that we have to start saving money. Tighten our belts. Cook more, eat out less. Cancel call-waiting. Return the new shoes.

2. Maybe Miri, my twelve-year-old sister, saw a Mob hit man butcher someone and the DA wants her to testify and we're joining the Witness Protection Program and moving to Los Angeles. California would be awesome. Except that everyone in LA has implants. Who wants something foreign in her body? Braces were bad enough – they made me look like a robot. (Although I have always wanted a robot. Particularly one programmed to fold the clothes that are currently carpeting my bedroom floor.)

3. Maybe my mom's gay. Tammy's mother came out four years ago. Since both Tammy's biological parents remarried, now Tammy has three mothers – one biological and two steps. As if one mother isn't annoying enough. Nah. My mother isn't gay. I've seen her bat her long eyelashes and twirl her hair whenever she runs into Dave, the twenty-seven-year-old hunkalicious fireman who lives on the second floor.

4. Maybe, bite my tongue, my mother or sister has a terminal disease. But Miri is always hungry. Are you hungry when you're terminally ill? I think not. Not that I've ever hung out with someone who was that sick. I've never had the occasion. But in a TV movie I saw a few weeks ago, two boys made fun of this poor kid with leukaemia because he was losing his hair, and

it fully pissed me off. If I ever knew someone who was dying, I would be extra nice to her. My mother *is* looking pretty pasty, so maybe – omigod – she has cancer. Although her pale skin tone could be because of her ridiculously unhealthy eating habits.

Honestly, she eats marshmallows for breakfast. And not the good kind in Lucky Charms – she eats the white ones out of a bag. And she packs herself one lousy bagel for lunch. And then we have tofu-crap for dinner. She refuses to cook meat. Even my sister is a vegetarian now, so it's two against one. Obviously, I don't think anyone is really sick, or I'd be hysterical. And if someone *were* sick, I would have detected it. I notice stuff. Like my mother's birth-control pills. Fine, I found them in the secret side compartment of her make-up case – yet another reason I know she's not gay. I don't know why she takes them; she hasn't had a date in two years. I tried to sign her up on an Internet dating site, but she freaked out when she caught me Photoshopping her eye wrinkles from her picture and made me delete her entire profile.

This is turning out to be a really chaotic list. No wonder I never make lists. I'm so bad at them. They're too restrictive, like tights. Miri loves them. (I'm talking about lists, not tights – we both hate the latter, especially itchy wool ones.) I'm the disorganized, last-week's-socks-still-under-my-bed kind of girl, but Miri types and pins her *Things to Do Today! Packing List for Dad's! Reasons Why I'm Anal!* (just kidding on that last one) memos to the massive bulletin board above her desk. The rest of her room is covered in tae kwon do certificates. She's a brown belt,

9

which is two levels away from black. How nuts is that? She's only four and a half feet tall and she can beat up my dad. OK, fine, she probably can't beat up my dad. Definitely me though. I went to a class once, but all the kicking, bowing and focusing required was exhausting. Never mind the impossible no-talking rule—

I notice the sign on the building elevator: OUT OF ORDER.

Groan. I guess the stairs will be my exercise for the day. For the week, actually. All right, the month. I fly up the first flight. I stride up the second. By the fourth I almost black out.

Maybe I should have stayed in tae kwon do. Then I wouldn't be so out of shape. I'm not one of those girls who obsesses about the size of her thighs, but it's kind of sad that I'm so young and out of breath.

Maybe there's a sports team I could join.

Nah. *Puff, puff.* Exercise. *Puff, puff.* Is. *Puff, puff.* Too. *Puff, puff.* Hard.

By the time I insert the key in the lock of the front door, I'm gasping.

I hang up my coat in the front closet. 'Hello?'

'We're in here,' my mother calls from her room.

I wipe the bottoms of my funky new sneakers, turn on the kitchen lights and pour myself a glass of water. Then I pass my room, my sister's room and the bathroom and then enter the warden's. She and Miri are sitting side by side on the bed, their legs hidden under a faded purple quilt, their backs against the headboard. Both are in their usual sleepwear: oversized concert T-shirts.

'Why does it reek of smoke in here?' An ashtray overflowing with cigarette butts is stationed between the

10

humps I assume are my mother's feet. What's going on? She hasn't smoked in more than a year.

'Minor relapse,' my mom says with a hangdog expression. 'Won't happen again. Sit down. We have to talk to you.'

Uh-oh. I try to forget about the revolting butts and focus on the issue at hand. This must be really bad. If we'd won the lottery, she'd have greeted me with a smile and champagne. Fine, probably not champagne, since that stuff's pretty pricey. But maybe Chardonnay. Occasionally she lets me have a small glass of wine with dinner. Says she'd rather I try it with her than at an unsupervised party.

Not that I've ever been to an unsupervised party. (But if anyone *does* invite me, I'm game. You can call me on my home [not cell] phone or email me at—)

'Oh, Rachel,' my mom says. 'Where to begin?'

Miri's eating from a bag of sunflower seeds. Watching her is disgusting. She sucks one seed at a time, licks her fingers, then sticks her grubby, nail-bitten hand (a habit she picked up from my mother) back into the bag. One wet seed is clinging to a frizzy strand of her shoulder-length brown hair. Very appealing.

'Want some?' she offers.

Ew!

'Are you wearing shoes in the apartment?' my mother asks, peering over the edge of her bed.

'No.' I'm about to thank her for them again, but curiosity about what they need to tell me takes precedence over manners. So I untie them and place them neatly on the floor. Then I slide, baseball-style (see how made for each other we are, sweet Mick?), stomach first on to her bed. 'This had better be important.'

Instead of responding, my mother lights up.

'Hello? Enough with the smoking,' I say, but she has the nerve to ignore me, so I turn to Miri. 'Why are you still in your pyjamas? Didn't you go to school? Don't you have tae kwon do?' She gets to skip class when she's not even dying?

'I stayed home all day,' she says, exposing mashed-up seeds. 'Mom and I had stuff to discuss.'

'Don't talk with your mouth full,' I say. Being the big sister, I try to give Miri constructive criticism. Often.

She closes her lips, swallows, then says, 'Don't give me orders when I'm eating.'

My mother rubs her fingers against her temples, almost setting fire to her bottle-blonde hair with the tip of her cigarette. 'Girls, please. I can't handle fighting now.'

I get nervous again. 'Is everything OK? What's going on?'

A smile spreads across Miri's face. 'Everything's fantastic.' She peeks over the edge of the bed, eyes my new shoes, and giggles. 'Amazing!'

My mom shoots Miri a warning look. 'Looks can be deceiving, Miri. I meant what I said before.'

My family is more confusing to interpret than Tammy's underwater mime techniques. 'What are you talking about? And if things are so great, why am I here?'

'Rachel.' My mother takes a deep breath. 'Your sister is a witch.'

2

My Sister Takes Animal Rights a Tiny Bit Too Far

'**E**xcuse me?' I ask, shocked.

My mother repeats herself. 'Your sister is a witch.'

'She's not *that* bad, Mom,' I say in a hushed voice, coming to Miri's defence.

'No, you don't understand. A witch-witch.'

Miri nods. 'Think Sabrina. Hermione.' She squinches her forehead, thinking. 'Or like that sixties TV show, *Bewitched*?'

My mom frowns. 'That really isn't the best example.'

Tell me, what is a teenage girl supposed to do after her mother says something so crazy? 'I think you should consider returning to therapy,' is what slips out of my mouth. I mean, *come on*.

My mother bites her chapped lip. 'Remember what happened yesterday? With the dead lobster?'

OK, let me backtrack for a moment.

Last night my father forced Miri and me to have dinner at the home of his future in-laws, the Abramsons of Ridgefield, Connecticut. Yes, in-laws. On 3 April, he's marrying STBSM (Soon To Be Step-Monster), referred to as STB for short.

We call her Jennifer in person.

There is also an STBSMM (Soon To Be Step-Mini-Monster). In other words, STB has a five-year-old daughter, Priscilla, which is a ridiculous name. Miri and I call her Prissy for short.

Abramson family dinners go on *forever*. The adults don't care; they don't have biology homework. Plus, they go through a minimum of three bottles of wine, so they're all smashed, and, unlike my mom, they don't let us have any. And since Prissy is seated next to Miri and me, we are forced to cut her food and listen to her non-sensical five-year-old questions and ramblings about anything that pops into her head. ('Today at school Ms Kimmel gave us Popsicle sticks, did your teachers ever give you Popsicle sticks? Mine was broken and it was sunny . . .')

Anyway, when Mr and Mrs Abramson's housekeeper, Miss (yes, they call their forty-year-old married Filipina housekeeper *Miss* – don't even get me started), put a full lobster on my sister's plate, eyes and all, I thought Miri was going to hurl.

On the one hand, I was upset. Dad *knows* that Miri is a vegetarian. Why didn't he tell the Abramsons? Actually, STB knows too, and they're her parents, so she's even more to blame. The whole situation exposed the total disrespect STB has for my mother and the way she raised Miri and me.

On the other hand, *yes, lobster!* I'd had lobster only once, and it had been the most delicious few moments of my life. Since I hardly ever get to have it, my mouth automatically salivated when I spotted the heated butter and the shell crackers.

Miri turned an odd shade of lime green. Her gaze washed over the creature that had been prepared for her culinary pleasure. And that was when things got weird.

Her dead lobster moved. Yes. Moved. As in, it came back to life. Can you say *Pet Sematary*? The antennae started quivering, the eyes flickering, the claws snapping. Mr One-Pound Special began migrating towards her water glass.

I was in the happy process of squirting my own lobster with lemon when I noticed the resurrection on the plate beside mine.

'Ahhhh!' I screamed, shivering.

'Ahhhh!' STB screamed.

'Oh my!' Mrs Abramson (occasionally referred to as STBSG – Soon To Be Step-Grandmonster) screamed.

'It's alive!' Prissy screamed.

We were in the audience of a horror movie.

The lobster knocked over Miri's glass, flushing our side of the table with water. My father jumped out of his chair, grabbed the sea creature, ran to the front door and threw it into the yard.

Some neighborhood Fido was going to get his nose clamped off.

Total chaos ensued. Miri started crying, Prissy started crying, I started crying, and Mr Abramson spit what he was chewing into his napkin.

'Miss! Miss!' Mrs Abramson yelled.

Miss, looking startled, poked her head into the dining room. 'Yes, Mrs Abramson?'

'Why weren't the lobsters cooked properly?'

15

Miss fiddled with her apron in confusion. 'They were, Mrs Abramson.'

'No, they weren't! One just walked off the table!'

Luckily all the lobsters except Miri's remained dead, and after a few minutes everyone resumed their normal drunk/boring/rambling dispositions.

Except Miri. She spent the rest of the night staring wide-eyed at her empty plate. Miss hurriedly brought her a tomato salad, but she refused to eat.

Later at home, Miri pushed the bathroom door open while I was peeing. She still had that freaked-out look on her face.

'Do you mind?' I hate when she does that. Why does she have to follow me everywhere? 'What's wrong with you?' I asked, wrapping the toilet paper around my hand, bandage-style.

She leaned against the towel rack and nibbled the skin around her thumbnail. 'I made the lobster come back to life.'

I laughed. 'You're funny.'

'I'm not kidding.' Her eyes filled with tears. Uh-oh. I felt my own eyes liquid up. I can't help crying whenever someone else cries. Like how some people retch at the sight of puke. I'm like that with tears, especially my baby sister's. Cute at three, highly embarrassing at fourteen. I blinked back the waterworks and tried to focus on how ridiculous she was acting.

'I felt so bad for him,' she whispered, 'lying on my plate like that. I told him in my mind to come back to us. And he did.'

I laughed again. 'You can't *will* things to come back to life.'

'But I did. And it's not the first time. What about Goldie?' Goldie lives in a small glass bowl on top of the refrigerator because that is the only spot in the apartment Tigger, our cat, can't reach. 'Do you know any other goldfish that has lived for ten years?'

'No, but we take good care of it,' I explained. Then came the tricky part: attempting to pull up my undies without Miri getting a peek at my downtown hair. I'm very self-conscious about my body in front of my sister. Mostly because hers is far more developed than mine. Case in point: even though she's two years younger than me, she wears a B, one entire cup-size larger than I do. When she rubbed her teary eyes, I made a grab for my panties. Success!

'No,' she insisted, still rubbing. 'He keeps dying and I keep resurrecting him.'

'You've been studying too hard,' I said soothingly. Ever since Robyn, Miri's best friend, moved to Vancouver, Miri hasn't made much of an effort to find new friends. All she does is study, go to tae kwon do and hang out with my mom. Oh – and make lists.

I felt bad for her, but explaining to my sister that she wasn't the Messiah was *not* my responsibility. 'Mom!' I screamed through the bathroom door. 'Can you please clarify the workings of the universe to Miri?'

I thought that would be the death of the resurrection rigmarole.

Obviously not.

My mother takes another deep breath, this time with the cigarette still between her lips. 'I was hoping I'd never have to have this discussion with you.' She turns her head and exhales towards the window. 'Witchcraft is hereditary, and it blooms during puberty.'

Obviously, my mother is crazy. I debate calling 911, but decide that my best bet is to humour her. 'And who did she inherit this witch stuff from? Dad? Is he Harry Potter in disguise?' I say in my best patronizing voice.

She shakes her head, unamused. 'From me. I'm a witch too.'

If I didn't know better, I'd worry that she's been smoking something besides tobacco. I pat her hair. 'You should take a nap.'

'Rachel, I know this is difficult for you to understand. The powers Miri and I have are very special. They've been passed down through the bloodline, from mother to daughter.'

'Mom, you know you're Jewish, right? I don't think there's such a thing as a Jewish witch.'

'Being Jewish has nothing to do with being a witch, Rachel.' She gives me yet another weight-of-the-world sigh. 'I know this is going to be difficult for you, honey. That's my fault for shielding you from the truth for so long. But I wanted you to have normal childhoods. I was hoping that if I didn't nurture the powers, they'd remain dormant.'

Normal? I won't even go there.

Her eyes fill with tears. Like me, she cries at the drop of a (pointy) hat. Must be hereditary. Just like this so-called witchcraft.

'These powers aren't always gifts, Rachel,' she says in a tremulous voice. 'I hoped you both might be lucky enough to escape them. You didn't seem to gain any of my higher consciousness at puberty—'

'Gee, thanks, Mom.'

'—which thrilled me. Because all I ever wanted for you was a regular life. But now Miri . . .' She trails off into sobs.

'It's OK, Mommy. Don't worry about me,' my sister says, stroking my mother's hand with suck-up circles. 'I'm happy about it. I finally understand why I've always been different. Everything makes sense.'

Apparently, both my mother and sister are delusional. I scoot closer to the phone on the nightstand, in case I have to call an ambulance to take them to the cuckoo's nest.

My mom wipes her cheeks with the back of her hand and manages to give Miri a smile. 'But now your powers have awakened. It's my responsibility to explain the changes in your spirit. We'll start training this weekend.'

'We're going to Dad's tomorrow,' Miri reminds her, her shoulders sagging with disappointment.

Mom pats her knee. 'Then we'll start on Monday.'

Wait a second. This is an early April Fools' joke. Or maybe I'm an unknowing contestant on a new reality show – *Win a Million Dollars If You Can Make a Fool of Your Eldest Daughter*. Don't they know I hate reality TV? I scan the ceiling for protruding cameras.

My sister pops another handful of sunflower seeds into her mouth. 'See?' she says to me. 'I *knew* I brought the lobster back to life.'

'It's amazing you were able to do that without a spell,' my mom says, shaking her head. And then, taking the prank to a whole new stratosphere of ridiculousness, she leans over to the nightstand and heaves a heavy book on to the quilt. From its earthy green cover, the book appears normal size, but then I notice that it's at least two

19

feet deep. My nose wrinkles. The book looks and smells as if it's been left underwater for a few hundred decades.

My mom thumbs carefully through its thin yellowed pages. 'According to the spell section in *The Authorized and Absolute Reference Handbook to Astonishing Spells, Astounding Potions and History of Witchcraft Since the Beginning of Time*, resurrection is very advanced. The version here calls for rose petals, frankincense resin and—'

'Tell me you didn't bring props.' How long have they had this practical joke planned? Does she think I'm that naive? Couldn't she come up with a less preposterous name?

'It's Miri's spell book,' my mom says, giving my sister a protective-looking smile.

Miri's eyes widen to the size of DVDs. 'Really?'

'Every witch has one. My mother gave me mine when I first came into my powers.'

Grandma just rolled over in her crypt. I can't *believe* she's bringing her deceased mother into this absurd prank! 'What about Aunt Sasha? Let me guess – she was a witch too?' My mom and her sister got into a huge fight years ago, and we haven't seen her since.

My mother ignores me. 'What's amazing is that Miri didn't even need the book. I never had that much raw will when I was her age.'

'Raw will? Is that like The Force?' I laugh. Ha-hee-ha. See that, camera? You're not ruining my sense of humour! Oops. That was another *Star Wars* allusion and, even worse, it was caught on film. I slouch down, hopefully out of prime camera view.

To my surprise, my mom keeps the ruse alive. 'Yes. It is.' She turns back to Miri. 'Honey, as impressed as I am

20

with your ability, you mustn't do magic in front of non-witches. Exposing yourself to the masses leads to nothing but trouble.'

I've been reduced to the masses? That's so much lower than the B-list.

'I'm sorry. I won't do it again,' Miri says, licking her palm. 'Trust me, I didn't even know I had it in me. I'll have to learn my limits.'

'Exactly. Which the book will teach you.' My mom flips through the pages and squints at the headings. 'It's been a long time . . . I'm a bit out of practice. But I estimate your training will take at least a year. From what I remember, section one traces the history of witchcraft. Section two covers the ethics—'

That's it! I've had enough. I'm not going to sit here while my mom pretends to train her apprentice. 'This is great fun and all, being the butt of your practical joke, but I'm going to meet my friends now.' I hop off the bed and stomp towards the door. Then I realize I've forgotten my sneakers. And that's when things get creepy.

My shoes float off the floor.

One foot, two feet. Three feet high.

No one is wearing them, touching them or commandeering them in any way.

My brand-new green suede sneakers fly through the room until they are six feet above the bed, eclipsing the white porcelain ceiling lamp. My shoelaces, which were previously hanging limply, contort themselves into a triangle. And then a square.

And a pentagon!

A hexagon!

A heptagon!

'OOOOHHHMMMIIGAAAAAAAAAWD!' I scream, heaving my back against the door. I peek in terror at my mom. Her eyes are closed tightly, her lips are pursed and she's reciting something under her breath. *What is she doing?* Why is she making her putting-on-lipstick face while my shoelaces morph into haunted polygons? Why is it so cold in here? *What is going on?*

Suddenly, my sneakers crash back to the floor with a thud.

Oh. Oh my. Omigod.

Miri's eyes are wide, but she doesn't look like I do, which is scared stiff. The hairs on my arms are standing up like cactus needles.

My mother is a witch.

My *mother* is a witch. My mother is a *witch*.

My mother is a witch.

And my vegetarian, socially inept little sister is one too.

3

Anything My Heart Desires

'I didn't mean to scare you like that,' my mother says, looking sheepish. 'My magic is a bit rusty. I was trying to make a heart.'

My intestines start playing street hockey and my throat constricts like a broken straw. I feel nauseous, I can't breathe properly and my legs start trembling. How can this be?

No one speaks. The only sound is my mother inhaling on her cigarette.

I sit back down on the edge of her bed in case my legs give out.

'Someone say something.' My mother reaches under her quilt and pulls out a pack of cigarettes, then lights a fresh one. I watch the smoke slither across the ceiling.

Miri peers over the edge of the bed again. 'The sneakers are really cool. Do you like them, Rachel? I can't believe it worked! Those are the ones you wanted, right?'

My mind is blank. 'What?'

'The sneakers. I wanted to put you in a good mood. You know, for when you found out that I'm a witch and you aren't.'

She what? And I'm way too busy having a heart attack to be in a good mood. 'What about . . . is it . . . are you . . . are you going to get warts all over your face?' is all I can manage.

My sister's hands fly to her chin.

'She most certainly won't,' my mother says tartly. 'Nothing is going to change. Our noses won't grow and our hair won't turn to black straw. Those are myths.'

My sister's eyes widen again, and her long lashes touch the base of her eyebrows. 'Does Dad know?'

My mother shakes her head. 'I never told him. I decided in college that I didn't want to be a practising witch. When I met your father, I was embarrassed that I was different.' She crosses her arms. 'I chose to repress the parts of me he wouldn't understand.'

'An excellent basis for a marriage,' I say. 'No wonder you're divorced.' Omigod. Omigod. My sister is a witch. My mother is a witch. It's impossible.

It's true.

Omigod. Wait a sec. 'What do you mean, you didn't want to be a practising witch?'

'I preferred, and still do, not to use magic in my life. I excommunicated myself from the witchcraft community.'

Suddenly, the impact of this entire conversation hits me as if I've just been whacked with a broomstick. 'But . . . why not?' Is she crazy? She can have anything she wants. *I* can have anything I want. Zit-proof skin! A flying carpet! No hair on my upper lip!

'Magic isn't all ruby slippers and castles,' my mom says sternly, as if she's reading me a warning label. 'There are consequences to every spell. And as I told you, I wanted you girls to grow up having normal childhoods.'

Of course I'm not listening. Instead, my mind is whirring. Seven-day weekends! School? So yesterday. Knowledge will be automatically downloaded into our brains!

But . . . where would we meet boys?

'What was your childhood like?' Miri asks my mom, interrupting my happy fantasy.

She sighs and looks down at the quilt. 'Different. Difficult. One day I'll tell you everything, I promise.'

A time machine to see what our parents were like in high school! So we can make fun of their clothes!

Miri's face scrunches up. 'So I shouldn't tell Dad? Did your father know?'

We never met our mother's parents. They both died before we were born. 'He knew,' my mom says. 'My mother told him. But he didn't deal with it well.' She bites her thumbnail. 'You'll have to make the decision about whether to tell your father. It's your choice.'

My mouth feels sandpapery. 'Can one of you poof me up a glass of fruit punch?' This witch thing is going to make my life *a lot* easier.

My mother shakes the burning part of her cigarette at me. 'No way. This is exactly what I was talking about. Laziness is no excuse for magic. Trust me,' she says, and gets a constipated look on her face. 'I've seen the consequences, and I don't recommend Miri use magic to do homework. Or to ace tests. Or to get fancy clothes or toys.'

What toys? Am I seven? Did I ask for the deluxe Barbie Corvette?

Although I wouldn't *mind* if my mother or sister poofed

up a *real* Corvette. A red one. Convertible. And a driver's licence. 'What consequences? What's the big deal?'

'We don't need to talk about everything tonight,' my mom tells us. 'But am I being clear, girls? Miri is not allowed to use her spells for trivial matters.'

I'm so confused. 'What *is* Miri allowed to use her powers for?'

My mother stubs out her cigarette. 'Every witch has to decide what's right for her. Including Miri. That's why I'm training her; so she'll be able to make an informed decision. I've chosen not to use my powers. Some witches take advantage of them for personal gain. Others use them to illuminate a path, and show people the way to goodness. A witch could try to make the world a better place by putting suggestions in people's minds to end various wars. The problem with that is that sometimes a spell meant for good ends up causing unintentional disastrous consequences. One witch I knew once tried to end an African heat wave and ended up causing an ice storm in Kansas City. After Miri's training is complete, she'll have to decide for herself whether or not she wants to pursue her witchdom. And if she does, I'm hoping she'll take the altruistic route. Carefully, of course.'

'Mom.' I tut-tut, shaking my head. 'Is it fair to make a twelve-year-old feel responsible for world peace?'

My sister smiles serenely. 'I understand what Mom means. If I choose to use magic, I can will people to do good deeds at school and stuff. Maybe if a bully is about to beat up a smaller kid, I can mentally *suggest* to him how he would feel if the tables were reversed. And then maybe he won't be mean.'

I eye Miri warily. She *so* isn't going to make the most of

this. This is a girl who does all her homework *on the day it's assigned*. Magic will be wasted on her. Like boobs. She's not even excited – I'd be bouncing off the floor like a basketball. She's definitely going to need some sisterly steering. 'Hello? Miri, can you get psyched, please? You have *magical powers*.'

She shrugs her small shoulders. 'I am excited. But I always suspected something was different about me. Like how Tigger always obeys me, and why no one ever found me during hide-and-seek.'

Tigger always listens to Miri. She says, 'Tigger, I'm freezing. Will you bring me a blanket?' and the fat fur ball digs his pointy little teeth into the purple afghan and drags it across the room. And me? Nothing. I can call 'Here, Tigger, Tigger' for centuries and that cat won't even blink. He'll squat on my biology textbook despite my waving my arms and screaming that I have a test the next day. Does he care? Does he move? No. I assumed cats just didn't like me. I didn't realize Miri could communicate with them.

And now that I think about it, I could *never* find her during hide-and-seek. I would cover my eyes, count down from twenty, then look in the traditional places: under the bed, between the coats at the backs of the closets, behind the couch. No Miri. Not even my father could find her. My friends couldn't. Dave the fireman couldn't. (Although my mom might have asked him up just to ogle his hotness.) 'Where did you hide?'

'In the bathtub. But I would *suggest* to you not to look there, and you wouldn't. See? I always wondered what was different about me, and now I know. And anyway, I've had some time to let the news sink in. Mom and I talked about this all last night and today.'

Excuse me? 'You knew this since *yesterday*? Why didn't anyone tell me?' I heard them talking, but I thought they were discussing pollution or something, not anything *important*.

My mom puts her arm around Miri. 'I wanted to see how she felt. And emphasize that she's not allowed to use any magic at all, until she's fully trained.'

She said that will take at least a year! Reading my mind (*really* reading my mind?), my mom gives me a serious look. 'I didn't want anyone to tell her otherwise.'

'But . . . you zapped me up new shoes,' I say feebly.

'I did that when you called to ask if you could go for pizza, before I knew the rules,' Miri admits. 'I wasn't sure it would really work. Mom said you were excited that you were invited, and I thought I'd give you something to show off.'

I guess that's why I didn't notice them all day. They only appeared on my feet after French class.

'Miri didn't tell me what she had done,' my mom clarifies. 'So when you called back to thank me, I couldn't have you run around the city in magic shoes. What if they disappeared and left you barefoot in the restaurant, or on your way home? The sidewalks are cold.' Then she shook her head at Miri. 'I knew we needed to talk.'

Miri picks up a sneaker and squeezes it like an orange. 'Seems fine.'

'Still,' my mom reminds Miri and me for the hundredth time, 'no more magic until you've finished your training.'

She can remind me five zillion times. There is no chance I'm waiting 365 days to test out Miri's magic!

Obviously, I'll have to have a word with my sister in private. My stomach grumbles. 'So conjuring up cupcakes from Magnolia Bakery is out too?' They're delicious.

'No Magnolia Bakery,' my mother says, exasperated.

'But they don't deliver!'

Miri is shaking her head in disbelief.

I narrow my eyes. 'If she starts *suggesting* to me that we switch rooms, that's completely unfair. I'm older and I'm entitled to the bigger one.'

My mother and Miri sigh in harmony.

'Good thing Miri is the one with the powers,' my obnoxious mother says.

So now it's three in the morning, and I can't fall asleep. I keep flipping my pillow over, trying to find the cold side, but both feel like chairs that have just been sat on.

I prop myself up on my elbows and stare at the pyramid-shaped reading lamp on my night table.

Reading lamp . . . turn on!

Nada.

Reading lamp . . . make it light! I wiggle my fingers at it.

Stupid lamp.

I know the witch stuff sounds insane, and I wouldn't blame anyone for not believing me. If it wasn't my own crazy family, I wouldn't buy it either.

But . . . it *is* my family. And the more it sinks in, the cooler it is. With Miri's help, I can have movie stars on my speed dial. A jacuzzi in my closet. A boyfriend. She'll zap my room clean. (Who needs a robot?) Give me bionic hearing. Poof me up a new wardrobe. The possibilities are endless. Endless!

And I'm not waiting a year. Nice try, Mom. I got Miri

29

to watch the Lord of the Rings trilogy with me four times in a row during my Tolkien phase; surely I can convince her to whip me up a spell or two. Where to begin?

Hmm.

Watching them fly around on Halloween will be nerve-racking. But this is the most kissed-by-a-prince/win-the-lottery/so-amazing-it's-unbelievable type of thing that has ever happened to me.

Ahhh. I lie down and pull the covers over my head. Then, for the first time, realization washes over me.

It's not the most amazing thing that has ever happened to me. It's the most amazing thing that has ever happened to . . . Miri.

Witchcraft, an ability normally passed from mother to daughter, has skipped me. As with breasts, nature has decided I don't qualify.

By four thirty I still can't sleep, so I decide that my mother shouldn't either.

Her ghastly early-morning breath wafts over me as I poke her in the shoulder. Unfortunately, that's a trait I did inherit. I'm sure my future husband will appreciate it.

'What's wrong?' she asks, sitting up. She's still in her ratty concert tee. You'd think a witch could spruce herself up a bit. Give herself a free makeover or fake nails. Get her roots done. She has a blonde ring orbiting her brown roots, as if she's Saturn.

I crawl into bed beside her. 'You owe me an explanation. Why can't I resuscitate lobsters? Do any witches get magic later in life?'

She switches on her bedside lamp. 'Normally magical powers appear during puberty, but some witches come into them when they have their first child.' She narrows her eyes. 'Don't get any ideas.'

'Mom!'

'Just saying. Anyway, one woman I knew traumatized herself and her husband when she levitated their baby right out of the crib.'

A balloon of hope fills me. 'So it can still happen?'

She nods. 'It can.'

Fantastic!

And then she adds, 'But it might not. Some daughters never become witches.'

My balloon pops and sags lifelessly to the ground. 'That's so unfair. Why does Miri get powers and not me? She didn't even finish the first Harry Potter and that was the shortest one. I read them all!'

'Honey, I know you think witchcraft is all fun and games, but it comes with serious responsibilities. Maybe when you're more mature and responsible—'

'What do I have to do?' I whine. 'Keep my room clean and make hundreds of useless lists like Miri?'

'It's not about specific actions. It's more of a mental state.'

'Oh,' I say, not sure whether I want to pout or cry at the unfairness of it all.

'Miri looks up to you, and I expect you to help her deal with the changes in her life and to guide her to do the right thing.'

Help Miri, guide Miri, blah, blah, blah. Miri gets everything.

I rest my cheek against the pillow and look at my mom. 'Remember in fourth grade when all the girls in my class were invited to Krissy Backer's sleepover and I wasn't?' I ask, feeling sad at the years-old memory. Then indignation fills me. Looking like a dork with those braces? Totally unnecessary. That haircut that had total strangers gasping with pity? Completely avoidable. I blink back tears.

My mom studies me. 'I know what you're thinking, honey.'

'Well, why didn't you?' I blurt out. 'You could have made my life a zillion times better if you had only used a smidgen of magic!'

My mom smoothes back my hair. 'I understand how it could seem that way to you. But trust me, magic isn't all that it appears to be. I wanted you and Miri to experience *life* – with all its joys and its sorrows – not some artificial world that I created to make you happy.' She kisses my forehead. 'I love you, Rachel. More than you'll ever know.'

'I love you too, Mom,' I say, sniffling. After a few minutes of witch-daughter bonding, I sit up. 'Did Miri use magic to give herself boobs?'

She smiles and shakes her head. 'I developed early too. You take after your father. He didn't have his growth spurt until he was seventeen.'

Life is so unfair. 'So I guess you can't put a spell on me to become a witch.'

'Afraid not,' my mom tells me. 'If you're meant to be one, you will be.'

I get up and walk to the door with a sigh. 'Well . . . can I at least keep the shoes?'

My mom hesitates, then smiles. 'I'll make an exception just this once.'

With that victory in hand, I drag my bare feet back into

my bed. But instead of sleeping, I spend the next two hours trying to levitate my duvet.

Unsuccessfully.

4
Fly, Miri, Fly!

It's only quarter to nine on Friday morning and the day is already a disaster.

First , I cornered Miri in the kitchen, begging her to zap away my horrendous under-eye circles.

'Did you listen to a word Mom said? No!'

'I was up all night digesting *your* witch news. Take some responsibility!'

But noooooo.

Then, she borrowed my new sneakers without asking, and, since my black boots have been MIA since the switcheroo, I had to wear my smelly gym shoes. If she ever takes them again without my permission, I'm fully dropping a house on her.

Except she's the one with the powers, so I can't even do that.

Third, because I'm still in a trance from yesterday's news, I tripped between the third and fourth floors and banged my knee on a metal stair. The bruise ain't gonna be pretty.

Fourth, Tammy went on and on about how fantastic yesterday's pizza excursion was for the entire twenty minutes of homeroom, and she made me miss all the announcements.

(I'm getting so much better at these lists. Maybe now I can have my powers?)

'I really had the best time at Stromboli's,' she says, for the eighty-seventh time, while unsnapping her lock. Her locker is right next to mine, because we're in the same homeroom and our last names both start with Ws. I'm Weinstein and she's Wise.

'So who was there?' I ask.

'Everyone.'

She must see the look of dismay on my face, because she quickly wrinkles her nose, which makes it look big (I'll admit it's a bit on the large side, even though I always swear to her it isn't), and adds, 'I mean, not *everyone*. It wasn't a big deal. You didn't miss much.' She wobbles her right hand, which is her so-so signal.

I don't need psychic abilities to know she's trying to make me feel better. 'Was Jewel there?'

'Um . . .' She pulls her green binder off her top shelf. 'Yeah.'

'And Raf? And Mick?'

She bows her head. 'Mick was. We sat at the same table.'

Ouch. An oversharpened pencil spears my heart. 'He would have been at my table if I'd been there,' I moan.

'I hadn't realized he was such a nice guy,' she says, intensifying the chest stabbing. 'I stuck my elbow in tomato sauce and he was the first one up to get me a napkin.'

So unfair. It should have been *me* staining my shirt.

35

'Maybe I'll find out where they're going tonight,' she says.

'No point,' I say, and sigh heavily. 'I have to go to my dad's.'

The most annoying part of having divorced parents is spending every second weekend in Long Island. I love my dad, and I want to spend time with him, but the packing, train taking and missing out on all the weekend festivities are a massive disruption to a fourteen-year-old's social calendar.

Of course, if I have an important event – bat mitzvah, school function, shoe shopping – I can stay in Manhattan, but then I burn Miri by making her go to Long Island alone. My sister says STB nags her more when I'm not around. ('Stop biting your nails!' 'Don't pick at your food!' 'No practising your karate in the house!') I don't doubt it. STB never nags us when my dad is there. She pulls a Jekyll and Hyde every time. When he's there, she's supersweet and helpful: 'You're so creative, Rachel!' As soon as he walks into the next room, she instantly becomes evil: 'Why are you such a slob?'

My dad hates it when we miss a weekend. But now that he has STB, he can't switch dates easily. She's always got something up her wrinkle-free sleeve – dinners, theatre tickets, trips to the Caribbean.

We never went to the Caribbean when he was married to my mom. We never even went to the Jersey shore. To be fair, he wasn't a partner in his law firm then and didn't have as much money. We drove to Florida twice and took some weekend ski trips to Stowe, but we never left the country (unless you count World Showcase in Epcot). Those car rides were long. We'd play Geography, the game where you name a city/state/country that starts with the final letter of the place last named.

'Vermont,' I'd start.

'Texas,' my dad would say.

'Salem,' my mom would complete.

And I thought it was her travel career that gave her the unfair advantage.

All the signs were there. I just didn't speak witchcraft.

Maybe one day my dad will take us to an island. Miri and I could learn to scuba dive and then I'd be able to better communicate with Tammy.

Hmm. Maybe not. Aren't witches allergic to water? The wicked witch in *The Wizard of Oz* melted when Dorothy drenched her. Does Miri have to stop bathing now? Super. Something else to look forward to.

Tammy eyes me with pity. 'I'm so lucky my moms and dad all live in the city.' She is surprisingly well adjusted regarding her mother/stepmothers situation. On Mother's Day she even buys three cards. 'Tomorrow, all of them are coming over for Valentine's Day dinner. Can you believe they all get along?'

'You're lucky.' Since my parents' divorce, I don't think they have even volunteered to be in the same room. It's not that they fight – they're always civil – they're just awkward. I get the feeling that, to them, being in proximity to each other is like listening to nails scraping against a blackboard.

I guess I should be grateful that they don't fight. They never fought. My dad just realized he was no longer in love with my mom. They had gotten married young, the day after they graduated from college, before he knew what he wanted. For weeks after they discussed divorcing, he stayed in our apartment until they worked out the financial arrangements and he found a place of his own. And not even during those weeks did I hear them argue.

'You spending Valentine's Day at your dad's?' Tammy asks me, interrupting my trip down Divorce Lane.

'*Mais oui.* Unfortunately. No hot date for me.' No potential change in my Frenching status this romantic holiday.

Tammy gives me a comforting shoulder pat as we head toward maths. 'Let's stop at the bathroom,' she says.

'I have to ask Ms Hayward something before class,' I lie, and continue walking before she has a chance to renege.

Explanation: I'm ditching Tammy in case Jewel gets to class early and saves me a seat. Maths is the only time she's nice to me these days.

OK, OK, I'm a horrible person.

But if it weren't for accelerated maths, I'd never spend any time with Jewel. And I see Tammy all the time because we have practically every class together.

Enough said.

As I follow the stairs up to the third floor, I try to talk myself out of my traitorous behavior. Why should I be nicer to Jewel than to Tammy? Forget it! Jewel can sit alone for once.

I open the classroom door. Jewel is in the back row, her furry pink pencil case on the desk next to her, saving me a spot. She waves me over.

So what am I supposed to do? Not go? I can't be *rude*.

'Hi, sweetie!' she sings as I slide into the plastic chair beside her.

'Hi,' I say, admiring her gorgeous, frizzless mahogany

curls perfectly perched on top of her head with two silver hair sticks. (I'd feel stupid with chopsticks in my hair, but they look great on Jewel. She's tall enough not to have to worry about poking out someone's eye.)

She's tried to teach me her frizz-busting technique ('Comb it in the shower, insert gel immediately post gentle towel dry, scrunch and diffuse within ten minutes or all is lost'), but I can never get my boring brown just-past-my-shoulders hair to look right. It's not straight, not curly. Just wavy. I'm an ocean head. And as I sit down, a single hair stands up straight to the ceiling.

Jewel giggles.

I lick my finger and rub the strand, trying to encourage it to stay with its friends. 'Remember when we used to rub balloons on our heads to make our hair staticky?' I say. I like to remind Jewel about our shared past in the hopes she'll remember we're supposed to be best buds.

'Mmm-hmm,' she says, and opens the magazine on her desk.

Jewel and I have been friends since pre-school, when we wore matching pairs of white leather sandals. During playtime we discovered we could attach our bands and pretend to be contestants in a three-legged race.

I'm dying to tell her about Miri. She would freak out. I'm freaking out. It's all I can do not to stand on my chair and scream at the top of my lungs, *'My sister's a witch!'*

I know, I know, it's not my secret to tell.

If I were a witch, I would blab to the world. Although . . . then everyone would know I was putting spells on them. Where would the fun be in that?

I'm also dying to tell Jewel because it would give us something we could bond over. It would be just like old

39

times, the two of us whispering secrets. We always had other friends, but we were the team. Occasionally, the three-legged team. Maybe one day we'll be a team again. It's not as if we had a fight, I remind myself as she flips a page. She's just really busy with her fashion-show friends.

I spot Tammy at the front of the room, looking for me. I motion hello, but the thing is, the seat next to me is already taken. She finds a spot two rows ahead of us, next to Janice Cooper. Janice hardly ever talks in class, and she always looks very serious when she takes notes. Tammy is friends with her, and she sits with us at lunch. She wears her straight long brown hair half-up in a gold barrette every day. She's a bit geeky, but that's all right.

'Which do you like better?' Jewel whispers twenty minutes later while Ms Hayward is explaining the surface area of the polygon on the blackboard. She slips me a stack of glossy pages ripped from months' worth of magazines. All feature A-list-looking models in barely-there designer dresses.

Jewel doesn't pay much attention in maths class. Why should she, when she knows I can explain it all to her later?

I'm really good at maths. I mean, really good. Geometry, trigonometry, algebra, whatever. Numbers make sense to me. I get a little rush when I crack a problem. And I always get the highest grade in the class. I know I always get the highest grade, not because I ask my fellow students what they got, but because Ms Hayward always makes a big deal of it. I'm not sure if she does it to be nice or just to embarrass me. 'And once again, surprise, surprise, the highest grade in the class goes to . . . little Miss Back-of-the-Room, Rachel Weinstein.'

Ms Hayward is not one of my biggest fans. Mostly because I spend her entire class passing notes instead of listening to what she has to say. I still get the highest marks. What's the point in paying attention? Everything she says is plagiarized directly from the textbook.

On the other hand, she can't seem to help showing the tiny nugget of respect she must feel for me. She can't hate her prize pupil. Who else will she send to the state maths competition?

All right, yes, I went to the state maths competition in November. And – geek alert! – I placed in the top five. I came in second. I am going to kick serious butt on my PSATs.

My dad wanted to know why I didn't come in first. He won a maths competition in high school and lets me keep his triangular silver trophy in my room at my mom's. He draws immense pride from his theory that while other daughters wasted their time playing with dolls, I entertained myself by playing with his calculator.

Which is true. Except that I was playing a game I used to call Barbie's Office, and the calculator was used solely as a prop.

Since my dad never had a boy, he tries to use me as a replacement for traditional father–son activities. It worked for *Star Wars* and calculators. Not as much for baseball.

'You throw like a girl!' he'd yell at me in Central Park.

'I am a girl!'

Maybe one day, Mick will be able to teach me. Sigh.

Anyway, I hate it when Ms Hayward focuses on me. That's why I don't participate in class. Who wants to look like a know-it-all? (Answer: Doree Matson, a fashion-show annoyance who unfortunately is in most of my classes – not this one thankfully – always sits in the front row and has her hand permanently stapled to the ceiling.)

So, instead of paying attention, I flip through Jewel's fashion options. I point to a knee-length dress in electric blue. 'This one.' It's a dress by Izzy Simpson, who is my absolute favourite. Not that I own anything designed by Izzy Simpson. Her designs are way too expensive. Jewel's family isn't rich, but her mom always buys her the best clothes.

She raises a thick, perfectly arched eyebrow. 'Yeah? Maybe.'

'What's it for?'

'Spring Fling.'

She's already shopping for Spring Fling? I don't even know when it is, let alone have a date.

Every year JFK throws four dances: Fall Ball, Winter Mixer (apparently the administration thinks that rhymes), Spring Fling and the prom. But the prom is only for seniors and, of course, the hot freshman, sophomore and junior girls whom the senior boys want to hook up with.

These dances are big deals. Major big deals. And no one goes without a date. But that's not a school rule. The administration makes a point of telling us again and again that no dates are necessary, but the unwritten mandate is no date, no go, which I am well aware of.

Fall Ball: The fashion show tryouts were two weeks away. Watched *Star Wars* trilogy with Jewel (who had yet to be let through the gates of high school coolness). Popcorn! Pedicures! Pyjama party!

Winter Mixer: Jewel had a date. New friend Tammy had strep. Me, home alone, with Miri.

Spring Fling: Me at the dance. Cinderella-style, I will gracefully sashay into the gym, professionally blown-out hair swaying over my strapless, sparkling, dewy shoulders. I will dance, I will dip, I will dazzle. I will have a handsome A-lister on my arm. Preferably his name will be Mick or Raf.

I'm going to Spring Fling. I am *not* missing another dance. I don't care who I go with, but this time someone will ask me. I know, I know. I should ask someone myself. But what if I ask and he says no? I'm not being antifeminist. Just chicken. But do you know what I'm even more chicken about?

The dancing part. Did I inherit witchcraft? Oh, no. I've inherited my mother's *total lack of rhythm*. Jewel used to spend hours with me, trying to show me how to move my butt without looking as if I were being electrocuted. Nothing worked.

But people don't really dance at dances, do they? Besides the slow ones, of course, which I can do. That's all about the sway. The school dance is more about the outfits, gossiping and making out. Dancing is completely secondary.

'Do they know the date yet?' I ask.

'Will told me—'

I blink. Jewel is on a first-name basis with the school president? To Tammy and me he's William Kosravi, the gorgeous and unapproachable senior, and president of the student body. He's also the older brother of Raf, aka one of the Loves of My Life.

'—that it's April third, the night after the fashion show. The Saturday kicking off spring break.'

Oh, no. No, no, no. 'That's the night of my dad's wedding.'

Jewel looks disappointed – for a millisecond. Her lips make an O. 'Well . . . it's just a dance.' This coming from the girl who has already put together a portfolio of clothing options. 'I'll show you my pictures,' she says as a consolation.

'What time is the dance?'

'Nine.'

I'll never make both. The wedding starts at six, but the torture will carry on until at least midnight. And it's in Port Washington, Long Island, which is at least a thirty-five-minute train ride away.

Ms Hayward says in a loud sing-song voice, 'Rachel, I know you don't feel that paying attention in class is worth your while, but perhaps you could stop yapping so your fellow classmates might benefit from my instruction?'

Then she winks at me. See? It's a love/hate relationship.

I space out for the rest of the class, but this time it's because all I can think about is that way back in October, before Jewel forgot we were best friends, I invited her to the wedding (my dad said I could invite two friends) and she said she'd be there.

Guess she forgot that too.

As the bell rings, I pile my books. 'What are you doing after school? Want to come over?'

Jewel carefully inserts her pen, purple calculator and bunny-shaped eraser back into her pencil case. 'Can't. I'm hanging out with Liss.' Liss is Melissa Davis, my red-headed, snobby A-list replacement. Her nose is so turned up, I don't know how she sees where she's going. Her mother choreographs music videos, so – do you have to ask? – Liss automatically gets to be in the fashion show. 'But definitely another time,' Jewel promises, squeezing my arm. And then she takes off.

And that, ladies and gentlemen, is me getting a first-class burn.

A burn that would have been more pronounced if I'd given her the bumblebee-shaped 'Won't you bee my valentine?' card that has her name on it in my schoolbag.

I swear it's not as pathetic as it sounds. When we were nine, Jewel threw her flip-flop into a beehive and we each got five stings. We spent the day crying and consoling ourselves with ice cream.

OK, it's pathetic.

Tammy, at least, is waiting for me at the front of the classroom.

I can't believe I am going to miss Spring Fling because of my father's horror-show wedding. I spend the entire train ride to Long Island freaking out. Which might be slightly premature, considering I don't even have a date yet, but what if someone asks me?

It's completely selfish to prefer an inane high-school dance to the celebration of my father's nuptials, but . . . but . . . STB is annoying and she doesn't love him as much as my mother did.

'Spring Fling is just a stupid dance. Get over it.' Miri's a tad annoyed that I keep interrupting her reading. She's been hunched over her grotesque-smelling encyclopedia of a book since we got on the train.

'Wait till you're a freshman. You'll see,' I tell her. 'And I'll stop obsessing if you let me look at the magazine you're not even reading.' On the glossy cover is the gorgelicious face of Robert Crowne, the new twenty-one-year-old singer/songwriter. His single, 'Sixteen Shades of Love', is on the radio 24/7.

Miri rolls her eyes. 'I need it to disguise *The Authorized and Absolute Reference Handbook to Astonishing Spells, Astounding Potions and History of Witchcraft Since the Beginning of Time.*'

'Are you going to say the entire name every time?' I yawn. 'It's putting me to sleep.'

'What should I call it?' she asks. '*Authorized and Absolute?*'

'*A-squared.* That sounds cooler.' I gaze at the cover. 'Where did that book come from, anyway? Is there an Amazon.witch?'

'Noooo,' she enunciates. 'Mom put a spell on hers to produce one for the next generation. But I like the new name. *A-squared.*'

'Let me see it.'

'I'm reading.' Miri lets out an amazed giggle. 'It even updated the language to be appropriate for a young, twenty-first-century witch.'

'Fine. It's not like I care.' Yeah, right. I spent all day attempting to kick-start my magical powers, whenever my thoughts weren't otherwise occupied with my Spring Fling obsession.

Like when I willed my combination lock to revolve itself.

Believe me, if it had worked, I would not be on this train.

And then later, when I spotted Raf in the cafeteria line, spooning mashed potatoes on to his plate, and I willed him to park that cute butt of his beside me.

46

He sat next to stuck-up Melissa Davis. She already stole my best friend; did she have to hijack Raf too?

'So,' I say, 'how was school? Put any spells on your teachers?'

'Noooo. First of all, I don't know how to use any of the spells, and second, for the hundredth time, I'm not doing any magic until I've finished my training.'

Blah, blah, blah. If I were her, I would have made dear old Liss choke on her celery sticks. 'What a waste. You could bet I'd use my powers if I had any.'

'Maybe that's why you don't.'

Look what witch has already become a diva. 'What's that supposed to mean?'

Miri leans back in her seat, holding her ticket. 'Mom says that some people get them when they're ready for them. Maybe you're not ready.'

'Excuse me, Miss Maturity.' I push her book and magazine out of her hands, and they tumble into the aisle.

She rolls her eyes. Does she think *she's* the older sister?

I bet she used her powers to make me do that just to illustrate my immaturity.

'You up?' I ask Miri.

My father has enough money to build a pool and sauna in his new house, but not enough for Miri and me to have our own rooms. STB decorated ours in yellow. She thought it was cute. I feel like I'm drowning in a lemon meringue pie.

'No.'

I throw a sunflower-shaped pillow at her. 'If I were a witch, I would never sleep. I would zap myself perma-awake and spend the night flying around.'

 47

She sighs. 'Maybe I'll zap myself asleep so I can stop staring at the ceiling.'

'Hey, there's a full moon. You want to borrow STB's Swiffer for a quick spin around town?' I giggle.

'Ha ha.'

'Can you fly?'

I see the outline of her head shaking in the dark. 'No.'

'So you've tried?' I say, psyched to have found her out.

'Mom told me that flying is a myth.'

'And you believe her?' I tsk tsk. 'You can bring lobsters back to life, make yourself invisible when playing hide-and-seek, but you can't fly?'

She sits up and her eyes glow in the dark. Not in a creepy way, but because it's dark in here and she's always had really white eyeballs. She can do tricks with her eyes too, such as crossing them, and making both eyeballs look outward. Mom hates it when she does that, and is always warning her that one day they'll stay like that and she'll have only herself to blame.

'I don't get how I did that lobster thing,' Miri confides. 'And I didn't make myself invisible. I projected my thoughts on you.'

'Does that mean I have a weak mind?'

'Maybe.'

'Shut up.'

She throws the sunflower pillow back at me. 'I don't think you're weak-minded.'

I feel creepy crawlies up my spine. 'Do you make *suggestions* to me a lot?' Fantastic. My own mother and sister constantly control my thoughts, without my even realizing it. How do I know what I'm really thinking and what they're telling me to think?

Is Miri telling me what to think right now?

'I'm not telling you what to think.'

'Omigod! You're reading my thoughts! Stop it!'

'I can't read your thoughts, moron. You're slamming your palm into your forehead.'

I pause in mid-slam. Oops. 'I'm on to you, young lady.'

STB calls Miri young lady. Miri once called her old lady in retort, but that didn't go over well.

'I don't know what I can or can't do,' Miri admits. 'I have to start my training. And study the spells. And I've decided not to tell Dad. At least for now, until my training is complete. So don't mention anything, OK?'

'Of course not,' I say, distracted. I wonder if I can use one of these spells to make Liss roll around naked in poison ivy. 'Will the spells work if I say them too?'

'I don't think so. Mom says it's not the spells themselves that work. They need to be performed by a witch.'

That is so unfair. Witches get everything. Ruby slippers, talking cats, flying brooms, their own TV shows.

I have an idea. 'Stand on the bed.'

'Why?'

'Just do it.'

She kicks off her covers and stands up on her bed.

'Now jump off,' I say.

'Why?'

'Just do it.'

She swings her arms back and jumps. She lands with a thud on the floor.

Maybe I *do* have the power of suggestion. Or maybe I'm just a big sister whose little sister listens to almost everything she says.

 49

Miri massages her right ankle. 'Ouch. What was that for?'

'I wanted to see if you could fly.'

'I told you I can't! I'm not Peter Pan.'

Hey. Wait a sec. I feel a rush of cold air, and suddenly my pillow is raising my back, as if I'm in the dentist's chair. Now it's . . . it's . . . moving away from under me and floating into the air! It's smacking me on the chin! On the head! On the shoulders!

Miri's eyes are closed and her lips are pursed, and she's attacking me in a magic pillow fight.

I try to grab the top two corners, but they wiggle out of my grasp like a wet bar of soap.

'Stop it!' I howl. Smack. 'This is so unfair!' Smack. Now the sunflower pillow is in on it too, slapping my legs.

Pound, pound. Uh-oh. Someone's at our door.

'Yes?' I say in my most ladylike voice. Smack. Giggle.

Miri's eyes widen, and the pillows drop lifelessly into my lap. She doesn't have time to return to bed, and the door opens while she's splayed across the carpet.

STB is wearing her silk cleavage-exposing bathrobe, and an eye mask is dangling around her neck. 'Miri, I'd appreciate it if you got back into bed. Other people are trying to get some sleep.'

'Sorry.'

'You girls will be exhausted for your fitting.' We have dress fitting number 738 tomorrow morning for our horrifically ugly pink powder-puff bridesmaid dresses. STB is batting her eyes furiously, as if looking at us is making them tear. She has gorgeous eyes. They're wide and warm and a kaleidoscope of blues and greens. The rest of her is OK. I mean, she's definitely pretty. She has smooth blonde hair that rests on her shoulders, creamy perfect skin, and straight, Liquid Paper-white teeth. She's slim and always dressed in tailored designer blouses and pants. But her eyes are incredible. I bet that's why my dad fell in love with her.

How can someone with those eyes be so horrible?

Miri snorts. 'We'll certainly need to be well rested to stand there like mannequins.'

I laugh.

STB does not. 'Enough with the mouth, young lady. And I wish you would leave those dingy T-shirts at your mother's and wear the Gap pyjamas I bought you. Now please go to sleep.'

The door makes a loud cracking sound as she slams it. We hear a nasal moan from the room next to ours. 'Mommmmmmy, the door woke me up.'

We giggle for a few minutes before trying to fall asleep. I'm hoping to return to the dream in which I'm voted the most popular girl in the universe at the school dance.

And that's when a plan bursts in my brain, like a kernel into popcorn.

Miri just did magic. She is therefore willing to break the rules. All I have to do is give her a worthy reason to do it again.

Our dad's happiness = worthy reason.

Like me, Miri wishes our father would find his *real* soulmate and live happily ever after. And the *only* way to make that happen is to put a spell on him.

We have to act now. If we wait until the end of training, it will be too late.

We must use magic to stop him from marrying STB.

Yes! Yes to the power of three! Yes x yes x yes!

Of course . . . since my calendar will be clear, there's no reason she can't whip up a quick potion for something minor . . . like making me the most popular girl at JFK. Jewel will be my Best Bud again and someone will ask me to Spring Fling.

A tiny snore escapes from Miri's nose.

My nose starts to twitch.

My creativity + Miri's magic = the end of STB + the A-list for me!

5

Glinda, the Good Witch of Long Island

Today is the worst Valentine's Day ever.

'STB doesn't actually think this is nice, does she?' Miri whines. She's standing, legs spread a foot apart, as Judy, the middle-aged dressmaker (she's at least twenty-five), contorts the heinous pastel-pink material around Miri's overdeveloped body.

I shake my head. 'Of course not. She *wants* us to look like pink doilies. That way she's the only one who looks good.' And she will definitely look amazing. She spent ten thousand dollars on her wedding dress. I heard her bragging about it to one of her friends.

Miri looks seriously fed up with being prodded. 'I bet Prissy doesn't have to wear this. Hers is probably adorable.'

'Actually,' Judy says, taking a pin from her mouth and making us realize she is listening to our conversation, 'her dress is a miniature version of yours. Your arms are so toned, Miri. You must be an athlete.'

'She's a brown belt in tae kwon do,' I brag. 'She'll probably be a black belt within a year.' She could be one tomorrow if she wanted to. Wait a minute. With Miri's help, *I* could be one tomorrow!

Miri squirms. 'Why are there rods in the material?'

'It's boning, to shape the dress over your breasts.'

'How can anything shape this get-up? It's so ugly.'

The bells on the door chime and STB and mini-STB glide inside. STB normally stops to get her morning iced coffee en route, but because we were running late, STB dropped us off first and then doubled back to Starbucks. (I was trying to figure out how to use STB's blue liquid eyeliner and ended up making squiggly lines all around my lids. The removal required multiple washings. Naturally, STB waited until we were in the car and out of my dad's earshot before she yelled at me for ruining her schedule.)

'How are we in here?' she asks now. She's asking Judy, not us. She doesn't care how Miri and I are doing. Since I'm still in my jeans, I'm enjoying myself. The more annoyed Miri gets at STB, the better chance I'll have that she'll go for my Making STB Disappear plan.

'I look revolting,' Miri tells her.

Yes!

STB almost chokes on her coffee. 'What kind of thing is that to say? How can you insult Judy like that? Judy, I apologize.'

Personally, I think it was the material Miri was insulting, not the craftswoman, but hey, why defuse a situation that's working in my favour?

Prissy is sitting cross-legged on the floor, caressing the bottom of Miri's dress. 'It's so pretty and pink and pink is pretty and my friend Nora has a pink dress and a purple dress and . . .'

STB motions for Prissy to be quiet and then turns to me. 'Let me guess; you're not happy either.'

Actually, I'm in a terrific mood. 'Hard to tell before it's finished,' I say diplomatically.

Miri gives me the evil eye in the full-length mirror. She'd better not retaliate and suggest I fall on my butt.

'But,' I add, 'I'm not sure if I'm crazy about the material.'

Both Judy and STB gasp. 'What do you mean?' STB asks. 'It's lace and raw silk. The material alone for each dress cost three hundred dollars.'

Three hundred dollars? For doilies?

'Money,' Miri says, 'which could have been better used in Somalia to help feed starving children.'

Or to purchase an Izzy Simpson dress.

STB ignores her and fingers a swatch of the material. 'Rachel's right. You can't judge the dress before it's finished. You'll both look adorable. Like dolls.'

Does she realize that doesn't help?

'I have sixteen dolls,' Prissy pipes up, and then starts counting on her fingers. 'Sandy, and Mandy, and Randy and Dandy and Princess.' When she runs out of fingers, she stops reciting and remains quiet, contemplating her dilemma.

'Fantastic,' Miri snaps. 'I've always dreamed of looking like Barbie.'

I wouldn't mind that. Barbie has excellent measurements.

STB takes a long swig of her coffee, then places it down on a table. 'Miri, how are your fingers?'

Miri clamps her hands shut. 'Fine.'

STB picks up Miri's right hand and prises it open. She does another one of her gasps. With all her heavy breathing, you'd think she was on the StairMaster. 'What am I going to do with you?'

Miri shakes her off. 'They're my nails, and I can bite them if I want to.'

She's getting angrier by the second. This is amazing! My sister doesn't dislike anyone the way she does STB. Before my dad started dating STB, I don't think I ever heard Miri tell anyone off.

STB and Miri embark on a stare-down worthy of a Hollywood action movie. Neither blinks.

Meanwhile, Prissy has finally stopped talking to herself and is now doing what she always does when she thinks her mother isn't looking: carefully picking her nose. It's kind of cute to watch because she has such small fingers. You'd think STB would be more concerned with that than with Miri's nails.

Suddenly, I feel the newly familiar rush of cold, and I look back at Miri and notice that her lips are doing that pursed thing. Uh-oh. I twist my head back to STB as her iced coffee slowly rises from the table beside her. Yikes! I leap toward the plastic cup and haul it down to safety before anyone can see.

The stare-down is over, because everyone's eyes are now on me.

I take a long sip. 'This is delicious,' I say while narrowing my eyes at my blushing sister. 'My turn to change now, right?' And then, before anyone can respond, I hurry to the dressing room.

Crisis averted. And minus the STB cooties, the coffee was tasty.

I take off my jeans and drape myself in my very own pink life-sized doily. Despite the hideousness of the dress, the truth is I'm finding the whole from-material-to-dress process intriguing. Maybe I'll learn to sew. How awesome would that be? I'd be able to make anything I want, rip off all the hottest designs. People would think I spent hundreds – no, *thousands* – on my outfits. I gingerly kick off my shoes so I won't step all over the material. I could even make my own labels – *Rachel* – and sew them inside. Or on the outside like all the expensive designers do. *Rachel* would come to mean chic. *Vogue* would feature my creations, and I would become internationally famous. Jewel would beg to be included in my televised prime-time biography.

Ouch. It feels as if I just stepped on a pin. Ouch, ouch, ouch. That killed. I hate anything that pricks the skin. How am I supposed to become a world-famous seamstress when I hate pins?

Maybe I'll get Miri to poof up the designer clothes for me, since magic is practically flying out of her these days. But I suppose she'll want to share the glory. Fine, we'll call the label Michel. I step outside, careful to avoid more pin foliage.

Miri gives me a sheepish smile as I pass her.

She's definitely almost primed for the plan.

'Arms out,' Judy says when I stand in front of her. I comply like a scarecrow. The truth is, I'm relieved to report, my reflection isn't that scary. The dress makes me resemble Glinda from *The Wizard of Oz*. I look kind of pretty. Except for a small zit above my eyebrow, my complexion is relatively clear. My nose is small. My eyebrows have a nice arch. I wiggle them in the mirror. My eyes are pretty big. Too bad they're boringly brown. My teeth are straight and white, so despite my too-thin lips, I have a niceish smile.

57

'We don't need boning for you,' Judy comments, interrupting my critical analysis.

'We don't?' I ask, watching myself purse my lips. That's how I'll look when I'm finally kissing someone. Or casting a spell when my powers kick in. 'Why don't we?'

STB sighs. 'Because you don't have breasts.'

Well, I never! 'But I might have breasts by the time of the wedding.'

STB snorts. 'Rachel, it's in seven weeks.'

'These things happen fast, you know. One day you're flat and the next day, boom, you're bursting out of your double-D bra. Do what you think is best, but don't get angry at me if we have to scrap the dress and start again at the last minute because of my inevitable blossoming.' These people need to have some faith.

STB throws up her hands. 'Give her boning.'

'Can I have some too, Mommy?' Prissy asks. 'I want boning!'

'Yes, sweet pea, you can have whatever you want.'

If she gets breasts before I do, I'll use the boning to make myself a noose.

The nails argument resumes the moment we're in the car.

'I want you to try that special polish again, the kind that tastes bad,' STB tells Miri.

I'm sitting next to STB in the front seat, Prissy is singing some highly inappropriate pop-music lyrics to herself in the back, and Miri is sitting behind me, staring vacantly out the window. 'No,' she answers. 'It doesn't work.'

'If you stopped biting, it would. I don't know how you nibbled through that polish.'

It was pretty gross. Well, I had to try some, didn't I? I just put a drop on my thumb and licked it. And then again on my pinkie, in case size affected taste. 'If she stopped biting,' I explain with forced patience, 'then it wouldn't need to work.' Come on, STB, you can be meaner than this. 'But it's not just the biting that's the problem,' I say, goading her. 'She rips them too.'

STB gasps. Miri kicks the back of my seat.

'You rip them? They're not old cheques; they're your precious hands! This has *got to stop*.'

Miri stays silent for a few seconds and then explodes. 'Why do you care so much? They're my nails! Mine! And I can do whatever I want with them!'

Yes!

STB reaches over her seat and wags her finger at Miri. 'No, you can't. You don't always know what's in your best interests.'

Since Miri could turn STB into a toad at any moment, STB obviously doesn't know what's in *her* best interests.

'You can't tell me what to do,' Miri grumbles. 'You're not my mother.'

Ah. The infamous not-my-mother line. Silly Miri. Turning her into a toad would be far more original.

When we return to the house, Miri runs up to our room and slams the door. I'll give her some space to seethe privately. Get her really worked up. Maybe a half-hour or so. And then I'll strike with Part One of The Plan. (Insert evil laugh. I would do one, but I've tried it and I sound like a constipated frog. My dad can do a great one, but this is hardly the time to ask him, and anyway, he's at the office, even though STB hates for him to work when we're here. She hates having to entertain us all day

59

without him. Not that she'd ever tell him that. Oh, no, she prefers to fume silently as though it's our fault.)

I decide to give Miri thirty minutes, tops, of solo stewing time. Maybe I'll watch some TV. I plop myself on to the couch in the living room and turn on the tube. Flip. Flip. Flip. Nothing but infomercials, reality TV and reruns. Hey, maybe *Bewitched* is on. I'll be able to give Miri some pointers. Nope. Just *Buffy the Vampire Slayer*. Forget that. I don't want to give her any dangerous ideas. What to do, what to do? I guess I could start my homework. I have an English assignment for Monday. I'm supposed to analyse Yeats's poetry for techniques such as alliteration.

Dull, dreary, drudgery.

Plight, plan, plot.

I know it's been only six minutes but, honestly, I think Miri has had more than enough time alone. I enter the room to find her lying on her bed, legs straight up against the wall, A^2 propped upright on her lap. I know this is a weird way to read, but we've both been doing it for years. It does seem a little batlike, now that she's a witch.

'I can't believe Dad is marrying her,' she complains as I lie down beside her.

Perfect. She's primed for Part One. 'He doesn't *have* to marry her,' I say in my casual voice.

She smirks. 'Then when will we wear our pink doily dresses?'

Aha! Here's my opening. 'If the wedding is cancelled, we will never have to wear them. Ever. Except on Halloween, if we're so inclined. You can dress up as Glinda, the Good Witch of the North.'

She raises an eyebrow. 'And why would the wedding get cancelled?'

When I was seven, I begged my mom to let me dress up as Glinda for Halloween, but she insisted that the Glinda costumes were all sold out and that I'd have to settle for going as a fairy princess. At the time I believed her. Now I know different. She was afraid that if I dressed like a witch, I would somehow *will* my magic into being. I can't believe she tried to thwart my powers! I can't believe a lot of what my mother did. Or didn't do.

She's a witch. She could have cast spells to make me happy. Like the time I wanted to get tickets to a concert at Roseland, but they were sold out. She could have whipped up two more. Plus backstage passes! She should have stopped me from ever getting hurt! She could have stopped my dad from divorcing her. The back of my neck stiffens. I haven't forgotten that early-morning conversation about experiencing the good and bad, but still . . . why not make life picture-perfect?

'Because,' I say now, taking a deep breath, 'we're going to put a spell on Dad.' If my mom wants to ignore the tools available to her, then that's her problem. Not mine. And not Miri's, if I can help it.

Miri raises the other eyebrow. 'We?'

She has to rub it in, doesn't she? 'Fine, *you* put a spell on Dad.'

'How did I know that would be your solution?'

'Because you're psychic as well as a witch?'

'Or because Mom warned me that you'd try to get me to use magic.' She shakes her head. 'No. I can't do it. I can't use spells to manipulate our father. It's not right.'

Strike out.

OK, no need to panic. Obviously, a goody-goody like her needs time to let the idea seep in.

And plenty more STB aggravation is sure to come.

I don't have to wait long.

Later, when we're called downstairs for what we assume is dinner, STB and Prissy are sitting, arms perfectly crossed, on the white suede couch. My dad is sitting in a chair, wearing a hideous red-and-brown striped shirt. He has the worst taste in clothes. He always asks us how he looks, and we all say fine, because none of us wants to be the first to tell him he has bad taste.

'What's going on?' I ask. They're acting creepy. I swear, if they tell us they're witches too, I am seriously going to lose it.

'Miri,' my dad begins, rubbing the shiny bald spot on the back of his head, 'please take a seat.'

My eyes meet Miri's and we sit down. Uh-oh. Did they hear me scheming? Did Miri inadvertently put a hex on STB? Is she no longer able to speak, but capable only of high-pitched ribbits now?

'We are very worried,' my father says, his forehead crinkling in actual concern, 'about the health of your fingers.'

Miri flushes bright red. I laugh. It's a nail-biting intervention.

'Chewing your fingers,' my father continues, 'can lead to damaged cuticles and infections. Not to mention all the germs you allow into your mouth because they were on your hands.'

I bet STB looked that up on the Internet and scared my dad. The woman will stop at nothing to get what she wants.

Miri's eyes are quickly filling to the rims with water, like clogged toilets.

'I want to help you, honey.' At this point he pats my sister on the head. 'We've considered treatments, and Jennifer has come up with an excellent plan.' He points his chin towards the coffee table, where a box of Band-Aids lies.

STB runs her perfectly manicured nails through her coiffed blonde hair, then says, 'We're going to wrap each of your fingers so you don't bite.'

That is *so* embarrassing. Perfect! God, I really hope Miri can't secretly read my mind.

Miri opens her mouth, then closes it. I think she's too upset to speak. She's looking like Drew Barrymore in *Firestarter*, and I'm getting nervous that she might set the house aflame telepathically.

Prissy rocks back and forth in her spot. 'Miri, biting your nails is yucky.' She fans out her little French-manicured fingers. 'Don't you want pretty nails like me?'

It's too much. Too awful. I have to help. 'Dad, I hardly think these drastic measures are necessary.'

'Don't start, Rachel,' he says, shushing me.

'They are. Now, Miri, give Jennifer your hands so she can wrap your fingers.'

STB smiles a toothy victory smile. 'And I don't want to see you picking them off.'

'Dad,' Miri whines, 'I don't think—'

'But I do,' he says. 'And I want you to start taking the B-complex vitamin biotin, which strengthens nails.' Did I mention that my father thinks vitamins are the cure for everything? 'And I'm your father. I *can* tell you what to do.'

Oh, burn. STB totally told on Miri.

STB opens the Band-Aid box and grabs Miri's hand.

'Could be worse,' I whisper, rubbing Miri's back. 'At least they're plain. She could have listened to Prissy and bought the Disney Princess ones.'

After dinner, Miri and I are lounging in front of the TV when I flip the channel and realize that *Star Wars*, *Episode IV*, the first one ever made, is just about to start. 'Dad!' I shout. '*Star Wars* is on television! Come watch! Dad! *Star Wars*!'

'This is awesome,' Miri says.

My dad runs down the stairs, full of energy. 'It is? Make room for me, girls.' He squeezes in between us on the couch. I unfold a multicoloured blanket and toss it over our legs. He puts an arm around each of us and we lean into him.

When the electric-blue words come on-screen, we all recite, 'A long time ago in a galaxy far, far away . . .'

Then we hold our breath. Wait for it . . . Wait for it . . .

We belt out the music as loudly as we can, like we always do.

STB, followed by Prissy, marches down the stairs. 'What are you doing? Why are you making so much noise? Daniel, I thought we were going to review the wedding place cards tonight.'

'We can't,' my dad says, not taking his eyes off the screen. '*Star Wars* is on.'

'But we have the DVD. Can't we do the place cards first and then you'll watch it later?'

'Watching it on DVD isn't the same as watching it on TV,' I explain.

'She's right,' my dad says. 'We can do the place cards tomorrow. Come watch with us.' He pats the space next to me.

STB shakes her head. 'I was never into this movie,' she says, and then disappears up the stairs.

How can he possibly marry her?

My dad waves Prissy over and she sits on his lap. 'What movie is this?' she asks, bouncing. 'Who is that? Why is she wearing cinnamon buns on her head? Why—'

'Shhh,' my dad says. 'No talking except during the commercials.'

Prissy tries watching for a few minutes, but then starts to squirm and heads back upstairs.

And it's just the three of us. The way it should be.

The second our father deposits us on to the train back to the city, Miri rips off the Band-Aids.

'She' – thumb off – 'is the' – index finger off – 'most miserable' – middle finger off – 'woman' – fourth finger off, no idea what that one's called – 'in the' – pinkie off – 'entire world!'

'She is quite evil,' I happily agree. 'Too bad it's about to become official. If only there were something we could do.' La, la, la.

Miri stares steely-eyed ahead. Then she nods. 'OK. You're right. We need to get rid of her. I can't have Band-Aids applied to my fingers for the rest of my life.'

Yes! Part One in motion!

I give her a nice big-sisterly squeeze. She's so tiny. Not that I'm so huge. Maybe after we're done rescuing our dad, I'll get her to make me taller, like five foot two. A giant!

I pull A^2 from her bag, and she promptly starts biting

her thumbnail. What, does she think I'm going to drop it or something?

Plop. Oops. I pick it up off the grimy train floor. 'Sorry.' Tee hee. 'Here you go. Start looking for an anti-love spell.' I put the book into her freshly bitten hands before either of us can do more damage.

She flips through the pages. 'I don't know if there are anti-love spells. I haven't finished the first section yet.'

'Isn't there an index?' There must at least be a glossary.

'No.'

Sigh. 'What you really need is the spell book on CD-ROM.'

Miri taps me on the head. 'Can we focus here? We need to get that witch out of our lives.'

Witch, huh? I can't stop the grin. 'You'll have to learn to watch your word choice. You can no longer use the word *witch* as a negative description.'

She slaps her hand over her mouth.

'How can I help?' I ask. I won't even bug my sister for the popularity spell today. I'll let her concentrate.

'Just let me read.'

I should start my poetry homework. But first I'll read about Robert Crowne's new tour. Then poetry. 'I'll leave you alone so that you can work your . . .' What's the word I'm looking for here? Oh. Right. 'Magic.' Tee hee. I really crack myself up.

She taps me on the shoulder. 'What we're about to do is a big deal, huh?'

We lock eyes. 'Huge.'

'Giant,' she says.

Maybe she *can* read my mind.

6

Project Popularity +
Greedy Sister = More Chores

As soon as I find a seat in homeroom, I frantically begin my poetry assignment. *Autumn is over the long leaves that love us.* I have no clue what that means.

'Morning.' Tammy slides into the empty chair next to me.

'Hey. How was your weekend?'

'All right. Hung out with the moms.'

'Nothing from *Aaron*?' I mouth his name in case anyone is eavesdropping.

'No.' The edges of her lips droop, but she quickly pulls them up. 'No card. Or date. I called to see what he was up to, but his mom said he was at Mick's party—'

There's a roaring in my ears. Mick had another party that I wasn't invited to. And it was probably the most incredible party ever because it was Valentine's Day weekend. Lights dimmed, romantic music, candles, chocolates . . . the entire A-list.

That's it. I have to get Miri working on the popularity plan pronto. I wonder if I can page her at school. No, she'd hate that.

I'll probably miss another party tonight. I'll probably miss one at lunch.

I'll worry about it later. If I finish this poetry assignment before maths, I can have the period free to chat with Jewel. I don't want to waste lunch on it, and it's too obvious to do in bio or gym. I hate gym. I have to wear my uniform puke-green sweatpants and too-long puke-green T-shirt. This month our phys ed instructors are teaching us meditation and yoga. They think it'll teach us to concentrate.

Now, what was I doing? Oh, right. Poetry!

I find Miri lying on her stomach across the kitchen table. Pages of printer paper covered in scribbles are piled next to her. Our mother is still at work. Ever since two years ago, when she and her friend Bonnie started HoneySun, she doesn't get home until six thirty at the earliest. At least she likes her job now. She especially likes being her own boss. I can relate. I wish I didn't have anyone telling me what to do.

I have to ask Miri. Today. I can't take not being popular any more. Calm down. I have to wait for the right time. I climb on to the table so I can see what she's up to. 'What are you doing?'

'An anti-love spell isn't going to work,' she says, bursting my one dream of happiness. 'I can't do it. It's too advanced.'

'Don't try. Just do,' I say.

'No, I'm serious. See the five broomsticks next to this spell?'

I see five miniature icons of broomsticks. 'Yessssssss.'

'That means it's advanced. One broomstick is for

beginners. I don't think the first spell I try should be a five-broomer. And this one looks particularly intricate. I'd need a black candle, a small cauldron, Dead Sea salts and something called *Achillea millefolium*. Oh, and a lock of the person's hair.'

'Dad doesn't have any to spare,' I chuckle. 'He's pretty bald.'

'That's another problem.'

'You can do it.' This is the same girl who figured out that if we suspended a hanger over our television, we could get thirty-two channels and not have to pay for cable. I'm sure she can figure out a teeny-tiny anti-love spell.

Miri shakes her head. 'I don't want to start with a five-broomer. When we tried snowboarding in Vermont, we started on the bunny hill, not the advanced. What if it doesn't work?'

'Then you'll turn Dad into a rabbit?'

Miri doesn't laugh. 'Not funny. Really, it's too advanced. And I don't even know what *Achillea millefolium* is or where to get it. Is it a food? A spice? A lizard? And anyway, the anti-love spell is temporary. It only lasts a few weeks. Most of the spells that have to do with people's emotions are temporary. So eventually he'd snap out of it and reschedule the wedding.'

'You don't know that. Maybe by the time the spell wears off it'll be too late,' I wishful-think out loud. 'He'll have figured out that he doesn't love her after all. Infatuation isn't love. So, for a while you'll remove the blinders, and once he sees the truth, he'll never go back.' I sigh. I can tell that Miri isn't buying my reasoning. 'So what are you saying? Don't tell me the plan is off.' No, no, no!

69

'I'm trying to find an alternative.'

Phewf. 'You're so good. And smart. I bet you could do anything you set your mind to.' Here it comes. The moment of reckoning. The witching hour. I give her my big-eyed-little-girl innocent look. 'I bet you could even find me a tiny little popularity spell while you're searching.'

She snort-laughs. 'Nice try.'

'Oh, come on! Please, please find a popularity spell for me? Please? Please, please, please?'

She shakes her head. 'There is no make-me-popular-in-high-school spell.'

'Why not?' I flip on to my back, leaning my feet against the apple-patterned wallpaper to get comfy. I probably should have taken off my shoes. Oops. Do black smudges come off?

'Because the book was transcribed in 1304,' Miri says, leafing though the pages. 'High school didn't exist.'

'It doesn't have to be *high school* popularity, precisely,' I say reasonably. 'Is there a spell for winning popularity among the peasants? Can't you whip up something that would make the knights and vicars think I'm cool?' I hop off the table in search of a cleansing solution. 'I thought the book was modernized!' The footprints on the wall would lead one to believe that I can walk sideways. Hey, how awesome would that be?

'It's the language, not the content, that's modernized,' Miri says. 'Do you even know what a vicar is?'

'You're the one doing the research.' Must I do everything? I begin to swipe at the telltale smudges.

'Fine, I'll keep an eye out, but I make no promises.'

Yes! 'Thank you, thank you, thank you!' I give her a big wet kiss on the cheek and then continue cleaning.

You'd think she could offer to zap the stain. Which leads me to a pertinent question. Why do witches have broomsticks? Can't they just raw-will the dirt away?

Two hours later Miri opens my door. 'I got it.'

'Don't you knock?'

'Don't you want me to get rid of you-know-who?'

I'm stretched across my pink carpet, doing my maths homework. The carpet used to be orange before Tigger managed to bring fleas back from wherever he runs to when we hold the door open too long. At first, we didn't even know we had fleas. All we wondered was why we had small red bites around our ankles. The whole experience was pretty vile. Anyway, the exterminator left my blinds open by mistake and the sun bleached my carpet. Now my room fully clashes. I have a sherbet orange dresser, duvet and desk, and a candyfloss carpet. The various pairs of jeans and sweaters that hang over every available item of furniture don't help the decor.

Miri shuts the door behind her. She presses her finger against her lips as a warning to be quiet, as Mom is in the kitchen cooking spaghetti and tofu balls. Miri sits down next to me, the book in her lap.

'You figured it out?' I ask, excitement rising. 'Did you figure out a popularity spell too?'

'Forget about your cool spell for now, OK? I'm concentrating on Dad's issue. And I half figured it out. Since we can't put an anti-love spell on Dad, we have to use a spell that will make him realize how awful STB is so he'll fall out of love with her on his own.'

Perfecto. 'What kind of spell?'

She shrugs. 'That's all I got.'

'That's it?'

'I had homework, and tae kwon do to practise too,' she huffs. 'Besides, I can't come up with *all* the ideas.'

Now is not the time to argue. 'Well . . . what can STB do that can make Dad stop wanting her? What if she robs a bank?'

'Should I wish for a pistol or a machine gun?' Miri gives me a you-left-your-brain-at-school look. 'I'm trying to make the world a better place, not more dangerous.'

Maybe that was a bit much. I rub my thumbs against my temples. 'Let's think. What does he see in her?'

'He's attracted to evil?'

'Get real, Miri. He's attracted to her looks. Those eyes, that skin, the smile . . .'

Miri claps. 'That's it! We hit her with an ugly spell.'

'But is Dad that superficial?'

'He must be,' Miri says. 'What else could he possibly like about her? He's blinded by her—' she pretends to gag '—beauty, and he can't see what an evil person she is. The spell will cast her in a new light. We're looking after his best interests. What happens when she gets old and her face sags? Is he going to get divorced? If he's re-marrying, he has to love the woman for who she is inside, right?'

Wow. That was some speech. 'Right.'

'So, let's do it,' she continues excitedly. 'I saw something that might work.' She flips frantically through the book. 'Here it is. It's called the Mask of Repulsion. Sounds good, huh? Let's make a list of the ingredients we need.' She jumps up, ready for action.

Does having magical powers excite Miri? Oh, no. But making a list? Be still my heart!

'Mir, we don't have to do it this second,' I say, remembering my maths homework. 'We're not going back to Dad's until next weekend.'

She narrows her eyes. 'Do you think it's going to be easy to locate these ingredients? I don't have a clue what *Taraxacum officinale* is. And we have to practise.'

Scratch, scratch. Scratch, scratch. *Miaow*. 'Your groupie is trying to scratch his way into my room,' I say. Wait a sec. 'Who are you practising on?'

She winks at me.

Is she crazy? 'No way! You are *not* using me as your ugly-spell dummy. I can't be A-list looking like an ogre!'

She opens the door a crack, and Tigger dashes inside and plops himself directly on A^2.

The halogen bulb in my brain flicks on and I see my next play. 'I understand that you're nervous,' I say, backpedalling. 'You could turn STB into a tree by mistake. So . . . why don't you practise doing another spell on me? Like say, perhaps, a popularity spell.'

She waves her arms like white flags in defeat. 'All right, fine. Whatever you want. I'll find you a popularity spell. But, for the record, you're being pathetic.'

Touchdown! 'Yes, I'm pathetic. Pathetically happy!'

'And,' she says, smiling, 'you're going to owe me. Big.'

Ah, the witch turns mercenary. Isn't that always the case? 'What do you want?'

She whips out a typed list from the spell book. Apparently, she's been waiting for just the right moment to spring it on me. 'For the next two weeks you will, one, set the table and clear the dishes.' My mother has us on an alternating schedule of setting and clearing the table, so we're both only supposed to have to do one each day. I wonder if dear old Mom will notice if I take over both duties. Probably not. 'Two,' Miri says, 'you're on trash duty.'

'Sure, sure, whatever.' It's not as if anyone can tell whether I recycle properly. I can cut a few corners without her catching me.

'And you can't cut any corners with the recycling.'

I give her the evil eye (essentially squinting with my right eye while raising my left eyebrow) to ward off future mind-intrusion spells. 'I'm on to you.'

She ignores me. 'Three, you have to come with me to the peace rally on March twentieth in Washington Square.'

'Can't Mom take you?'

'I'd rather go with *you*. It'll be fun,' she pleads.

'I doubt it.' I hate rallies. My mother has dragged me to a slew of them. All you do is stand there and freeze your butt off. 'You sure you don't want me to take you shopping? We can go to Bloomie's. I'll buy you that every-day-of-the-week underwear you've always wanted,' I add, dangling the only carrot I can come up with under the circumstances.

'Peace rally. Final offer.'

Any way you add it up, it's worth it. 'Deal.'

We shake on it. Hip, hip, hooray! I'm going to be popular! I do a little victory dance.

'Don't do that. You look like you're drowning.'

Humph.

'And you can't ever tell Mom we traded,' she adds.

Is she nuts? 'We can't tell her about any of this. She'd

turn us both into frogs. Or cats.' I nudge Tigger with my foot. 'Maybe she had another daughter before me. And she did magic. And Mom turned her into a cat. A male cat, just to be mean.'

Tigger miaows.

'Why would she turn her into a male cat only to have her neutered?' Miri asks.

'Girls!' my mother hollers from the kitchen. 'Time to set the table!'

It's Monday and therefore . . . my turn. But it's worth it. Every time I doubt that, I'll just think of my name at the top of the A-list.

Tigger follows me into the kitchen and almost trips me while I'm taking the plates down from the shelf. Hmm. Who knows? What if I wasn't far off about Tigger? What if he really used to be human and was cursed by my great-grandmother to spend eternity as a not-too-bright feline? Creepy. Especially considering how many times the perv has watched me change.

My mother licks tomato sauce off a wooden spoon while she checks the garlic bread in the oven and stirs the pasta. When she makes dinner, she looks like the Tasmanian Devil. She's an excellent multitasker. She's the same at work. I've seen her type, fix the jammed fax machine, make coffee and book a trip to Costa Rica on the phone simultaneously. And that's without using magic. Imagine if she did – her clients would all have sunny, turbulence-free vacations. She's crazy for not using it. What's the point? Why not? Why not be happy? Why not have a perfect life?

When she was married to my dad, she used to take better care of herself. She used to get manicures and visit the hair salon. Now that she's so busy working, she seems to have decided that she'd rather spend the energy on her new agency, and on us of course, rather than on what she looks like. But why shouldn't she have it all? 'Mom,' I blurt out, 'why not use your magic to have great hair?'

'Why are there black smudges all over my kitchen walls?' she asks.

'Tigger's been acting up.'

Tigger miaows, wraps his body around my leg and tries to bite me. Bet you wish you were still life-sized so you could tell on me, big sis (or evil nemesis of my great-grandmother).

'Bad Tigger,' my mother scolds, waving the wooden spoon at him. 'Will you clean him off? He must have stepped into mud on the stairwell. And I told you,' she says, and waves the wooden spoon at me, 'magic isn't a game, Rachel. I won't use it unless it's absolutely necessary.'

You'd *think* saving her marriage to my dad would have been absolutely necessary, wouldn't you? Maybe it's minor in the grand scheme of witchcraft, but still. You'd better believe I would have kept him around. (And poofed him up some hair and clothes from this decade.)

I open my mouth to tell her what a mess she's made of our lives, but then close it. Because it seems kind of stupid. Why am I angry at her when my dad's the one who left? Because she could have stopped him and she didn't? It's his fault. He should have stopped himself from leaving.

I pick Tigger up and carry him to the bathroom. He starts circling the sink as I turn on the water. Cats hate water, right? Not Tigger. He'll jump into the toilet bowl if it's open. He's also been known to dig his teeth into the end of the toilet paper and make a run for it, tee-peeing the living room, kitchen and all three bedrooms.

I know I keep joking that he used to be human and female, but it might be true. What if Mom meant to put a prosperity spell on us, and it went horribly wrong? Maybe tee-peeing our apartment is her – now his – revenge. What if Miri's currently unknown popularity spell goes wrong? What if I become Tigger's feline emasculated pal?

I take a deep breath to calm myself down. That's what we learned in gym today – deep breathing. Miri won't screw up. Inhale. She won't. Exhale. The yoga's not working. I bet the technique is only for people living in rural areas with fresh air.

I wash Tigger's already clean paws (thankfully my mother didn't check them) in the sink, then let him down. As soon as his feet hit the ground, he lunges for the toilet paper, bites into the end and makes a run for it out the door. Stupid cat.

I hope my younger sister has more sense than my older one.

7

Two Boys Are Better Than One

A week later, I'm in the middle of a truly fantastic dream in which Mick and Raf are fighting over me at Spring Fling, in a *Matrix*-y slow-motion battle with lots of 360 turns and backflips, when I feel a poking in my cheek.

I open one eye. Miri is hovering over me, shoving her index finger into my face. I close the eye. 'Do you mind?'

'Trying to wake you,' she whispers.

No kidding. I open the eye and see that the clock says 5:07. 5:07! Did she bump her head on a cauldron? 'Why are you waking me at five-oh-seven?'

'Here, take this,' she says, and shoves something into my mouth.

I sit up, suddenly energized. 'Is that my popularity potion?'

'No. A breath mint.'

Humph. 'If you don't like my morning breath, don't wake me in the morning. Or in this case, the middle of the night.'

'Do you want me to make you a spell or not?'

Yum, peppermint. 'So, lay it on me. What did you find?'

She shakes her head. 'I don't think I'll be able to do a popularity spell.'

'What? You promised!' I kick my duvet off and sling my feet over the side of the bed. What kind of witch is she? She can't do an anti-love spell, and she can't do a popularity spell. She can't even do a spell that will take care of chores – why else would she have to make that deal with me? What good is being a witch if she can't do anything fun? 'I don't appreciate you waking me in the middle of the night for no reason except to give me more under-eye circles.'

Miri takes a step back and pouts. 'It's not my fault. There is a popularity spell, sort of, and it's only two brooms, but it would need me putting dried cinnamon into the entire student body's water supply. I don't have a clue how to do that.'

'That does sound tricky,' I admit, scooting over. Miri sits down next to me.

'We don't want to get caught putting anything in the Manhattan water supply.'

'True.' I sigh with disappointment. 'So what now? Nothing?' Are my dreams over?

'That's the best way for mass popularity. The other way is to collect hairs or nail clippings from everyone in the school—'

'Seems unlikely.' I can't see myself running through the halls with hair and nail scissors. Unless I opened up a makeshift salon in the cafeteria and offered free manicures and haircuts. As if people would let me near them with scissors. Anyone who went to middle school with me would remember the time Jewel and I decided to get rid of our fringes and I played barber. Not a pretty sight. 'There must be another way.'

'I found a love spell, if you want to try that instead.'

Now we're thinking. 'Tell me more.'

'It's only three brooms. And all I'd need are a few minor ingredients.'

That could so work! Awesome! If Mick or Raf falls for me, not only will one of the Loves of My Life be my boyfriend, but I'll become A-list by default. Yes! 'How long does it last?'

'I'm not sure. A few months, tops.'

'Maybe by the time it wears off, he'll be madly in love with me, anyway. He'll realize I'm smart and fun and cute and—'

'Full of yourself?'

Ha ha. 'By the time it wears off, at least I'll be firmly rooted in the A-list.' This is an outstanding plan. Instead of becoming popular to have a boyfriend, I'll get a boyfriend to become popular.

I bounce on the bed and let out a scream.

'Shhh,' Miri whispers, and tugs at my ankle. 'Mom will kill us both if we wake her up. We were up really late last night doing my training.'

'Oh yeah. How did that go?'

'Great. Do you know that witchcraft has been around for over twenty-five thousand years? When there were cavemen, there were witches. Later this week we're going to talk about the spread of witches across Mesopotamia and then Europe . . .'

My eyelids start to feel like bricks, and I lie down. 'You're putting me back to sleep here.'

'Sorry. Oh yeah, the reason I woke you up was to tell

you that if you want to do a love spell, you have to buy some yogurt and borrow something that belongs to your guy. Like a piece of clothing.'

Oh, is that all? 'How am I going to do that?'

She shrugs and climbs in beside me. I move over so she can share my pillow.

'Tell him you're cold and ask to borrow his sweater,' she says.

Sweet, naive Miri. 'Why, hello, Raf. Chilly today, isn't it? Would you mind taking off that woolly sweater?' He'd think I was a psycho. Although . . . within a week he'd be in love with me anyway, so maybe it doesn't matter. But a pencil would be easier. That I could swipe when he's not paying attention. 'Can it be a pencil? Or a notebook?'

She sighs. 'Rachel, what happened when you didn't have the right ingredients to make chocolate brownies and you made them anyway? Remember when you used baking soda instead of flour? And they tasted like sawdust?'

'True.' But has anyone eaten sawdust? For all we know, it's delicious and tastes like brownies. Or not. 'Guess we shouldn't take chances on this first one.'

'We don't want to end up with the pencil falling in love with you. Or writing on you.' She giggles.

I giggle too. 'Or turning me into a pencil.' I do love the feeling of a newly sharpened number two poised over a maths quiz, though.

We pull the covers over our heads so we won't wake our mother. I can't believe I convinced Miri to put a love spell on anyone. She must be really antsy to test out her magic wings.

At 7:02, I wake up freezing, with sunlight spearing my

81

eyelids. I open one eye and see Miri waving her hands at my window, her eyes closed and her lips pursed.

'What are you doing?' I ask. The left side of my blind is pulled up and the right side is hanging diagonally, still covering the window.

'Using magic to open your blinds. But I screwed up and now one half is stuck.'

She's more antsy than I thought. She'd better figure out what she's doing before it's my turn to go under the wand.

In homeroom, I vary the plan slightly. Why have just one boy fall in love with me when I can have two? If I can get my hands on clothing belonging to Mick and Raf, then they'll both fall head over heels in love and, just like in my dream, they'll fight over me. How romantic! I'll open my locker and find two love notes. They'll both want to help me with my coat, so I'll let each of them remove one sleeve. Mick will piggyback me to class while Raf carries my books.

When the bell rings, I hurry back to the second floor so I can stalk the boys and analyse their attire for something to steal. Raf's locker is right by Mr Silver's classroom. I spot Raf's handsome frame as he snaps his locker closed and heads to class. He's wearing a blue button-down shirt, jeans, a brown belt and brown shoes. I nibble my lip. If he were wearing a sweatshirt, maybe he'd take it off, but a shirt? I don't think so. And I can't think of any reason he would take off his jeans or belt. Unless he has gym this afternoon. Yes, gym! I can break into the boys' locker room after he's changed and . . . I'll get caught and the entire school will think I'm a perv. If only Miri could whip me up one of those Harry Potter invisibility cloaks.

No, wait, I've got it! I can just borrow his gym clothes from his locker. Brilliant! All I need to do is catch him opening his locker and scope out his combination.

I miss him after second and third periods, and then I finally spot him in action just before lunch. Freshmen and sophomores have lunch from eleven to eleven forty-five. Tell me, who's hungry at eleven? It's ridiculous. That's why I'm looking forward to junior year. Not because I'll get my licence. Not because of prom. Because I can't wait to eat at twelve like a normal person.

Anyway, Janice, Annie Banks and Sherry Dollan are congregating by Tammy's locker. They all know each other from middle school, where they were a foursome. Now it's Annie and Sherry, me and Tammy, and Janice is kind of on her own.

'I'm starving,' Annie says, peering into her lunch bag. Annie is in our homeroom class, but always sits next to the door, because she supposedly has an extra small bladder and has to go to the bathroom at least once every class. She also has long brown hair and the biggest breasts I've ever seen. Honestly, they must be at least a triple-D. At the moment, she's wearing a red turtleneck, and they look like two beach balls. If only she could share the wealth.

Sherry's in our English class and is Annie's best friend. 'Hi-ee girls!' she says now, while chewing a lock of her blonde hair. 'How is your day-ee?'

Her tendency to add the sound *ee* to every word gets ver-ee annoying. And the fact that she sucks on her curls grosses me out. But she is very friendly and has decent opinions in class. So I try to overlook these things.

I focus on Raf. All he has to do is move over a little and I'll see his locker. Come on, Raf. Your wide manly shoulders are blocking my view! He snaps the lock open and I've missed my chance. He puts on his jacket, gloves and hat. Maybe he'll drop a glove on his way out for lunch and then, presto, my work here is done.

Raf goes out for lunch a lot. And it's never with other fashion-show people. He's also friends with some football players and some sophomores who are in a band called Illuminated. Such random friends.

Tammy and I never go out for lunch. We always eat with Annie, Sherry and Janice in the cafeteria, on the left side of the room, fourth table from the back.

Until I can sit with the A-list (table at the back near the window), this crew will have to do. Not that I'd drop Tammy. I would do my best to make sure she'd have a seat right beside me. Jewel on my left, Tammy on my right and Raf and Mick directly across from me. A trapezoid of happiness.

Raf manages to hold on to his gloves. And then the redheaded, ever-annoying Melissa blocks his path and whispers something to him. If only I had superhuman hearing. Is that too much to ask? One measly power?

He says something, and Melissa points down the hall at three other A-list fashion-show girls, who are buzzing around, manicured hands waving. In my steal-clothes excitement, I've missed whatever crisis is taking place in fashion-show land. Last week the Eiffel Tower that the student set designers were building cracked in half and the cast members were all in a tizzy. The theme is Citygroove, which means that each number will feature a different city. According to Jewel, the Eiffel Tower is for the freshman and sophomore formal-wear number. The song is 'Come What May' from *Moulin Rouge*.

I'm distracted again when Mick saunters through the hallway. He's wearing jeans and an untucked sweater. I follow him so I can see better. He approaches his locker, places his fingers on the lock, slowly turns the dial . . . seven . . . twenty-two . . . eighteen . . . bingo!

Seven, twenty-two, eighteen! Seven, twenty-two, eighteen. Seven, twenty-two, eighteen. Seven, twenty-two, eighteen. Why don't I have a notepad to scribble this on? Seven, twenty-two, eighteen. I open my locker, rip out my geometry textbook and write the combination on the cover.

Yes!

'Rachel?' Tammy asks, linking her arm through mine. 'When you're finished stalking, do you want to come for lunch?'

Busted. 'I was just—'

She laughs. 'Daydreaming. I know. He's hot. But I'm starving.'

Since I can't confide in her, I nod and secretly plot my next move. I'll have to take five minutes during class, when the hallway is empty, sneak back here, borrow Mick's hat or his puke-green gym shirt, hide it in my locker and then run back to class. The obvious choice is to miss English, since I'm in advanced and therefore supposedly know what I'm doing.

But French is boring.

I can barely keep my eyes open.

One of the reasons French is so boring is that I have no friends in the class. Tammy and Janice are in accelerated; Jewel and Sherry are in Spanish. Annie is in regular too, but she's in another class.

'*Je parle, tu parles, il ou elle parle, nous parlons . . .,*' Doree Matson recites. As usual, she's sitting in the front row and answering all the questions.

When she finally gets to the end of her conjugation, I decide it's now or never. '*Excusez-moi, je dois aller à la toilette.*' I hear a few titters from the peanut gallery in the front. They're so childish. I hope I didn't ask if I could pee on the floor.

Did I?

Madame Diamon nods and asks if anyone would like to conjugate *parler* in the conditional tense.

Doree raises her hand.

As I exit the class, I wonder what it's like to teach a language all day that no one understands. To have to listen to people sounding like morons. Staring at you as if you're not making sense. Asking if they can pee on the floor. I couldn't ever become a second-language teacher. Partly because I barely speak a second language. But mostly because I don't think I could teach.

Not that I have a clue what I *do* want to be. A businesswoman? A rocket scientist? I don't know what a rocket scientist does, but how fun would that be? To say you're a rocket scientist. 'It's not rocket science,' a sexy stranger at a cocktail party would say. I'd lean in closer, allowing him an eyeful of my extraordinary cleavage (this is way down the line, so glistening cleavage is very plausible, if not likely). 'Actually,' I'd say, 'I *am* a rocket scientist,' and gasps would ensue. *Mon dieu!*

Must concentrate on covert mission. James Bond music plays in the background. I really should have worn all black today instead of jeans, an orange sweater and sparkling green shoes. How un-covert can I get?

I skip down the stairs from the third floor. First stop, my locker. I need my geometry book. (When this spell is done, I should ask Miri to find one to improve my memory. I'd better write that down in case I forget.) Hmm. I probably should have noted which locker is Mick's. They all look the same. Metal and narrow.

I close my eyes and try to remember where he stood. Four to the left. No, five to the left. Six. Definitely six. This would be so much easier if I were a witch. I could purse my lips and make his locker glow.

I purse my lips. *Make the right locker glow!*

Nothing glows.

Must remember. I think I was right the first time. Four to the left. I peer down the hall to make sure no one is coming. All clear. Peer down the other side. Also clear.

I look at my textbook and see the seven, twenty-two, eighteen, then position myself in front of the fourth locker to the left. Here we go. I take a big breath and turn the dial to the right. Seven. Left, twenty-two. And then a quick eighteen. And . . .

No go.

I turn to the right. Seven. Left, and around once for good luck. Twenty-two. And then a slower eighteen. And . . . nope.

Maybe it was the fifth locker over and not the fourth. If only my brain were like a TiVo and I could skip back to the last episode. I try the fifth locker. And then the next one. And the next one. And the entire row. It isn't working. I need to concentrate.

I slide to the floor, rest my head against the locker behind me and breathe just like we learned in gym. In. Out. In. Out. Am I turning too fast? Do I have the wrong code? Why isn't my plan working? Why is it so hard to steal a piece of clothing? Maybe I'll tell Mick that I'm doing a project on shoes and that I need to borrow his. Or maybe I'll stand really close behind him and cut out a piece from the back of his sweater. It wasn't tucked in. He'll think he caught it in a door. Yes, that's what I'll do. I'll try to catch him when the bell rings. But right now I'm tired. So very tired. It's Miri's fault for waking me up so early. Maybe I'll just close my eyes for a second. They're so heavy. Yes, that feels good.

The next thing I know, I'm being tapped on the shoulder.

I open my eyes to see Mr Earls, JFK's vice principal, looming over me.

'Taking a nap?' he asks. His eyebrows are too close together, like Bert from *Sesame Street*. I've seen him at assemblies and lurking in the hallway corners before, but I've never had the pleasure of being this close to him until now.

'Just thinking,' I say. 'I'm on my way back to class. Sorry, sir.'

'There will be no thinking in the hallway on my watch. And I don't think you were thinking. I think you were napping. And skipping class.' He scribbles something on his notepad and throws it at me. 'Detention today after school. You can think then. But no napping.'

What? Detention? Me? I've never had detention before. Ever. 'Oh, please, sir. I was only here for two seconds.'

'Do you want detention again tomorrow? That's what you get for arguing with me.'

Gulp. Someone's on a power trip.

Blinking back tears, I walk to French. Mr Earls doesn't realize who he's messing with. One day I'll have magical powers and then he's so going to be morphed into a cat. A neutered cat. Yes, Mr Earls, do you understand? One day people will call you Fluffy.

As I return to my lonely seat in the back of the class, I feel a heaviness inside my lungs, like when I wake up some mornings and realize that Tigger is sitting on my chest. Life is so unfair. My mom has magical powers. Miri has magical powers and boobs. My dad has STB. Jewel is popular and has a new best friend. Tammy has . . . well, Tammy has Sherry, Janice and Annie.

And I have nothing. Nothing at all. Nothing . . . but detention.

8
Detained

I am such a detention novice that I don't even know where to go.

I head to the school office on the first floor. 'Excuse me.' I address the secretary. She's staring at her computer screen and doesn't appear to notice me. 'Where do I go for detention?' Is it like prison work? Do they chain us evil-doers together and force us to mop the gym? Repaint the halls?

'Room one-oh-four,' she says without looking at me. 'Next to the events board.'

I was hoping she'd cry out, 'Rachel Weinstein? A sweet freshman like you couldn't possibly have done anything to deserve this awful punishment! Don't be silly! Whoever gave you detention will be dismissed from his post! Go home and don't worry your sweet self for one more minute!'

I guess I'm dreaming. She wouldn't know who I was unless she checked out the trophy case outside the office. When I ranked second at the maths competition, I had mixed feelings about my placement being showcased. On the one hand, anyone who passes it will see my engraved

90

name. On the other hand, winning maths competitions is more likely to be the ticket to a *Star Trek* convention than to the kingdom of coolness. But I quickly realized that it didn't matter. My name is barely even visible. The trophy was shoved into the back, behind the bowling club's trophy. Yes, the bowling club. I would have assumed a maths competition would be considered worthier than a bowling match at a high school, but what do I know?

Anyway, the secretary doesn't know who I am. She doesn't care that I'm not the type of girl to get detention. Not that I can blame her. I don't know her name either. 'And, um . . . what am I supposed to do in detention?' I ask.

'Homework.'

I slither towards Room 104. Boring. The only thing keeping up my spirits is the possibility of a supremely hot rebel guy sitting near me in detention, à la the eighties movie *The Breakfast Club*. I'll be Molly Ringwald, all princessy and serene, and he'll be Judd Nelson, with that who-cares attitude. He'll be wearing ripped jeans and a stashed cigarette behind his ear. At first we won't speak. We'll just eye each other. And then he'll say something rebel-ish, like, 'Do you think we can smoke in here?'

I'll say, 'I don't smoke.' And then before the hour of detention is over, we'll be hooking up. I'm not quite sure how we'll get from my retort to the hooking up, but I'll let him figure it out since I've already done more than my share of the planning.

I hold my breath and open the door. Except for a scrawny teacher I recognize from the science department, the desks and chairs are empty. He looks up from his grading. 'You're Rachel?'

At least someone knows my name. I sit down in the back row. 'Yup.' I watch the front door for the rebel. I keep watching. Five minutes later, I raise my hand. The skinny teacher is scribbling all over the paper of some poor student and doesn't notice. I wave again. I'd like to call out, but I don't want to get another detention. I cough. Loudly.

He looks up, annoyed. 'Yes?'

'I was wondering where everyone else was.'

'You're it.' He looks back down at his papers.

I'm it? I was JFK's worst student today? The biggest school rule that was broken in the last twenty-four hours was no napping in the hall? Where are the drugs? The weapons? The kids who skip class? The rebel caught smoking in the bathroom, who still has the audacity to stash a cigarette behind his ear?

Bet this Mr Science Teacher hates me. If it weren't for my detention, he'd already be at home in his pyjamas.

La, la, la.

I would have closed the door if I had thought I was the only one coming. I wonder if I'll get a bad-girl rep if anyone sees me in here. I'll have to dye my hair pink and get a tongue ring.

In an attempt to suck up, I pull my bio homework out of my schoolbag. We have an assignment due on Friday.

Twenty minutes later there's a rustling of voices outside the door. 'They're not going to be able to find anyone,' a girl's voice says.

'But we have no choice,' says someone else. Someone who sounds like . . . Jewel?

'Putting these posters up is such a waste of my time.'

If I were just a fraction further up, I'd be able to see

them. I try to covertly scoot my desk up an inch. Nope. Another inch. One more. Five more.

Science Man glares at me.

I smile.

I spot Melissa's long red hair. Melissa and Jewel are outside my detention room.

'Stop whining, Bee-Bee,' Jewel says.

Bee-Bee? *Bee-Bee?* I feel nauseous.

'If they weren't good enough to get in the first time, they're not good enough to get in now,' Melissa snaps.

What are they talking about? The *click-clack* of their shoes tells me they're about to pass my door, and I quickly scoot my desk backwards so they won't see me.

I must see that poster.

The remaining thirty-five minutes of detention takes at least three hours. Finally, *finally*, the hands of the clock above the door say 4:00. Freedom! I grab my bag and launch myself like a rocket from the chair into the empty hallway. In the distance I hear the muffled voices of students with far more energy than I have.

As soon as I see the poster, I feel giddy, fizzy, like a soda can that someone shook and opened.

FRESHMAN FASHION-SHOW
REPLACEMENT DANCER
NEEDED TRYOUTS FRIDAY
AFTER SCHOOL IN THE CAF
CITYGROOVE

So that's the crisis. Someone dropped out. Or broke a leg. They're missing a dancer. Whoever the new dancer is, she'll receive automatic A-list status. She'll be able to hang around Jewel. She'll be able to hang around Raf. She'll definitely have a date for Spring Fling.

My heart pounds in my chest. I want to be in the fashion show. I want to have automatic A-list status. I want to hang out with Jewel and Raf. I want to be so cool that I don't have to capitalize.

I'm going to try out.

I clap with glee and do my hooray dance (which looks a lot like my victory dance) in honour of my new plan. In mid-twirl I trip and fall on my behind.

So what if I have six left feet and the show is primarily a dance show?

I know someone with a cure.

9

Rub-a-dub-dub, Green Slime in My Tub

I poke my head into Miri's room. 'Are you finished yet?'

She throws her pencil case at me and nails me on the head. Since she's started martial arts, her aim is much improved. 'If you'd stop harassing me every four seconds, I would be. Can't you just sit on the bed and wait?'

'Miri, it's been two days. The tryouts are *tomorrow*.' I close her door behind me so Mom won't see the trouble we're brewing in here. And I mean brewing, literally. Between Miri's smelly feet is a white plastic bowl. They make her go barefoot in tae kwon do, and I wouldn't let her waste any time showering until she finished the spell. 'What are you doing now?' I ask.

'Mixing.' She's sitting on her deep-green carpet, leaning against her bed.

The blinds are closed. Wow, she's even more paranoid than I am. Does she really think the sixty-year-old woman and her eight cats who live directly across from us care what we're up to?

Funny, the neighbourhood watch would definitely peg her as a witch before Miri.

I peek over the bowl's edge to see what she has going on. The mixture is a weird orangey green. 'You're using the popcorn bowl? Gross.'

'This *was* the popcorn bowl. It's now a cauldron.'

'Guess I'll be having chips for a snack tonight. You should probably buy a new popcorn bowl.'

'You get it, then. I'm doing this for you, in case you've forgotten.' She points to the spell book. 'I need you to help with something. What is eighteen twenty-fourths of a cup?'

'Three-quarters,' I answer automatically.

'Perfect.' She fills her mixing cup with some sort of crushed fruit. 'The spell book is like a deranged maths test with all these fractions.'

I take a sniff. Yum. 'It smells like an orange.'

'It is. And a cup of crushed pistachios and two-fourths of a cup of butter, which is a half, right?'

I nod. I got the maths gene while she got the magic gene. Not fair.

'And,' she says, dumping in the final cup, 'ground red pepper.'

Hmm. That actually sounds tasty. I do love pistachios. 'Need any more help?'

'I'll call you when it's ready.'

I find my maths homework. I'm suddenly in the mood.

While I'm clearing the table after dinner (of course I'm clearing the table – these days I'm always setting or clearing the table. 'Where's Rachel? She must be in the kitchen setting or clearing the table'), Miri sneaks up behind me. 'It's done,' she whispers, and hands me the bowl, which is now greenish brown.

'Am I supposed to eat this?'

She laughs. Actually, it's more like a cackle. Something I've noticed as part of her repertoire lately. 'Only if you want major indigestion.'

Witch humour? 'So what do I do with it?'

'Bathe in it.'

'Are you insane?'

She puts her hands on her hips. 'That's the dancing spell. If you don't want to do it, don't.'

'I'm just kidding, Mir,' I say, feeling guilty for giving her a hard time. 'Thank you. I appreciate your cooking it up for me.'

'You're welcome. Want to test it out?'

I smile. 'Definitely. So that's all I have to do? Bathe in it?'

'Yup.'

'Do you think Mom will wonder why I'm taking a bath for the first time since I was six?'

Worry clouds her face. 'Good question. What should we do?'

I have a plan. I finish putting the dishes into the dishwasher, then knock on Mom's door. She's under her covers, her face peeking out, reading a romance novel. My mother loves romance novels. I think she's waiting for Prince Charming to magically appear.

She *could* have him magically appear if she wanted to. Just poof him up. Tall, strong and a cleft in his chin. Why not, huh? What's wrong with her?

'Mom,' I say, 'can I take one of your pills? The robo whatever? My back is killing me.'

97

She rests her book against her stomach and waves me over. For a second I think she's on to me, but then she asks, 'Did you pick up something too heavy?'

'Um . . . yeah. My desk.' Why in the world would I pick up my desk? I am useless at coming up with believable lies.

She sighs. 'Rachel, you only get one back in life.'

'Thanks for the advice, Mom,' I say in my earnest voice. Under normal circumstances I would make fun of her for being such a cheeseball.

'The pills are in my medicine cabinet.' She resumes her reading.

'Thanks.' And now for the epiphany/performance of a lifetime . . . hands caressing back . . . eyes light up with an idea . . . eureka! 'Wait a sec. Do you think taking a bath would help my extremely sore back muscles?'

'Good idea,' she says, already lost on a beach with Prince Charming and no longer paying attention.

Mission accomplished. I back out of the room, making sure to close the door behind me, and then I run back to Miri.

'All set. Pass me the bubbles.'

'They're not bubbles,' she says, and hands me the pop-corn bowl.

I open the bathroom door and try to shut it behind me. She pokes in her hand.

'Do you mind?' I ask.

'I have to come in with you.'

'I prefer my privacy.'

She crosses her arms in front of her chest. 'Without my incantation you're just bathing in fruit salad.'

I let her in. 'Lock the door. And stay quiet. If Mom sees

98

you're in here, she'll know something's up.' I sniff. 'Gross. It smells like smoke. She's been smoking in here again. Why does she think she can hide it from us? It's so obvious.'

Miri shrugs. I don't know why she doesn't care about the smoke as much as I do. She never has. I was the one who used to cry myself to sleep because I was convinced my mom would die of lung cancer. I was the one who, when I was seven, found a pack of her cigarettes that she was hiding from my dad and broke each one in half and flushed them down the toilet. Miri never gets mad at Mom. They're always on the same page. I'm more like my dad. Maybe that's why I never get mad at him. How can I get mad at someone who's just like me?

'What do we do for the spell?' I ask.

'We fill the tub with water, add the mixture, then I recite the spell.'

I turn on the hot water. Miri shakes her head and twists the knob. 'The spell book says the water must be cold. Probably written before indoor plumbing and hot-water tanks.'

'I'm supposed to sit in a freezing cold bath in the middle of winter?'

Miri shrugs. 'That's the spell.'

I'm going to get sick for sure. 'Let's get this over with.'

She sits on the edge of the closed toilet seat and opens her spell book. Then she dumps the concoction into the bathwater and waves her hands over the tub.

I pass her my toothbrush. 'Do you want to use this as a wand?'

She shakes her brown hair. 'No.'

'Maybe a pointy hat? I can make one out of the tissue box.'

'What I need,' she says, 'is for you to be quiet so I can concentrate and access my raw will.' She closes her eyes, purses her lips and gets a constipated look on her face. After a few moments of quiet (as quiet as you can get in New York, with the constant honking and car alarms in the background), I feel the familiar cold rush as Miri chants:

> *From Heaven to Earth,*
> *From America to France,*
> *Let this potion*
> *Make Rachel dance!*

She opens one eye and peers at the water.

'You've got to be kidding me.' I burst out laughing. 'That's the spell?'

'That's what it says.'

'That's the worst spell I've ever heard! Ever hear of alliteration? And it barely even rhymes. No Pulitzer for whoever wrote that one. And how come you didn't say abracadabra?'

She gnaws on her thumbnail. 'Will you just get in the bath?'

'Can you leave now?'

'I've seen you naked a million times. We've taken baths together since we were born.'

'First of all, Mom will find it odd if we're both in here. Second, there are some things you stop doing as you mature,' I say haughtily. 'Such as biting your nails, for example.'

'Fine, I'll leave if you're going to be such a baby.'

'How long do I have to stay in here?'

'At least a half-hour,' she snarls, slamming the door.

I lock the door behind her and then undress. I decide to start small. I hesitate before dipping my right big toe in. Ahh! It's colder than snow. I take a deep yoga breath and drop my entire foot in. Ahhh! I whip it back out and then thrust it back in. Ahhhh! Does the thirty minutes count from now or from when I'm immersed? Slowly I put both feet into the water. And then my calves. And then my knees, my thighs, my butt, my stomach, my non-existent breasts. Teeth are chattering. Lips shaking. Fingers turning blue. My skin is tingling as if it's asleep, but I can't tell if it's from the spell or the frigid temperature. The water looks as if it's been mixed with green slime, and it feels sandy against my skin. Am I supposed to dunk my head? I want my head to have rhythm. I want to be able to swing my hair side to side. I'd better do it. I dunk, keeping my eyes tightly closed.

Cough, cough. Sputter, sputter. Oops. I bet I was supposed to close my mouth.

Miri pounds on the door. 'You OK?'

Cough, sputter. 'What happens if I swallowed some by mistake? Will my colon do the Macarena?'

'You'll be fine. You can get out now, if you dunked your whole body.'

'I thought I was supposed to soak for thirty minutes.'

'I lied. You were being annoying.'

I quickly rinse off, bolt out of the bathtub and grab a towel. When my shivering subsides, I empty the grossness out of the bath, rinse it out and return to my room and my sweats. Then I pull my hair into a bun and tie up my running shoes. I turn on the radio and position myself in front of the full-length mirror on my closet door. '*Me against the music . . .*'

When I try to do the Harlem shake, my shoulders wobble. Without rhythm. Like they always have. I try a body wave. Nothing. A simple butt groove?

Nope.

Abraca-rip-off! I storm out of my room and into Miri's. 'What's wrong? Why isn't it working?' My voice is rising and I'm starting to sound hysterical. I took the bath, didn't I? I can still feel pistachio remnants where the sun don't shine. What else must I be subjected to? What other indignities await? The madness must end.

Miri rolls her desk chair away from her computer and searches through A^2. 'I don't know . . . Maybe I didn't do it right . . .'

'Don't say that. What's going to happen to me? What if you made my arms become snakes, or elastics?'

'Hold on,' Miri says. 'There's a footnote. XI. Let me find XI . . .' She looks up at me. 'It says that the spell might take up to half a moon turn to take hold.'

'What does that mean? A half a month?'

'I think it's twelve hours.'

That's not too bad. It's eight now, so that means the spell will be up and kicking by tomorrow morning. 'Are there any other footnotes you forgot to read? Like how my skin turns to scales?'

'I don't think so. But guess what.'

'What?'

She rolls back to her computer desk. 'I just got another wedding update email from STB. This time telling us all about the song list.' She groans.

STB sends out weekly wedding updates to all of her

guests. About the caterer, the flowers, the anticipated weather. Like anyone cares. All they do is clog our in-boxes.

I check my own email on my computer. I don't even bother opening the wedding emails; they go right into the trash. Jewel still hasn't emailed me back about the last email I sent her, two weeks ago. Tammy's on IM, so I instant message with her for a half-hour, then decide just to call her.

'What's up?' she asks. I imagine her giving me the scuba thumbs-up.

'Nothing.' I wish I could tell her!

'The bio assignment took me forever.'

Whoops. Forgot to finish that one. After the call I return to my desk, and then at ten thirty I decide to hit the sheets early. Unfortunately, it takes me forever to fall asleep because I'm too excited. Just as I'm about to nod off, I give my behind a little shake to see if it's gotten its rhythm yet. Hard to tell.

At seven thirty the next morning, I bolt from bed. I shower, get fully dressed, flick the radio on and return to my spot in front of the mirror.

'*Me against the music . . .*' Again. I feel shivers down my back, like hundreds of ants have formed a conga line on my spine. That must be a sign. What are the chances of the same song being played?

So for the second time I try the Harlem shake. And my shoulders move. I mean *really* move. Then I try the body wave. And my body twists in a way it never could before. And then, finally, I shake my butt. And let me tell you, it gets down. All the way down. Touches the pink carpet, back up, and then back down again.

Oh. My. God. Omigod. My arms are flying, my head is soaring, my behind is grooving, and I do not look like I'm being electrocuted. I look like I know what I'm doing. Abracatastic!

'Miri!' I yell. 'Miri, come here!'

She runs into my room. I do the Macarena and even *that* looks good. She claps and jumps up and down. 'I can't believe it!' she shrieks. 'You can dance! And I did it!'

'Girls?' my mom asks from her marshmallow breakfast in the kitchen. 'OK in there?'

'Fine!' I say. 'Use your indoor voice,' I tell my sister. 'Be calm.'

But I can't be calm. Because I am good. So good. So good I could be the back-up dancer in a music video. Hey, I could *star* in a music video. 'How long does this spell last?'

'For good. Only emotion spells wear off.'

If it's me against the music, I'm kicking the music's sorry butt.

10
Rochelle/Rackelle/Ruth

Tammy keeps looking at me strangely, as if I'm wearing my jeans and scoop-neck black top inside out.

'What?' I ask as I moonwalk into world civ.

'What?' I ask as I moonwalk into world civ.

'Why are you jumping all over the place?'

I try to stop the rhythm flowing through my body, but it's tough. I'm like the Energizer Bunny. 'I'm not.'

'Yes, you are. You haven't sat still the entire day.' We claim two desks on the side of the room, right under the map of the ancient world that looks as if it may fall and smother us at any moment. 'Is everything all right?'

'Everything's terrific,' I drawl.

'Want to come over after school?'

'I can't. I have a *hmphsh*.' I mumble the last part and wipe my hand over my lips as if I'm removing a milk moustache.

'You have a what?' she asks.

'I'm trying out for the fashion show,' I admit.

Her mouth pops open 180 degrees, exposing her very narrow, very tall teeth. Her entire body is narrow, tall and straight. Except her nose, which is wide and a bit crooked.

Last month we tried to use some of my mom's make-up to shadow it, but she ended up looking as if someone had punched her. 'Why would you do that?' she asks.

'Because I want to be in the show?'

'No, you don't. You said that the show was elitist and materialistic and that it objectified women.'

'I never said that,' I lie. I may have said that. But that was when I couldn't dance and had zero shot of getting in.

She raises an eyebrow. 'So why didn't you try out last time?' It's amazing that Tammy can already see through me. We buddied up on the first day of ninth grade, when she warned me that I had a blue line on my face. Apparently, my new pen had leaked all over my hand and, unaware, I had scratched my upper lip. Would you believe, an exploding pen on the first day of high school, which led to a gorgeous Hitler moustache? Before our next class, Tammy led me to the bathroom and helped me scrub it until it was less noticeable. Slightly less noticeable, anyway.

'I've decided I need to get more exercise,' I say. 'To be healthy.'

Now she raises both eyebrows simultaneously. 'Healthy? Since when? You just polished off a movie-sized bag of M&M's after demolishing two slices of pepperoni pizza for lunch.'

What, does she keep records of everything I eat as well as say? 'And *that's* why I have to start working out.'

She shrugs. 'I didn't know you could dance.'

'Well, I can.' As of this morning.

'Lucky. I can't. But I'll watch you try out. For moral support. You know, Annie and Janice are trying out too.'

Yes, I know. They've been talking and practising all

week. I was trying to be low-key, so no one would ask me to show them my moves until I was magic-ready.

Annie's bustline hasn't helped my self-esteem. I sneak a quick look at her sitting by the door. I don't know how she dances, but I'm sure she'd be an asset if there's a swimsuit number.

When the bell rings, I rush into the bathroom one last time. I've gone in between every class to confirm that my booty can still move. I now check again (still moving), fluff my lame wavy hair, scan my outfit (these aren't just *any* jeans I'm wearing; they're my Perfect Butt jeans), then apply black mascara to accentuate my brown eyes (if only I had my sister's superhuman eyelashes) and pink lipstick. My heart feels like a crazed yo-yo. Ready.

Tammy is waiting for me outside the bathroom. I grab her hand. What if I bomb? What if the spell just makes me think I look good? What if I make a complete fool of myself?

'Rachel, you're not breathing,' Tammy tells me at the top of the stairs. 'Remember what we learned in gym? In, out, in, out.'

I breathe in too quickly and end up hiccuping.

'Deep breath,' she says, holding my hands in the air. 'When I'm diving, I have to always remember to breathe. Deeeeeep breath. Deeeeeep breath. Otherwise you could panic, pass out and get mauled by a shark.'

Is this how she tries to comfort me? I cling to her arm and slowly descend the three flights of stairs to the cafeteria. Maybe I'll get lucky and, except for Annie, I won't have any competition.

Wrong. A line of fifty wannabe dancers snakes along the wall toward the caf's entrance, which is being monitored by suck-up Doree. She counts off the first five girls in line, ushers them into the room and then closes the door so we can't see inside. I recognize most of the waiting girls, and I wonder who the *real* competition will be. Besides Annie, of course.

I remember the last tryouts. I came with Jewel and stood outside the door, and she was so nervous that she shook. A lot of the girls here today were at the first round too.

The music starts inside *(boom, boom, boom)*, and I can't help it; my feet start tapping. Tammy looks at me as if I'm nuts. The music stops, the five girls are let out and Doree escorts the next five girls in. A few minutes later she leads in another five.

Janice joins us. 'Ready?' she asks, looking very serious. I so can't picture her letting loose and feeling the rhythm.

I nod. Deeeep breath.

Tammy engages Janice in conversation instead of me. Obviously, she realizes how nervous I am. Five more girls go in. Why is no one coming out? Are they dying of humiliation inside?

I'm in the next group. Even if I'm the best dancer here, I still might not get in. What if I'm too short? What if they just don't like me? What if I'm not fashion-show material? A few of the girls behind me are whispering about Laura Jenkins, the girl who dropped out.

'I hear she was failing all of her classes and her parents made her quit,' someone says.

'I'm not surprised,' another girl answers. 'She's already in remedial everything.' I couldn't care less why she dropped out. I'm just happy she did.

The music stops.

'One,' Doree counts, tapping Janice on the head. 'Two. Three.' I'm three. 'Four.' She taps Tammy.

'Oh, I'm not trying out,' Tammy says. 'But can I watch? For moral support?'

Doree gives her the once-over. 'No.'

Tammy squeezes my arm and backs away. 'Good luck!'

As I pass through the cafeteria doors, I see the girls who just tried out exiting through the back door, and I feel nauseous. At the front of the room, the tables have been moved so there's a space for us to try out in. The eight freshman cast members (there are nine in all, but Doree's playing host) are sprawled on top of the remaining tables, waiting to watch us. Jewel and Melissa are next to each other, giggling over a magazine, too busy to notice me.

I have never felt more ridiculous in my life. It's like that dream when you're sitting in homeroom and you realize you forgot to put on your pants. Five masking tape Xs mark the cleared area, separated from each other by a half foot.

'Please stand on the third X,' Doree tells me without even a hint that she's in almost all my classes.

We line up, all five of us trembling, as if we're about to beg for our lives in front of a firing squad. *Don't look up*, I tell myself. Don't look up, don't look up. I look up. Raf is on a lunch table all the way in back, lying on his sexy stomach, possibly doing his homework. I think I might puke.

'Please tell us your names,' Doree says.

'Janice Cooper,' Janice says, since she's first in line. Her voice catches on the *p*, and the firing squad snickers.

Poor Janice.

'Ivy Lions,' says the girl next to me. She's wearing

 109

high-waisted jeans, glasses and a plaid scrunchie. I know without a doubt there's no way she's getting in. Two fashion show seniors whisper and laugh, and I can feel Ivy's humiliation radiate from her cheeks. I want to cry for her. I can't decide if she's gutsy or just stupid.

'Rachel Weinstein,' I say. Jewel's eyes jump up from the magazine at my name. I smile shyly at her.

'You didn't tell me you were trying out,' she mouths, looking slightly panicked. For the first time it occurs to me that she might see me as another Ivy. After all, she's seen me dance.

'Surprise,' I mouth back.

'All right, girls,' says London Zeal, one of the two producers. Every year two seniors who have been in the show previously are elected to produce. They're responsible for choosing the ten freshmen, ten sophomores, ten juniors and eight other seniors who will participate. Half are guys, half girls. And just because someone gets in one year doesn't mean he or she will make it the next. Everyone still has to try out. Usually the same people make it year after year, but last year one of the sophomore dancers, Kate Small, hooked up with London's boyfriend behind her back. Guess who got cut this year?

Mercedes Redding, London's cohead, is sitting cross-legged on a yoga mat. She is the skinniest person I have ever seen. Honestly, her jeans must be a size zero. Of course, all the guys think she's hot, even though she has the body of a ten-year-old. Or used to think she was hot. She chopped her long blonde locks to her chin over Christmas, and the response has not been favourable. Mercedes is a great dancer, but she doesn't talk much.

London, on the other hand, never shuts up, and you can

hear her coming down the hall from a mile away – her voice is so nasal it sounds as if she's holding her nose when she talks. You can also see her from a mile away. She dresses head to toe in one colour. Today she's wearing purple. Purple tank top, purple skirt, purple fishnets, purple high boots. Purple-tinged sunglasses. She's also lined the rims of her eyelids with purple eyeliner. It's very striking.

'Now, girls,' she says. 'I'm going to show you a sequence of moves from one of the dances that you would be in, and you're going to attempt to keep up. Then we'll invite some of you, or none of you, to come back for second rounds, which will be in about an hour. The show is in less than two months, so we have no time to waste. The rest of the cast has been working together since October. So whoever we choose has to be better than good. She has to be . . .'

Magical?

'. . . amazing. So, if you're wasting our time, just leave.'

The five of us stay frozen in our spots.

London snaps her fingers and someone starts the music.

I can do this. I can do this. I did it this morning and I can do it now *(boom, boom, boom)*.

London positions herself right in front of me. 'Five, six, seven, eight! Left arm up, right arm up, twirl, groove, bend, kick ball change . . .' She goes on. And on. The moves get more and more complex. She looks like a mosquito trapped in a small room, zigzagging perfectly in sync with the music from wall to wall.

We're supposed to remember all this? An eternity later, she stops, turns around and gives us a big fake smile. 'Your turn.'

I steal a quick glance at the other contestants. They look as if they're going to cry.

'All right then. Let's see who can keep up.' She turns her back to us and sings, 'Five, six, seven, eight! Left arm up, right arm up, twirl, groove, bend, kick ball change!'

And I'm right behind her. Following her every move. The girls on each side of me aren't doing too well (Janice keeps flapping her arms), and they're all smashing into each other like bumper cars, but I'm in the zone. My arms and legs and butt are in sync and can feel the music. Not only am I following London, I'm kicking higher, swooping lower and shaking faster.

I'm on fire.

For the first time ever I am totally lost in the music. All I feel is the piercing beat and the liquid movement of my body. When the sequence is over, I realize that everyone is staring at me. Not only London, Mercedes, Jewel and Raf, but the entire freshman cast as well as the other contestants.

I look up at Jewel. 'Wow,' she mouths.

London crouches beside Mercedes and whispers. Then London stands up and says, 'Rochelle, we'd like to see you at callbacks at five. The rest of you can go.'

Rochelle? That's me. Yes!

I wander the hall for the next hour. Wendy Wolcott, a freshman with short black hair that frames her face, is also wandering. We're walking in opposite directions and keep crossing paths in front of the second-floor water fountain. We don't speak to each other, neither wanting to get too close to the competition.

At 4:55, I return to the caf.

Jewel tackles me the second I walk in. She has a huge smile on her face. 'When did you learn to dance like that?'

I smile back, mostly because it's the first time in forever that she's voluntarily spoken to me outside of maths class. 'I've been practising.'

'No kidding. You were amazing. Like, superstar amazing.'

'Thanks.'

'Good luck,' she says, and pats me on the back. 'Not that you need it.'

In the corner, Wendy is tying her shoelaces. Annie walks in. I wave. I wonder if she has to wear a sports bra for dancing. All the boys in the show stop what they're doing and stare. The three of us line up.

London motions to the cast to find their seats. 'First we want to see you dance freestyle. Second, walk. Third, interact with your partner for the formal.'

Walk? I have to walk? I didn't ask Miri for a walking spell. What if I don't know how to walk?

'Mercedes and I make all the casting decisions, but we're allowing the freshman dancers to help us decide, since they're the ones who have to dance with you. So first, freestyle.'

She snaps her fingers, and the music pumps through the room. (How does she do that? Is the room set up with The Clapper? Is she a witch too?)

I start to move. My feet move, my knees move, my butt moves, my arms, my neck. I feel rubbery and alive and I couldn't stop myself if I tried. Wendy and Annie dance beside me, but they're watching yours truly out of the corners of their eyes.

When the music stops, everyone applauds, looking at me.

'Very good,' London says. 'Now, all of you please pretend you're on the catwalk and walk towards me.' She shuffles backwards and beckons to us, as if she's a father teaching his kids to ride a bike. Heel, toe, heel, toe. I remember reading that in a teen mag. I hope I don't need training wheels.

'Very good. Now, Rackelle and Anna, please sit down and let's see how Raf looks with Wanda.'

My heart leaps into my mouth. Raf! Why on earth did Laura quit the show when Raf was her partner? Who cares if she was failing school? And who in the world are Rackelle, Anna and Wanda? Oh, right, that's us. London's way too cool to remember our names.

Annie/Anna and I sit. I try to keep my back straight and model-esque by imagining a ruler against it.

Raf jumps off the table and joins Wendy/Wanda. She's only an inch shorter than he is, not a half-foot, like me, and my heart sinks. They look adorable together.

'Give her a twirl,' London instructs.

He gives her a twirl.

'Now a dip,' she says.

If only I could purse my lips or twitch my nose and make him drop her. Miri? If you can hear me, toss her to the floor like a pair of discarded socks.

London whispers something to Mercedes, and Mercedes nods. 'Thank you, Winnie. That was excellent. Ruth, you're up.'

That must be me again. I stand and try to heel-toe my way to the centre of the room. Heel, toe, heel, toe. Or is it toe, heel? And that's when it happens. I trip. I stumble and fall forwards on to my hands.

Everyone gasps.

'I'm fine!' I sing, trying to keep my voice light and fluffy. I force myself to laugh. 'No problem. Must have tripped on something.' Unfortunately, I realize that I tripped on my own untied laces. Stupid magic shoes.

'You OK?' Raf asks, arriving by my side. Our eyes meet. I know this sounds like something out of one of my mom's romance novels, but I can't look away. His eyes are liquid midnight. It's as if I'm drowning in them. He offers me his hand and I let him help me up, and his touch is hot, like the side of a whistling tea kettle. Omigod. I'm so in love. Really and truly this time.

When I've regained my balance, he lets me go. Damn. Maybe I should fall again. Or not. Everyone is staring at me. Just what they were praying for—a klutz who will trip on her own two feet during the show. Perhaps even fall off the stage.

'Let's see a twirl,' London tells us. Raf takes my hand again and I twirl into him. Please don't let go.

'Now a dip.'

I lean back in his arms. I could stay like this forever. His lips are only a few inches away, and he smells so yummy. If only he'd lean in a bit closer and kiss me. That would be so romantic . . . or not. My first kiss in front of the entire fashion-show cast?

'Thank you, Randy.'

That's it? Why didn't I get an excellent like Wendy did? Despair overwhelms me like a wave in the ocean. I'm not going to make it.

While the boys gape at Annie's assets, I wonder how

115

many weeks I'd have to set and clear the table for Miri to break both Annie's and Wendy's legs. Kidding. Kind of. What a terrible thing to joke about. I guess that's why Miri got the powers and not me. I'm an awful person. I must have the worst karma. My aura must be a revolting brown-green for trying to sabotage my father's wedding alone.

Annie's not a bad dancer. But I don't think she and Raf look like a match made in heaven or anything. She's too tall.

'Thank you for coming,' London says after Annie is done. 'The results will be posted on Monday. Try not to obsess all weekend.'

What? On Monday? I have to wait the entire weekend?

See? I knew I had lousy karma.

11

Pass the Benzoyl Peroxide

On the train ride to my dad's, Miri doesn't even pretend to care about the tryouts. All she wants to talk about is the spell for STB. 'He's going to take one look at her and run the other way,' she says gleefully. 'And then she'll finally be out of our lives.'

'Finally,' I repeat. Even though we can't perfectly imagine what life would be like with a single dad – he and STB were an item after six months of him being separated from my mom – those six months without her were much better than the time with her. We were the priority. He lived in the city in a building called Putter's Place. It's a popular building for Manhattan fathers when they leave their wives. On Sundays I'd see half the kids in my grade with their suitcases in the lobby.

Maybe he'll never remarry. Maybe he'll miss us and come home. The backs of my eyes prick. Maybe I should think about something more fun. Like the fashion show. 'And speaking of finally, on Monday I'll know if I made the cut. Do you think that my tripping screwed my chances?'

'Uh-huh,' Miri says. She's obviously not paying attention,

because the proper response would have been 'No! Of course not! Don't be stupid!' She pulls her new spell notebook out of her schoolbag (she's now making lists of her attempted spells and her observations in a navy blue spiral book that she doesn't let out of her sight), as well as a foot-long, inch-wide glass beaker filled with light orange guck. 'We have to get this cream on STB's skin.'

'Where did you get that beaker? It looks like something from science class.'

'That's where I got it.'

'You stole it from your science lab? I thought you were a good witch, not a bad one.'

She flushes. 'I'll return it on Monday.'

'Sure you will.' I shake my head with exaggerated disappointment. 'Two weeks and you've already gone over to the dark side.'

She pouts until I stick out my tongue and wag it up and down. As usual, my silly face makes her laugh. She crosses her eyeballs in response.

'So how are you going to get the concoction on STB's skin?' I ask. 'Hug her?'

'I would if that weren't completely out of character. She'd know something was up.'

'Why don't you mix it in with her moisturizer? You know the two-hundred-dollar mini-tube she special-orders from France and hides on the top shelf of their bathroom?'

'If I mix it with that, she'll get a rash every time she uses the cream.'

'Is that what's going to happen? She's going to get a face rash? We could have just put poison ivy in her room.'

'It's supposed to cause the ugliest of ugliest face conditions. Which I'm guessing means boils or maybe even jaundice.'

'It's not going to hurt, is it?' It's one thing to make her temporarily ugly, but I'd feel horrible if we caused her any physical pain. (I was just kidding about breaking Annie's and Wendy's legs. Sort of.)

'No. And I added horseradish, which is supposed to make any spell temporary, so it should only last a few days. Just long enough to make Daddy snap out of his fascination with her and cancel the wedding.' Miri stares into the beaker. 'Keep your fingers crossed.'

As soon as we step off the train, we spot our father.

'Hi, Daddy,' Miri says, and throws her arms around him.

I feel a lump in my throat, like I always do when I first see him. It really sucks to have divorced parents. I know I'm supposed to be mature about it (I'm lucky to have two parents who love me, et cetera, et cetera), but sometimes I can't help feeling sorry for myself. I don't want to be a hypotenuse stretched between two divergent parents. I don't want to see my dad only once every two weeks. I see my gym teacher more often than that. Is that normal?

My dad hugs me, and my throat slowly de-lumps. He takes our bags, and we follow him to the car, where STB and Prissy are waiting. STB waves as soon as she spots us. Prissy squishes her face against the back window.

STB turns her head to see us when we climb into the back, then gives us a big fake smile. 'Hi, girls, how are you?' There's no way she likes these weekends. Why would she? Who wants to take care of two teenagers?

'I get to sit in the middle,' Prissy says, settling back into her booster seat.

STB faces front again, admiring her reflection in the sun visor mirror. 'Did you have a good two weeks?'

'Yup,' I say. I bet she won't be admiring herself after tomorrow. And I bet as soon as my dad's out of earshot, she won't be this nice.

'That's great,' she says. 'Really great.'

As if she cares how our weeks went. Two can play that game. 'How were your weeks?' I ask.

She sighs. 'Long. Weddings are so difficult to plan, aren't they, honey?' She reaches over and pats my dad's bald spot. If she keeps touching it, it's going to get even bigger.

'And we'll have three more weddings to plan after this one, since we have three daughters,' my father says.

It weirds me out that Prissy lives with my father. At least she doesn't call him Dad. I wonder if she'll start to after the wedding. Her father lives in LA, so she only sees him a few times a year. I wonder why he and STB got divorced. I wish he'd share the reasons with my dad. I'll ask him for a top-ten list if we ever meet.

My father parks in front of Happy Palace, the neighbourhood Chinese restaurant, to pick up takeout. 'Honey, will you ask for chopsticks for me?' STB the show-off asks as he gets ready to run in. As soon as he's gone (OK, it was a few minutes later, but still, she's so rude), STB whirls around. 'Miri, how are your fingers? Have you stopped biting?'

Miri sits on her hands.

'Do we have to put the Band-Aids back on? And I won't have you giving me attitude like last time. Your mother

120

might let you get away with that type of behaviour, but it won't be happening at my house.'

Miri's face turns redder than a stop sign. I'm hoping she turns STB into a frog, but nothing happens. She must be exercising her self-control. It's one of the things they learn in tae kwon do. She'd be amazing on a diet.

'And, Rachel, I'd appreciate it if you could try to keep your room tidy this weekend. I'm not a maid.'

'Mommy doesn't like messes,' Prissy adds.

STB laughs. 'No, I don't. And sometimes your room looks like it was taken over by animals.'

I wish Miri were sitting next to me so I could squeeze her hand. Hard.

My father returns with the food. 'That was quick, honey,' STB says, smiling sweetly, all traces of evil gone from her voice. He hands her the food and kisses her on the cheek. How does he not see through her sickeningly sweet facade?

'Lemon chicken, General Tso's shrimp, Szechuan beef and crispy noodles with tofu for Miri,' he says while backing the car into the street.

'Did you get me chopsticks?' STB asks.

He slams his hand against his forehead. 'Oops.'

'That's all right. Next time.'

When we reach our driveway, I help my dad with the bags. Miri approaches our target. 'You have dirt on your cheek.'

STB wipes her face with the back of her glove. 'I do? Where?'

'I'll get it,' Miri says, and before STB can reply, Miri

121

dips her gloved finger into the vial behind her back and rubs a drop of the concoction on STB's cheek.

'Thanks,' STB says.

Miri smiles. 'Oh, you're very welcome.'

Score! I refrain from giving Miri a thumbs-up and lift my suitcase out of the trunk. Hah. I'll show her an animal. She's about to look like one.

The next morning, at some unearthly hour, we're awakened by a piercing scream.

Miri and I spring from our beds. A second later, we hear another, even more piercing scream.

'I guess it worked,' I whisper.

We open our door and poke our heads into the hallway. STB shrieks yet a third time.

We slowly walk to my father's room and knock. 'Hello?' I ask. 'Is everything all right?' Then I whisper in my sister's ear, 'Be subtle.'

My father opens the door, looking half asleep. 'Girls, did either of you pack any pimple cream? Jennifer broke out.'

I don't think benzoyl peroxide is going to do the trick this time, Dad.

'Can we see?' my not-so-subtle sister asks.

'What Miri means,' I say, elbowing her in the stomach, 'is that as teenagers, we're often afflicted with various unfortunate skin conditions. So perhaps we can help. Or at least empathize.'

This seems to make sense to my dad, as he nods and says, 'Jennifer, come show the girls.'

'I'm not a freak show,' she cries from their private bathroom. 'I must have had an allergic reaction. No more General Tso, I can promise you that.'

'Maybe the girls can help,' my dad says.

The bathroom door opens slowly. I see an arm, and then . . . a face covered in clusters of good old-fashioned zits.

That's it? Where are the boils? The rash? Are pimples the worst face condition a witch can come up with? There's hardly a day that goes by when I don't have a pimple. I'm finding this highly insulting.

'Any suggestions, girls?' STB asks.

'No,' we say in unison. I'm trying not to laugh. 'I'm sure they'll go away soon.'

'Exactly,' my father says. He pulls his precious fiancée into a hug. 'They're kind of cute. Makes me imagine what you looked like as a teenager.'

STB giggles and pats his bald spot.

I try not to gag.

Miri and I desert the lovefest and retreat to our room. 'Acne?' I whisper angrily. 'That's the best you could come up with?'

She shivers. 'I hate pimples.'

At twelve, she has yet to experience one and therefore sees them as the world's worst potential affliction. 'Well, they're not going to be enough to propel our father out of love with her! He didn't stop loving me when I had that massive zit on my nose last Christmas, did he?'

She shivers again. That zit (which I referred to as Santa's Gift – we joked that I must have been really bad last year) had freaked her so much that she'd started stuttering in its presence. I don't know how she's going

123

to manage high school. 'Maybe if he's not so mesmerized by her beauty,' she reminds me, 'he'll see her true self.'

I'm not convinced. 'Hey, did you ever find out what *Taraxacum officinale* was?'

'Of course. It's in the spell. It's a fancy name for a dandelion.'

'I'm going to the drugstore,' my father says through our closed door. 'I have to pick up some pimple medicine and some vitamin A. That'll be good for Jennifer's skin.'

I climb back into bed. What would be even better for her skin is packing up and moving out. Can we give her that in a pill?

A few hours later, at a normal waking time, I pass my father on the stairs. My stomach is growling from hunger, and my dad is getting ready to go to the office.

I can't believe he's working again on the weekend. Which means Miri and I get to spend the day with the Pimple Queen.

And then I notice it. The nasty fist-sized red zit on his chin. I stop him in mid-step. 'Dad, you're breaking out too.' I've never seen my father with a pimple. Fathers aren't supposed to have them. They're also not supposed to cry or show signs of weakness. Or leave you alone with a wicked STB.

'I am?' He touches his chin. 'I was wondering what that bump was.'

I race back to our room and close the door. Miri is reading the spell book shielded by her science textbook. 'He's breaking out too,' I whisper breathlessly.

'What?'

'Dad has a pimple on his chin. Is it possible it's a coincidence?'

124

She stares at me. And continues staring at me.

Then with a trembling hand she points at my nose. 'It's b-b-back,' she stammers.

No. No, no, no. No way. 'Don't tell me that.'

She drops her book and covers her face with her hands. 'I screwed up.'

I can't break out now! Santa's Gift lasted for two weeks! Raf or Mick will never ask me to Spring Fling if I have a massive boulder on my nose! I push Miri away and peer into the nearest mirror. 'No!' I cry, horrified. It *is* back. Bigger and badder than before. I thought sequels always paled when compared to their originals. And what's that on my forehead? 'How did this happen?' I shriek, spinning towards Miri. 'Did you put the spell on me too?'

Miri gnaws on her thumb. 'I don't know. Maybe it can spread. Maybe Dad touched STB with the potion and it spread to him and then you when he kissed you goodnight.' Her hand flies to her cheek. 'What if I get it too?'

She starts scribbling in her spell observation notebook.

I'm going to cry. What if it spreads all over? On to my hands, my neck, my stomach? Who knows what this spell is capable of? My entire body could become one big erupting pimple. I grab her shoulders. 'You need to fix this. Now.'

Her eyes fill with tears. 'I don't know how.'

'Figure it out!' I storm out of the room and knock on my dad's door. I expect to find him and STB in a state of hysterics, but instead they're lying on the bed, cuddling and, worse, *giggling*.

'I have it too,' I say, which for some inexplicable reason just makes them laugh louder.

'Let's see,' my dad says.

I stand over them and point to my nose. STB's face has worsened. Her forehead is covered in pus. My father's acne has spread to his bald spot.

'The pimple cream is in the medicine cabinet,' my dad offers.

As if that would work.

'We should call Harry,' STB says. Harry is my father's friend who also happens to be a doctor. 'In case it's shingles or the chicken pox. Or measles.'

'I think those spread to your whole body and not just your face,' my father says. 'But I guess I should call him.'

STB points to his blistering forehead and cracks up. They both start rolling on the bed, they're laughing so hard. Why isn't he repulsed and realizing how horrible she is? Apparently, like pimples, laughter is contagious. I back out of the room before I catch the latter, too, and run back to our room. We need a cure. Pronto.

I open the door to find Miri having a minor panic attack. A zit has appeared under her left eyebrow. I grab a paper bag from the kitchen and tell her to breathe into it so she won't pass out.

Then I start reading the book. Fixing this is obviously up to me.

'Aha,' I say an hour later, when Miri's cheeks have regained colour. 'There are two potential solutions. Spell reversal, or a new spell for clear skin.'

'Spell reversal,' she says, pacing the length of the room. 'No need to throw another unknown into the mix. We could end up translucent.' She trips over the pants I wore yesterday and gives me a withering look. Then she hangs them up.

'The only problem with spell reversal is that it's a five-

126

broomer. If you can't even handle an easy spell, how would you handle this one?'

Her face brightens. 'I could call Mom.'

'Are you crazy? She'd freak!' She'd be furious about our plan to make STB ugly, and she'd demand to know what other spells Miri has concocted. I'd lose my rhythm for sure. 'Keep Mom out of this.'

'Then I'll do the clear-skin spell.' She lies on her bed, sticks her feet up against the wall. 'Let me see the book.'

I pass it, lie down beside her and cross my big foot over her tiny one. She sighs. 'I don't know about these ingredients. We need a teaspoon of salt from the sea, two-fourths of a cup of lemon juice, and five-fifteenths of a cup of milk. What is that?'

'A third of a cup,' I say smoothly.

Miri slams her hand against the book in exasperation. 'Why can't these ancient sorcerers just say what they mean?'

'Maybe it got screwed up in the translation.' Or maybe it's the book's master plan to get me to help my sister.

'But where are we going to find salt from the sea? Do you think Dad will take us to the beach?'

Brainstorm! 'Remember before school started when I used STB's mud mask and I got all pissed because it took off my tan?'

She nods.

'That was a Dead Sea mud mask. STB has a whole collection of beauty products from the Dead Sea, including salts. They're in the back of the bathroom cupboard behind Dad's Vi—' There's probably no reason to share the Viagra finding with Miri. It freaked me out enough for the two of us. 'Behind Dad's vitamins. I'll get the salts.

 127

And there are lemons in the white pottery bowl in the kitchen.'

Miri shakes her head and starts biting the skin on her pinkie. 'Rachel, those are fake. Haven't you noticed they've been there for a year? And that they don't smell?'

'Why would someone showcase fake lemons?'

'Why are there drawers in the kitchen that don't open? Who knows? They have lemonade in the fridge. I guess that will have to do. And they must have milk.'

The skin on her pinkie is bleeding. 'They do, but since STB is lactose intolerant, it's all Lactaid milk. Do you think that makes a difference?' I take a breath, then frown. 'Can you please stop mutilating your fingers? It's grossing me out.'

She looks at her hand. 'I didn't even realize I was doing it.'

I throw her a tissue. 'You're lucky STB's been too preoccupied to make you wear Band-Aids. OK, let's get Operation Clear Skin in motion.'

The doorbell rings, and we join the rest of the family downstairs.

'It's not measles or shingles,' Harry says, scanning our faces. 'It looks like acne. But I have no idea why all of you have it.'

STB swats Prissy's hand away from her face, which is now covered as well. 'Stop scratching, honey. You're making it worse.'

Prissy looks the most ridiculous with her acne, but seems to mind the least. 'They're fun,' she says, poking her pimples. 'I can play connect the dots. In school we sometimes play connect the dots . . .'

I tune her out and watch Harry write us a prescription

128

for a new medicine called Xonerate. 'It should alleviate your symptoms by midweek.'

Midweek? This problem had better be history *tomorrow*. I can't go to school like this.

Thirty-five minutes later, while my father and STB go to the pharmacy to fill the prescription (STB is wearing a baseball hat and large sunglasses as a disguise – I couldn't believe she even went with my dad but she's probably wanting to get out of spending any extra time with the two of us), Miri cleans the beaker with boiling water, as the spell book directs. Then, in the bathroom – Miri by the sink, me on the rim of the tub – she mixes the lemonade with the lactose-free milk and the Dead Sea salts.

Prissy knocks on the door. 'Can I come in?'

'We're busy!' Miri yells. 'Come back later.' Sometimes she talks to Prissy the way I talk to her. Or the way Jewel talks to me, as if I'm a groupie.

I wonder what Jewel did today. I called her yesterday, but hung up when I got her machine, and called Tammy instead.

'Why not now?' Prissy whines.

Because then you'll tell your mother we're casting evil spells on her, and she'll make us see a shrink? 'We'll be out in a second,' I say through the door. 'I hope she doesn't set the house on fire while we're in here,' I tell Miri. We're the worst babysitters ever.

'It's done,' Miri says. 'Now be quiet.'

> *Skin so smooth,*
> *Skin like silk,*
> *Face like an angel,*
> *White as milk.*

I shiver from the cold and then snort. 'Honestly, I could write this stuff. What if the witch is African American? Or Hispanic? If it adjusts to the twenty-first century, shouldn't it be politically correct?'

She shakes the potion and then dabs it on her face. 'Did it work?'

'It's been a second and a half, so no,' I say, applying it.

She stares at her reflection in the mirror. 'I need it to work now.'

'You're certainly not the fairest of them all,' I tell her.

Prissy slams her foot into the door. 'Let me in! Please?'

I unlock the door and Prissy falls through. Oh, no. She's taken the connect-the-dots idea to a new level, having drawn black lines all over her face.

'What did you do?' I ask incredulously.

'I used Mommy's make-up.'

'I'm washing that off. Now.' I gingerly wipe her face with a washcloth, trying not to gag. Then I medicate her. Touching someone else's pimples is not a pleasant activity. I'd rank it up there with changing a baby's diaper or cleaning up someone else's vomit.

'Thank you,' she says softly, and blinks her big blue-green eyes at me. She has the same beautiful ones as STB.

My repulsion thaws. She's not so bad. Kind of sweet, actually. I hope she doesn't have the mean gene like her mother.

I rinse the cloth and when I face her again, her little finger goes up her nose. I can't help laughing. She laughs too, and wipes her hand on my wrist.

I laugh even harder.

'We should put the conconction into the Xonerate cream,' Miri suggests, tidying up. 'I don't care that

STB looks like a pin cushion, but Dad shouldn't have to suffer.'

When my dad and STB come home, Miri claims she needs to use the medicine first, grabs it and sneaks it into the bathroom to replace it with her concoction.

By Sunday morning, all five of us have clear faces.

'I'm definitely investing in Xonerate,' my father says over breakfast. 'It's a miracle drug. And I'm sure the vitamin A didn't hurt either.'

'You know,' I tell Miri on the train home, 'we could make a fortune if we sold your clear-skin potion at school.'

'No. And we need a new plan.'

'Why no? Try to see the big picture. We could be millionaires.' I'd make a great businesswoman. I can easily imagine myself walking down Fifth Avenue, screaming into my cellphone, high heels click-clacking against the pavement, hair flowing in the wind as I climb into my private helicopter on the roof of my office.

Miri taps me on the head. 'Can you stop daydreaming and focus on the new plan?'

'What new plan?'

'The new plan on how to get our father to cancel the wedding. Our first plan backfired. Dad didn't even notice how ugly she was.'

I laugh. 'She did look pretty ugly.'

Miri bites her thumb and I slap her hand away. 'I know,' she says. 'But he didn't care. In fact, he seemed to love her even more. How is that possible?'

'Well, he wasn't looking his best either.' I think for a moment. 'It's not enough to make her appearance ugly. We have to help him see her real personality, how awful

 131

she is. She's sweet in front of him, but as soon as he's out of the room, she morphs.'

Miri nods. 'So what do we do? Tape her with a hidden recorder and then play it for Dad?'

'Come on. You're a witch. You can do better than that. Otherwise, start thinking bridesmaid. As in dresses. As in putrid, puffy and pink.'

12

Crazy, Cool or Just Plain Good

Can't look. Must look. Can't.

It's first period, and I'm standing in front of the events bulletin board. I excused myself from homeroom as soon as I saw London walk past the door. I knew she was posting the results. I asked to go to the bathroom and then bolted to the board that holds my future in its thumbtack grasp. I'm too terrified to open my eyes.

If I got in, wouldn't Jewel have called to tell me? I so didn't get in. Maybe she wasn't allowed to tell me.

Maybe London threatened her. Told her she'd get booted out if she spilled the beans about the fashion show.

Maybe I did get in! My feet start tapping to an imaginary salsa beat. I picture myself as the star of *Dirty Dancing III: Manhattan Nights*.

Or maybe not. Maybe they chose Wendy. Maybe Jewel blackballed me. Maybe she's not too busy for me; she just doesn't like me any more.

Can't look. Must look. I'll open just one eye so if I don't get in, both my pupils won't be scarred.

First I see the words *freshman fashion show replacement dancer*. And then I see—

rachel weinstein.

I open both eyes to make sure it still says my name, then proceed to jump up and down. Abracarific! I'm about to moonwalk down the hall when I see the sadistic Mr Earls. I skip back to class before he has a chance to give me another detention.

Not that detention is such a bad thing.

Detention + eavesdropping = fashion show.

Did I mention that I love maths?

By the time we get to our lockers, the whole school knows.

On the way to my next class, Doree throws her arms around me. 'Congrats!' she squeals. 'I'm so excited to have someone in class to talk to about the show! This is so awesome!'

'Congratulations, Rachel,' William Kosravi says.

The president of our high school just talked to me. *To me*. He knows who I am. Now I can call him just Will too! Suddenly, everyone knows who I am. People I've never even seen are congratulating me.

This is so much more effective than a maths tournament.

Or even bowling.

'*Je suis très excitée de te voir danser!*' Madame Diamon says as she passes me in the hallway.

'*Enchantée,*' I murmur, sashaying past.

Tammy can't stop smiling. 'I'm so happy for you.' She gives me a thumbs-up. 'Want to celebrate after school? We can go for pizza.'

'Yeah, great,' I say. We turn into the second-floor stairwell, and before I know it, I'm being suffocated by arms.

'Congratulations!' London and Mercedes scream. Two of the most popular girls in school are hugging me. Unbelievable.

'Practice starts today after school,' London says, ignoring Tammy. Today she's in navy blue. Jeans, sweater, Yankees hat, boots and eyeliner. 'Plan on working your butt off. You have a ton of catching up to do. We expect you to be at practice every day after school except Wednesday for the next month.'

Like that's a bad thing? I can't think of a better way to spend my afternoons than with Jewel and Raf.

'What are we practising today?' I ask, trying not to appear eager.

London whips out her clipboard. 'Jewel volunteered to teach you the opening during lunch. It's extremely vital that you know what you're doing because the freshman girls start off the dance, which sets the tone for the entire show. All lunch practices are in the drama room.'

She offered to teach me? That's so sweet. She is such a great friend. See? She still likes me! 'After school, the cast is meeting in the caf to review the first dance,' London continues. 'It's a medley of music from *Chicago*.'

I knew there was a reason I bought Mom the DVD for her birthday. Besides her birthday, I mean.

'And tomorrow after school is the freshman and sophomore *Moulin Rouge* rehearsal. Raf Kosravi is your partner.'

I know! Hooray! Abracazam! He'll fall in love with me and invite me to Spring Fling!

'And the girls will all be wearing Izzy Simpson.'

Yes! Yes! Yes! 'Oh. Cool,' I say, shrugging.

'You have Wednesday off. Mercedes and I have Pilates.

Thursday is the practice for the all-girl freshman and sophomore dance. It's to Will Smith's "Miami" and I'm choreographing and it's going to be incredible. You'll be wearing Juicy. On Friday Mercedes will work with everyone on the closing, which is also the entire cast. It's to a dance version of Frank Sinatra's "New York, New York." Everyone will wear black Theory clothes.' She snaps the clipboard under her arm. 'Those are all the numbers you're in.'

Can you say *overwhelming*? That sounds like a lot of work. Not that I'm going to complain. London seems to take this show *very* seriously.

'Oh wait – there's also the all-freshman Vegas dance. Melissa put together a stripper theme that was fantastic, but the administration heard about it and said it was inappropriate. So you didn't miss anything because she's redoing it. Later,' she concludes without ceremony, and they slink off.

Why is Melissa choreographing? And somehow I missed what label we'll be wearing, but who cares? I'd wear something by Judy if I had to.

Well, maybe.

'Wow,' Tammy says. 'Guess we're not going for pizza after school today.'

'Guess not,' I say, vowing to do it as soon as the show is over.

Tammy and I start walking. 'But how amazing is it that designers let you model their clothes?' she says.

'So amazing,' I say. 'I guess they do it for the publicity. And rumour has it we get our hair and make-up done for free the day of the show,' I add, half guilty.

'Lucky,' she murmurs. All right, three-quarters guilty.

When we get to maths, Jewel waves from the back. 'I'll see you later,' I say to Tammy.

'Hi, hon,' Jewel says. 'I'm so excited for you!'

I can't stop smiling.

'I was dying to call you this weekend. *Dying*. But London told me I had to keep it under lock and key.' She makes a zipping motion to her mouth. She should be making a locking motion, but I don't want to call her on it. 'Aren't you thrilled?'

'Thrilled,' I repeat. 'So how long do the practices last?'

'Not long. And then we go out for food.'

Is it possible I'll be privy to the after-school hang-out? The bell rings, signifying the beginning of class. Ms Hayward slams the door and starts to set up her books.

'So you have to tell me,' Jewel says, leaning over her desk towards me. 'When did you learn to dance like that?'

'I must have picked it up.' Or bathed in it. Whatever.

'But how? I couldn't get over you. No one could. You were all anyone could talk about at Mick's.'

'At Mick's?' Mick isn't in the show. He definitely wasn't at the tryouts.

'At his party on Friday. Honestly, we were all totally bowled over. Mercedes said she was glad that Laura Jenkins dropped out, because you're ten times better than she is. She couldn't understand why you didn't try out in October.' Jewel shakes her ringlets. 'Me neither.'

Ms Hayward bangs her ruler against the desk. 'Rachel, do you think you and Juliana can stop talking long enough so that I can teach my class?'

I open my textbook, the smile still on my face. Even Hayward can't ruin this perfect day.

*

'That foot spin at the end took me two weeks to learn, and you got it in two secs,' Jewel tells me at fashion-show rehearsal. I'm at *fashion-show rehearsal*! Raf and Jewel and London and thirty other A-listers are wandering around and I'm not dreaming. At least I think I'm not. I'd pinch myself but that would look weird. The entire cast is in the cafeteria and we just did a run-through of the opening number that Jewel taught me at lunch.

'Thanks,' I say demurely.

'It's true,' says Stephanie Collins – Stephy to those in the know. She's standing on the other side of me and must be the only girl in school shorter than I am. She's under five feet and has long silky blonde hair that she wears in two low pigtails. Her nose, eyes and lips are so small, they look like miniatures. 'I don't want to stand next to you. You're going to make me look bad.'

Whoever said cool girls were mean is crazy. I've gotten nothing but compliments since I got here.

'Are you two going to Snack Shoppe after practice?' Stephy asks us.

Jewel winks at me. 'Is that where everyone is?'

Stephy double-checks the text message on her pink cellphone. 'Uh-huh.'

'Rachel, you want to go?' Jewel asks.

'Sure.' If I'm dreaming, I never want to wake up.

I feel like Cinderella. And Raf is my prince. My spell had better not run out at midnight.

I follow Jewel and Melissa to a booth at the back of Snack Shoppe. A booth where Sean Washington and Mick are seated. Yes, Mick. I've forgotten about Mick since being paired with Raf, but he's still extremely hot

138

and has excellent boyfriend potential. I sit down across from him and try not to stare. He looks as if he belongs in an Abercrombie & Fitch catalogue, but with more clothes. Sean is another super-hot guy. He has dark skin, a buzz cut and the brightest, whitest smile I've ever seen. He's in the fashion show, too, and dancing with Jewel in the formal.

'Hey, dancing ladies,' Mick says, and shoves a fry into his mouth.

'Hey,' Jewel and Stephy say.

My mouth is too dry to speak. It feels as if someone attached a Dustbuster to my tongue.

Jewel orders an iced tea from the waitress. Then Melissa orders an iced tea. Then I order an iced tea. As if I need the caffeine. What I could use is water. Like this second. My mouth is a desert and I'm afraid it'll crack if I open it.

'What's going on?' Jewel asks Mick.

'Just hanging out. Crazy party on Friday, huh?'

'Totally wild,' Melissa says.

'This weekend is going to be even crazier,' Mick says. 'Nat's in town.'

'Excellent,' Jewel says.

I have no idea who Nat is (girl? boy? cat?), but I nod as if I do.

'Rachel, you going to come this week? Show off the moves everyone's been talking about?'

He's talking to me. He knows my name. He invited me to his party.

He's talking to me. He knows my name. He invited me to his party.

139

He's talking to me. He knows my name. He invited me to his party.

Omigod.

'Hello? Rachel?' he says.

Super. We're on speaking terms for four seconds and I've already screwed it up. Way to go.

'She doesn't talk,' Melissa says. 'Just dances.'

Well, *that* was pretty rude. 'Sounds cool,' I say. Is *cool* still a cool word to say? Does saying it take away from its cool nature? Should I have used *crazy* like he did? Or *awesome*? Or what about plain, reliable *good*?

Mick smiles and gobbles up another fry. He has beautiful plump lips. They remind me of ripe, juicy grapes.

Maybe he'll let me fan him and feed him a few?

The waitress brings our drinks and I take a big gulp. I need to be seriously cooled down. Seriously crazied down?

I feel a strong squeeze on my shoulder and spin around. Omigod.

It's Raf. Touching me. Squeezing me. Mick is across from me, talking to me with his beautiful plump lips while Raf, with his electric hands and deep-sea dark eyes, is touching me. Did I already say that this is the best day ever?

This is the best day ever.

'Hey, partner,' he says.

'Hi,' I squeak.

He pulls up a chair from the table next to us and joins our group. 'Ready for tomorrow?'

Am I ever. 'Definitely. I hope I can keep up.'

'Don't worry, you'll be fine. Why don't we meet at lunch and I'll go over some of the moves?'

'Great!' I agreed a little too quickly. But who cares? I have a lunch date. A lunch date! Yes! Isn't dancing kind of like cuddling standing up?

'Where do you want to meet? I'll get the music from Mercedes.'

'Your locker?' I say.

'Sure. It's—'

'Right by Mr Silver's class.' Did I just say that? What reason could I have for knowing where his locker is except for being a psycho stalker? 'I think,' I add. Everyone's staring at me. Mick's staring. Sean's staring. Melissa's staring. Jewel's staring.

'Yeah,' Raf says. 'It's down the hall from yours.'

Excuse me? He knows where my locker is? Why does he know where my locker is? He's never said one word to me. Is it possible he's a psycho stalker? My psycho stalker? How cool would that be? How cool! Crazy! Awesome! Good!

Raf pushes back his chair. 'See you tomorrow, Rachel.' And then he pops over to a table in the back where some senior football players are sitting. He is so cool. He's comfortable talking to everyone.

I gulp down my iced tea. I'm concerned that if I don't weight my body down with liquid, I might float to cloud nine.

Have I already mentioned that this is the best day ever?

I am in Raf's arms.

No, really. And I'm not dreaming. (This time I did pinch myself to make sure.) I am fully awake, at school, and in his arms.

It's lunchtime on Tuesday, and Raf and I are in the

drama room, practising for the formal. Basically the dance goes like this: ten boys strut down the T (the catwalk), then ten girls follow, then we stand in front of our partners. They twirl us, they dip us, we do a few sexy moves, we all walk back down the T to the stage, and then each couple walks down the T for a thirty-second romantic duet. Afterward we return to the stage for another minute of dancing.

The show is going to take place in the school auditorium, on the same catwalk that they put up every year. Unfortunately, we hardly ever get to practise in the auditorium, except during the week before the show. The drama club gets priority. It's highly unfair. They have a *drama room* to rehearse in. They claim it doesn't give them enough space. It's all kind of a joke, because being in the school play is nowhere near as cool as being in the fashion show, but teachers think the play is more educational, so, whatever.

At the moment, we're practising our duet – basically Raf pretending to kiss my outstretched arm. Oh yeah, we're fake making out. I can't believe actors get to fake make out every day. Maybe I should become an actor. Not in high school, obviously (not cool), but later on in life. Maybe I should just ask Mercedes to choreograph a real kiss into the routine. Is there a suggestion box?

'That's the end of our duet,' Raf says. 'Now we walk back up the T, and it's Melissa and Gavin's turn.'

'Got it,' I say as he spins me out of the twirl. Gavin is in my English class. His clothes are all black. He spends class drawing cartoons in the margins of the novels we're studying and has always been too cool/

awesome/crazy/good for me to approach. But not any more!

Raf twirls me one more time and then we're done. 'Do you feel comfortable with the moves, or do you want to try it again to make sure?'

Hmm. That's a tough one. 'I guess one more time wouldn't hurt.'

During the after-school practice, Raf whispers, 'You going to Mick's this weekend?'

I sniff him before answering. He still smells so delicious. Like soap and boy. Yum. 'Yes. You?' Please say you're going, please say you're going!

'Yeah. Mick's is a fun night.' We walk off the pretend T (Mercedes made it with masking tape) and take our position on the fake stage. His arms are wrapped around my shoulders.

Sniff. Yum.

Maybe he'll ask me to go with him. I know I'm invited on my own, but what do I do, just show up? What time? No one's mentioned a time. I can ask Jewel, but I don't want to remind her that I don't know.

Sniff. Yum.

'Do you have a cold?' Raf asks.

'No, why?'

'You keep sniffling.'

Super. Now he's worried I'm going to get him sick. Just what every guy dreams about. An infectious partner.

'Allergies,' I respond. Must stop sniffing and concentrate on his other attributes. Like his gorgeous dark liquid eyes, his wide muscled shoulders, his clear smooth skin . . .

143

'Rachel?' Raf says, nudging me and snapping me out of my reverie. 'We're supposed to walk offstage now.'

Right. I might have to beg Miri for an anti-love spell. I'm never going to be able to concentrate on the show.

13
Always Lock the Door

When I stretch my arms up to pull on my top, my entire body aches. Dancing is a killer workout. Who knew? All that aside, with my new buff bod, I'm ready for my big night. Yes, ladies and gentlemen, the day has come. After only one week of schmoozing with the important people, I, Rachel Weinstein, am going to an A-list party.

I spent most of the week panicking – what time am I supposed to be there? Should I ask Tammy so I won't have to walk in by myself? – but then today during maths, Jewel turned to me and said, 'Hey, can we go to the party tonight together?'

'Sure,' I said, as if it were no big deal. 'When do you want to meet?'

'Nine?' she said, rolling one of her curls around her finger. 'At our spot?'

Our spot was at the corner of Ninth and Fifth, right outside the neighbourhood ice-cream parlour. We've clocked up many hours, and even more calories, at that corner.

Thank goodness I didn't ask Tammy. I was hoping all

week I wouldn't have to. In fact, I mastered the art of changing the subject every time she brought up the weekend. For example, on Wednesday I interjected with an 'Omigod, did I tell you about what happened at practice yesterday?' and then dived right into some random anecdote about London, like when she was practising a jeté and accidentally kicked Doree in the butt.

I know I'm not being nice. But I can't tell her about it and then not invite her, can I? And I can't tell her to come along, because this is the first time I've been invited and how do I know what Mick's guest policy is? He didn't say, *Come to my party and please bring a friend.* What if there's a head count? What if Mick is only allowed to invite thirty people and Tammy would make thirty-one? This isn't like Stromboli's Pizzeria; this is a *private gathering.* If he wanted Tammy to come, wouldn't he invite her himself? He knows her. He brought her a napkin when she got tomato sauce on her shirt!

The thing is, if Tammy tags along, I'll be tied to her the entire night. I need to be able to roam unattached.

I pretend Miri's room is a catwalk and sashay inside. 'What do you think of this outfit?' I'm wearing jeans and a tight red top, carrying my black slinky blouse as a back-up.

She's lying on her bed, feet up, immersed in A^2. 'Just as good as the last seven.'

'Don't exaggerate. I've only tried on six outfits.'

'Whatever. They all look the same.'

'Exactly. They all look the same because the shirt I wanted to wear tonight, my tight white V-neck, smells like BO because *someone* wore it after tae kwon do without asking if she could borrow it.'

She grimaces. 'Sorry.'

'It's OK. I know how you can make it up to me. You see, the other reason these shirts all look the same is because I'm flat-chested.' I examine myself in the mirror above her dresser. 'I'm not asking for much. Maybe half a cup size. Or a full one. Two if you want to get crazy.' Truth is, two might be a little obvious. If you're an A-cup Friday in world civ, you can't be a C-cup Friday night. People might notice.

'No boob spells, but I'll wash your shirt.'

'You're no fun.'

'I'm trying to find a truth serum,' Miri says, frowning.

'I don't think that'll help me. No guy should hear the truth. If I tell Raf or Mick how hot they are, they'd get massive egos.'

'Not for you, you freak,' she says. 'For STB.'

I perch myself on the edge of her bed. 'That's our new plan?'

'*Our* new plan? You mean *my* new plan. You've been too busy with your dancing to help me.'

I've been at rehearsals practically every day. I guess I have been neglecting my sister. 'Sorry, Mir. I'll spend tomorrow helping you.'

'Yeah? That would be great. I want to stock up on some ingredients. Can you take me to get them?'

'Tomorrow's perfect. I don't have rehearsal until Sunday.' See? I'm a good sister. 'So explain *your* new plan to me.' I hold the black top over the red and look in the mirror. Hmm. Maybe I should change.

'OK.' She spins around and leans her back against the wall. 'He has no idea what she's really like. So if we give her a truth serum, guess what happens.'

147

The red. No, the black. Which complements my complexion? I think I should go with the red. Miri is staring at me expectantly. 'I don't know, Miri. Unlike you, I'm not psychic.'

'I'm not asking you to be. I'm just asking you to pay attention to me for two seconds!'

Oops. Maybe I *am* the worst sister ever. I pat her knee. 'Let's not get cranky. Tell me your plan.'

She sighs. 'Once I give her the truth serum, she'll say what she really thinks in front of Dad. He'll see the horrible person she really is and then break up with her. See?'

For someone so young, she certainly is clever. 'Ingenious. And tomorrow we'll buy the ingredients. But tonight I must look gorgeous. So what do you think? Red or black?'

I choose red. And then black and then red again, and then Miri throws a black marker at me, which she doesn't realize is open. It leaves a huge blob in the middle of my shirt. So I choose black. Then I try to line the inside rims of my eyes the way London does, and I almost poke my pupils out. Then I apply blush to the apples of my cheeks, like the beauty experts recommend. One stroke, two strokes. Uh-oh. I look like a clown. I wash my face and try again. One stroke, two strokes. Still clownish. And now the wet eyeliner has streaked down my face. I wash it thoroughly and reapply my eyeliner. It's in my best interests to go blushless.

'Going to the party!' I scream to my mom and Miri. I'm meeting Jewel at nine, and I have only two minutes to spare.

It's so cold that I can see my breath. When we were younger, Jewel and I used to wear matching earmuffs.

Over the past five months, every time I've reminisced about Jewel (like about the time we wrote a play and had her father video it, or the way we used to make ice pops with orange juice in the summer), it's made me sad. But not today. Today she's meeting me. Today we're hanging out. Life is good.

When I reach the corner of Ninth and Fifth, I glance at my watch. Nine o'clock. I'm right on time. Ten minutes pass. She's always late. Like twenty to thirty minutes late. I used to give her a fake time of twenty to thirty minutes earlier so I wouldn't have to wait. Like telling her the movie started at ten after nine when it really started at nine thirty. But this time I forgot. And now I've been standing here like a moron for eleven minutes. The little hairs on my upper lip that I've contemplated waxing have frozen into needles. Maybe I can just snap them off now. Good thing I don't have a boyfriend who wants a kiss hello.

If only it wasn't too cold for ice cream.

Twenty minutes later, I spot Jewel's curls bouncing down the street. 'Hi, Bee-Bee!' she says, taking my hand.

It's just like the old days.

I love brownstones. My father's mother, my bubbe, used to live in one before my dad moved her into a retirement home on Long Island. She shared the building with three other tenants and lived on the top floor.

Mick's family has two, and I'm not talking about tenants. They own two full brownstones. They broke down the dividing wall and now occupy the largest mansion I've ever seen.

149

When Jewel pushes open the unlocked door, I try to keep my mouth from hitting the floor. 'Crazy place, huh?' she says. We both start giggling. 'Coats go in there.' She points her chin at the walk-in closet.

The house smells like beer and pizza. The lights are dim and a low bass is blasting through the floor and ceilings. I recognize some sophomores and juniors sprawled on a beige leather couch. And . . . is that a senior? There are seniors here! And not the loser kind who don't have friends their own age. Some even look older than seniors. How cool is Mick?

'Do you know all these people?' I whisper to Jewel. I'm looking for Raf, but I don't see him. I can't believe I'm here.

'Some of them,' she whispers back. 'They're friends of Nat's.'

Ah. The infamous Nat. Why does everyone assume I know who Nat is? Jewel must notice the confusion on my face, because she adds, 'Mick's sister. She's at Penn but comes back some weekends.'

We hang up our coats, and then I follow Jewel to the second of four floors. Jewel looks as if she's stepped right out of a music video. She's wearing jeans so low that her thong peeks out. How is wearing dental floss up her behind comfortable? Jewel is also wearing a tube top that exposes her . . . 'Jewel, when did you get a belly-button ring?'

She peeks down at her navel. 'Over Christmas. You like?'

Two months ago? I can't believe I didn't know that. When Sean pats her behind as we walk into the living room, I wonder what else I need to catch up on.

A crowd of people is sitting on an L-shaped red leather couch. Music blares from speakers perched on every wall, and it sounds as if the band is in the room with us instead of on the wall-sized flat-screen TV. Who knows, maybe they are. From what I can gather, Mick's family has enough money to fly a group in.

Mick jumps from his seat. 'Hey, gorgeous,' he says to Jewel, wrapping her in a bear hug and lifting her off the ground. He puts her down, then turns to me. 'Hey, gorgeous,' he says, and picks me up. Hey, gorgeous? I love him!

Maybe Miri secretly put a love spell on him as a surprise favour. Or maybe, I think as I inhale the scent of booze breath, he's dipped into his daddy's liquor cabinet.

He eventually puts me down and takes off for greener pastures. When I look around the room, I realize that Jewel has taken his seat, and I now have no idea what to do with myself.

Maybe Jewel will introduce me to the blonde girl she's talking to, and the three of us can engage in stimulating conversation. Nope, she doesn't seem to be in any great hurry to include me. Jewel? Um, Jewel? Hello?

There are bags of spilt chips on the marble coffee table, and I pick up what I think is a plain one and pop it into my mouth. Ew. Vinegar. Should I sit on the floor? I'm the only one standing. The shaggy red-and-white carpet looks pretty comfy. I think I'll take another chip.

Yup, I'm very busy here eating. Who needs people to talk to or a place to sit? I can eat. I eye a can of soda. Ooh, I can drink too. I pop it open and take a long sip. And then another. And again.

'There you are!' squeals a high-pitched voice, and I

look up to see Melissa waltzing into the room. 'Scoot that sexy ass over,' she says to Jewel, and squeezes herself a spot. 'Who did you come with?'

Why didn't I think of that? I could have just squashed myself in.

'Rachel,' Jewel says, twirling a curl.

'Who?' Melissa asks, a blank look on her face.

Oh, come on. She knows who I am. Hello? I'm standing right here.

Jewel peers around the room as though trying to remember where she put me. 'You know. Rachel. There you are,' she says, finding me.

Melissa fixes her beady eyes on me. 'Oh, right. Her. How are you, superstar?'

'Fine.' I'd be better if I were in your seat. Melissa's eyes burn into me and I take another long sip.

'How sad were those tryouts?' Melissa says, rolling her eyes. 'I don't know why all those pathetics bothered showing up. They couldn't dance the first time. I don't know why they thought they'd get in the second time.'

Jewel laughs. She stands up and waves her arms like a chicken. 'Who am I?'

'Janice Cooper,' I say, and then instantly feel ashamed. I take another soda.

Melissa cracks up.

'Good call,' Jewel says, then scoots over. Apparently, there's more space on the couch than she let on. 'Why don't you sit with us?'

I'm in. Physically and metaphorically.

Thirty minutes later my bladder feels as if it might explode. I'm terrified that my seat will be gone by the time I return, or that Melissa and Jewel will disappear and

I'll have to search the entire house, pretending to be busy until I find them. 'Save my seat,' I say, trying not to appear anxious. Notice how I suavely don't mention where I'm going. Above all, I resolve, I must maintain an aura of mystique and sophistication. I head off in search of the can.

I find it on the deserted third floor. Only one problem: the lock doesn't work. Super. What do I do now? Go back and find Jewel and ask her to watch the door? There's no time for that. My bladder won't make it.

I'll just be quick. The door is on my right, so I can hold it closed with my hand.

Obviously, as soon as I pull down my jeans, someone turns the door handle. I slam my arm against the door to stop it from flying open and scream, 'I'm in here!'

The door closes. Oh, man. I really hope that was a girl.

'Sorry,' says a low, boy's voice.

A familiar-sounding voice. Raf's voice.

I am never coming out.

Raf is waiting outside the bathroom door. How am I supposed to pee with Raf less than a foot away? I can't. Not with a guy I like within earshot. I can barely pee when my dad is on the same floor.

Maybe if I take a while, he'll go away. Or he'll think I'm . . . you know. Having female issues. Or worse, stomach problems. Oh, gross. I'd better hurry up. Don't want him thinking *that*. Must pee. Now. Come on. Nothing comes. Where is the tinkling sound? How is this possible? I was bursting a second ago. The only sound I hear is the ticking of my watch. No, it's my heart pounding. I'm panicking. I shouldn't panic. I have to stop panicking.

Breathe in, out. In, out.

I know. I should turn on the water. The sound will mask the tinkling sound. The only problem is that the sink isn't within grasping distance, so I'll have to get up to turn the water on. Which will be fine, as long as Raf doesn't try to open the door when I'm in mid-grab. Not that he would. A horrifying thought occurs to me. What if in this excruciating silence he worries that I've drowned and bangs down the door to save me?

I'm going for it. Three, two, one. I hurl myself towards the sink, throw the water on and fly back to the toilet.

Ah. I hope this is quick. Of course it isn't. It's the longest pee ever. He's probably long gone. I've been in here at least an hour.

Finally, I'm done. I flush and wash my hands, then open the door.

Oh, no. Oh, whoa.

Raf is leaning casually against the wall, looking hot in his low baggy jeans and a worn, soft-looking green T-shirt. Out-of-control hot. Hotter than the sun. Hotter than the sun on fire. Hotter than the sun drenched in gasoline, then set on fire. Hotter than—

'What's happening?' he asks, patting me on the shoulder. 'I was wondering where you've been hiding.'

He was? And now he's found me. In the bathroom. Super. 'I've been here. I mean, downstairs. You know.' I could use that invisibility cloak right about *now*.

'I just want to use the bathroom,' he says. Of course he does. I've been hogging it for hours. 'And then, maybe you and I can catch up or something?'

'Sure,' I say, admiring the ease he displays regarding his bodily functions. I mean, you have to be pretty confident to come right out and say, 'I need to use the bathroom.'

He smiles and disappears inside. He wants to catch up! Yes! Not sure what we're catching up on, since we've only known each other for a week. Any chance that *catch up* is a euphemism for *hook up*? Is he going to kiss me? Am I finally going to have my first kiss? Am I supposed to wait? I don't want him to think I'm stalking the bathroom. What should I be doing right now? For the first time I understand Miri's strange relationship with her nails. This would be a good time for me to start biting. If anything, it would give me something to do.

Luckily, being a guy, Raf is done two seconds later.

'Let's find somewhere to sit,' he says as we head downstairs. He smiles at me, and my heart does somersaults. He has such a nice smile. Why didn't I notice his nice smile before? His teeth are so white and straight. I know I've noticed his wide shoulders and yummy smell and beautiful eyes.

I follow him into the living room and look around. Melissa and Jewel are gone. Thanks for waiting for me, girls. In fact, except for a passed-out sophomore, the room is empty. I hear group laughter from downstairs, which is fine by me. Alone time with Raf.

He hands me a soda and lounges on the couch. 'So what do you think of the show so far?'

My knee is only two inches away from his. 'It's fun.'

'Yeah? How come you didn't try out in October?'

'How do you know I didn't?'

'You would have gotten in if you had.'

Was that a come-on? I've never heard one before, but from what I've garnered from the movies, it might classify. 'I wasn't sure I'd have time for everything.'

A huge smile overwhelms his face, crinkling his eyes into half-moons. 'Too busy winning competitions?'

Does he know about the maths competition? Is there a hole for nerds where I can bury myself? 'What are you talking about?'

'I spotted the trophy by the office with your name on it.' He nods. 'Pretty impressive.'

I'm not sure if I should be dying of embarrassment or puffing out my chest. On the one hand, winning shows I'm smart.

On the other hand, it's maths.

Maybe he didn't read the trophy carefully. Maybe he thinks I won a cheerleading competition. Rah-rah.

'Quick, what's the square root of two hundred and eighty-nine?'

So much for that theory. 'Seventeen,' I answer automatically.

He takes another sip of his drink. 'Five hundred and fifty?'

'It's not even, but it's around twenty-three point four . . .' I laugh.

He looks at the ceiling and pretends to calculate. 'I'll take your word for it. Smart and talented. Impressive.'

Yes! He's impressed! I've impressed the hottest male specimen on the planet! 'Not really. Just in maths. I can't conjugate a French verb to save my life. Madame Diamon wants to kill me. Who do you have?'

'Monsieur Parouche.'

'Who else do you have?'

'Henderson, Wolf.'

Wow. All accelerated classes. Why does there have to

be more than one accelerated class for each subject? Why couldn't he be in mine? 'What's your elective?'

His cheeks turn pink. 'Creative writing.'

He'd be turning bright red if he knew that I'm currently picturing him serenading me. I'll be at my window, and he'll be on the street, standing beside the monthly parking garage, reading his poems. Bet he's a better rhymer than A^2. 'Don't be embarrassed. That sounds fun.'

'I guess you're right. It's far less geeky than winning a maths competition.' A wide grin stretches across his face. 'Kidding.'

Just then a group of seniors passes by, and Will jumps on Raf. 'Are you flirting with a girl?'

How cute! Brothers wrestling.

'I was until you sat on me,' Raf answers from beneath his brother, sounding annoyed, but pleased that his big brother is paying attention to him.

Will puts him in a headlock, messes up his hair and then faces me. 'So you're his new partner, huh?'

'Yup.' I'm on the couch with Raf, the love of my life, and Will, the president of the student council. This must be heaven.

'His new girlfriend too?'

Raf turns the colour of the couch. I'm pretty sure I match. You'd think the class president could be a little more mature. Not that I mind. Say it again! Say it again!

'Will, I'm going to kick your ass later,' Raf mumbles from beneath his brother.

Will laughs, messes up his hair again and takes off.

'Brothers,' Raf says, shaking his head. 'I have two. Mitch is in his third year at NYU. They're both pains. What about you?'

'One sister.' Hopefully Prissy will never make it to that level. And I don't want him to know anything about any potential wedding. No way. My schedule is wide open. Or it will be once Miri's spell works.

'What's she like?'

'She's . . .' Magical? Focused? A brown belt? 'Full of surprises.'

We talk for the rest of the night. Or at least I think we're talking. It's hard to tell what's going on from cloud nine. The conversation seems to revolve around school, friends and television. Turns out he hates reality TV as much as I do. (See? We are so made for each other.) Around midnight, Raf glances at his watch. 'I've gotta head out soon. I'm playing hockey at 7 a.m. How are you getting home?'

He's a genius, a poet, gorgeous, a fantastic dancer . . . and athletic? Is it possible? 'I'll get a cab with Jewel.' I should be going home soon too. I have no curfew, but it's understood that I'll be home before twelve thirty.

He fidgets with his fingers. 'Um . . . I was wondering . . . what are you doing for the rest of the weekend? Do you want to come to a concert tomorrow night? My dad got me some comp tickets, and I have an extra one. Do you like Robert Crowne?'

Omigod. Omigod. He's asking me out on a date. I seriously think my heart just exploded. Oh, wait. I just forgot to breathe. Must focus. In, out. Out, in. Oh, no, I'm screwing the order up. 'O-OK,' I stammer, before I pass out from lack of oxygen.

He smiles that adorable smile. 'Why don't I call you around one tomorrow and we'll make a plan?'

I nod, too happy to risk speaking. I write down my

number for him while trying to catch my breath, and we go downstairs to find Jewel.

I can't stop the smile from spreading across my face. Having a date feels amazing. Like my back is being tickled, I'm biting into a brownie and I'm floating all at the same time.

I bet this feels even better than having magical powers. I spot Mick picking some girl up off her feet and it doesn't even bother me. From now on all of my energy will be focused on Raf. Sorry, Mick.

I have a date.

14
My First Ever Quasi Date

Raf has obviously changed his mind and decided to take someone else to see Robert Crowne.

It's one thirty. He has not called.

'Can we go now?' Miri whines. She's already in her coat and boots, waiting by the door.

'Ten minutes,' I say.

'You said that ten minutes ago.'

I ignore her and continue wandering around the kitchen, pretending to be busy.

'I know you're pretending to be busy.'

I sit down on the tiled kitchen floor. 'He said he'd call at one.'

Ring!

I leap to pick up the receiver, but all I hear is a dial tone. 'Hello?' Weird.

Miri is bent over and howling. 'Sorry, I couldn't resist.'

'Huh? You did that?'

'Yeah,' she says between giggles.

My hopeful expression morphs into an annoyed scowl. 'How?'

'I'm not sure. I kind of suggested that you hear the phone ring. Isn't that funny? It didn't even ring.'

I wag my finger at her. 'Not funny. Don't do that. Why isn't he calling?'

'He's a boy. He's late.'

'What do you know about boys?'

'More than you, if you're expecting him to call on time. He'd better hurry up. I'm overheating.'

Just then the phone rings. I eye her with suspicion. 'Is that you?'

'No, I swear, it isn't.'

'Are you forcing him to call?'

'Don't be crazy. What's the big deal, anyway? You said it wasn't even a date. That he got free tickets and has no one else to take.'

I grab the phone. Then I drop it and grab it again. 'Hello?' I did say that. If he got the tickets for free, then is it more of a friend thing than a date?

'Hi, is Rachel there, please?' It's him! It's him! It's him!

'Speaking.'

'Hey, Rachel, it's Raf.'

I try to infuse my voice with surprise. 'Oh, hi, Raf. How are you?'

'Good. Just making sure we're still on for tonight.'

'Definitely.' Yes! He doesn't want to cancel!

'Great. It's at eight. Where do you live?'

I tell him my address.

'Hey, you're right on my way. I'll come by and pick you up?'

That is such a date thing to do. A friend doesn't pick a friend up. A friend meets a friend. Like how I met Jewel. 'Sure. If you want.' I say goodbye and hang up the phone. 'I have a date! Kind of. Do you think it's a date?'

'If he's meeting Mom, it's a date.'

'He's only meeting Mom because she's on the way,' I clarify. Obviously, I don't want him to meet my mom. It will not improve my chances of future kind-of dates.

Miri pushes me out the door. 'We can discuss this en route. We have a lot of shopping to do. Did you bring your Hanukkah money?'

'Looooooong gone. I've bought shoes, jeans, make-up . . . But I have twenty bucks on me from leftover allowance.'

Miri blinks at me. 'I have two hundred saved up from my birthday and the holidays.'

How did she save two hundred? Oh, right. She borrows my stuff instead of purchasing her own.

As soon as I lock the door behind me, I ask, 'So where are we going? Some mystical secret market? Is there a Diagon Alley in New York like in Harry Potter? Will we have to ride the four and a half subway line?'

'You're being crazy again,' Miri says. 'We're going to the supermarket. And we'd better hurry, because Mom said she'd only be running errands for a few hours.'

'The supermarket?' That is so uninspired.

We enter Food Emporium and push our cart down the aisle. 'We should stock up,' Miri says, thinking out loud. 'So I don't have to keep stealing ingredients from Mom's kitchen.'

'What's on your list?'

'Almonds, apples, basil, butter, chamomile, cherries, chile peppers, garlic, ginger, honey, horseradish, lemon, mint, mustard, onions, salt, tomatoes and yogurt.'

Any more food and we'd have a buffet.

'And maybe some mozzarella.'

'Why? What spell is that for? Are you going to make us taller?' I start laughing. 'Get it? Because it stretches?' Maybe I should be a comedienne.

'Ha ha.' She leans against the wall and almost knocks over a display of cereal that's placed under a giant cardboard strawberry. What is it these days with the dried fruit in cereal? Are we astronauts? Too lazy to cut up our own fruit? 'No,' Miri says after she catches her balance. 'I'm in the mood for pizza. And Mom might be suspicious about why we went to the grocery store. If we make dinner, she won't grill us. Following?'

'Like our offering to make dinner won't be suspicious?'

She casts me an accusatory look. '*You* offering to make dinner would be suspicious, not me.'

'You are so very clever,' I say, and throw a candy bar into the cart. Yum.

'Don't get that,' Miri says. 'The manufacturer makes South American children work in sweatshops.'

I almost take it out. But, really, would one little candy bar make a difference? Bet Mir got that from some conspiracy theory website anyway.

'Let's get some bath salts for Mom,' Miri says. 'Maybe she'll like them. And maybe we'll need them.'

I pick up the honey and the almonds. 'So tell me, what do these things do? Honey makes you sweet? Almonds make you nuts?'

'All these herbs and foods and, um . . . condiments have magical properties. They send vibrations into the cosmos when combined with my raw will and the spell.'

'I have no idea what you just said.'

'You know how a smell will make you feel a certain way?'

Like Raf's smell. Yum. 'Yeah.'

'It's the same thing. The spell, the ingredients and my power all work together to make what I wish for happen.'

'Cool.' I push the cart down the frozen-food aisle. 'But why does it get cold whenever you do magic?'

'I'm not sure. Maybe the energy in the room is being sucked into the spell?'

'Can everyone feel the temperature change? Or maybe just other witches?' I ask hopefully.

'Everyone. That's why Mom says it's especially dangerous to do spells in public.'

'Oh.' We head towards the meat-and-poultry section. Wait a sec. 'You said the spell works with the ingredients and your powers. But you made the lobster move without a single word.'

'But I didn't have any control over what I did. These spells allow me to be in control of what I wish for.'

I hurry her towards the baking aisle, *away* from the dead animals, just in case. 'So what do spices do?'

'Well, chamomile is a calmer. Salt is a cleanser. Garlic is a protector.'

'What are we using for the truth spell?'

'It's easy. All we need for that are water, almonds and a little mint to give it some kick. And there aren't even any crazy fractions to confuse me.'

'Kick?'

'Yeah. Mint is an activator.'

In the vegetable aisle I peruse the onions. Cipollini, Mayan, red, red pearl, white pearl, yellow, Maui. 'Is there a specific type you had in mind?'

She looks mildly afraid. 'I don't know. Can't we just get a regular one?'

'What's a regular one?'

She points at a beige one. 'That looks like the kind Mom uses.'

I toss it into the cart as though it's a basketball. Score! 'Hey, any ingredients we can add to make me irresistible tonight?'

She shakes her head over the shopping cart. 'Don't you want him to like you for you, and not because of a spell?'

'You're the one who made him call me.'

'No, I did *not*. I would never do that. It wouldn't be right.'

Wouldn't be right unless I agreed to set the table for a whole year, I think, but refrain from saying. I wouldn't want her to get mortally insulted and accidentally-on-purpose sabotage my date tonight.

'Besides, you're already irresistible,' she adds, making me smile. 'I'm just a beginner at all this hocus-pocus, remember? Why risk what you already have?' She pushes the cart toward the condiments.

I plop a container of yogurt into the cart. 'I already know Raf likes me for me. He asked me out, didn't he?'

Although, before I got into the fashion show, he'd never even talked to me. If Miri hadn't cast that dancing spell, I'd be watching TV tonight with Tammy.

So what? Maybe sometimes love needs to be kick-started. You know, laced with a little mint.

'I can't believe you girls made dinner!' my mother exclaims, swallowing another mouthful of pizza. While we were at the grocery store, we also picked up pizza crust, lettuce and a loaf of French bread. Are we not the best daughters ever? 'I might put you two girls in charge of cooking once a week. Who knew? How much did all this cost?'

'Only fifteen dollars,' Miri says. The pizza stuff alone came to fourteen. The rest of the bill came closer to fifty. The nonperishables are hidden in Miri's closet, and the fruits are buried behind larger items in the fridge.

'Well, dinner shouldn't be coming out of your allowance.' She reaches into her wallet. 'Here's a twenty.'

Maybe that's how Miri still has so much money. Our mother is lining her pockets. I have to give my sister credit. It was a pretty good idea and the pizza is tasty. Except for the sunflower seeds she for some reason thought would make a good topping. I keep piling them on to my napkin.

'Rachel, Tammy called.'

'Oh yeah?' I'm dying to tell her about my date. She's going to freak. But spilling the boy beans means I have to come clean about Mick's party, and how can I do that without looking like the World's Worst Friend?

I'll deal with it on Monday. I'll call Jewel instead.

'Girls, I'll do the dishes. Rachel, you go get ready for your date.' She does a big freakish wink. It's weird; when she winks, her open eye doesn't move at all. Most people's eyes widen, but not my mom's. Creepy. She's pretty excited about this milestone occasion. Ever since I told her, she's been winking and patting my head. Could be worse. She could have said that I couldn't go, or that I was too young to date or something lame like that. I wouldn't have put it past her.

'It's not a date, Mom.' Even though he's picking me up and not meeting me somewhere, he never used the word *date*. So my mom can't either.

'Sorry, your quasi date.' She gives me another one of her freakish winks. 'Do I get to meet this quasi date?'

'Not if I can help it. I know this is my first quasi date, but let's try to keep it low-key.'

'Does that mean no pictures?' Miri asks, exposing the pizza in her mouth.

'Ha ha. Video camera only.' And then, just in case either of them takes me seriously, I clarify, 'No camera.'

'Is he paying for the tickets?' Mom asks.

'What difference does it make?'

She scrapes a piece of cheese off her plate with her fork and deposits it in her mouth. 'If he's paying, then it's a real date.'

'What are you from, the 1950s? Guys don't pay for dates any more.'

'Yes, they do,' she says stubbornly.

'I'd hardly qualify you as a dating expert, Mom. Anyway, the tickets are comps, meaning he didn't pay for them. What are you two doing tonight?' I ask, hoping to change the subject. I'm nervous enough without the inquisition.

'Continuing with Miri's training,' Mom says, scratching another piece of cheese with her fork. 'We're almost done with the history of magic.'

Miri's eyes light up like two candles. 'So, we're going to start practical magic now?'

Mom quickly shakes her head. 'No. Not yet. Next we're learning about consequences and ethics. Don't worry. You'll get to use real magic eventually.'

Miri almost chokes on a piece of pizza. If Mom only knew.

'I'm going to get ready,' I say, and push back my chair.

My mom makes smooching noises. 'Do you think he'll kiss you at the end of this quasi date?'

'Wouldn't you like to know,' I say, and run off to shower before they see how red my cheeks are. If I had one wish, it would be for him to kiss me. No, I take that back. If I had one wish, I'd wish for him to ask me to Spring Fling.

I turn on the hot water and step under it. It feels amazing. You get so much more pleasure from a shower when you do it at night rather than first thing in the morning, when you're half asleep and would rather be in bed. Today I think I'll even shampoo twice, just like the bottle suggests.

I know my evening plans are causing *mucho* excitement around here, but that's because no one has gone on a date in two years. After the divorce Mom went out with a slew of men whom she met through work (not that I met any of them – she only dated on the weekends when we were at my dad's, but I saw their names on caller ID), but she didn't like any of them. Eventually, they stopped calling.

The truth is, I think she still has a thing for my dad.

She kept his shirt. It was his comfy sweatshirt, the grey one with the soft worn-in neck and blue pen stain on the sleeve. The one he'd wear when we all hung out and watched TV. That was before he made partner and worked all the time.

I asked my mom if she'd seen it, but she said no. And then, a year later, when I woke up at seven one morning and couldn't fall back asleep, I sneaked into my mother's room to borrow a romance novel and saw her sleeping with it cuddled in her arms. Not wearing it. Just . . . holding it.

I went back to my bed and cried myself to sleep. Being in love with someone, marrying him, having two kids with him and then being abandoned by him has to be the most tragic thing ever. He started dating STB only six months after he left, before the divorce was even final, but sometimes I wonder if maybe she was in the picture a wee bit earlier than he likes to admit. Like maybe while he was still living here. Maybe that's why he 'didn't feel the same'. Who knows?

I would have thought my mom would hate him, but she never says one bad word about him. Ever. She just cuddles with his sweatshirt. I'm hoping she's washing it occasionally for hygiene reasons, but it's really none of my business.

By 7:20, I'm all dolled up. I'm wearing my second-best pair of jeans (sucks that I wore my best pair last night) and a green shirt that hopefully accentuates my eyes.

At 7:25, Raf buzzes up.

'Your quasi date is here!' my mother yells from the living room.

'Can you please stop saying that?' I yell back.

Two seconds later he rings the doorbell, and I run to greet him before my mother can. Unfortunately, both my mom and sister instantly appear behind me in the hall. How did they get here so fast? Did they beam themselves over? I'll have to keep a closer eye on those two.

I open the door. Raf smiles. He looks so cute. He's wearing jeans, the same jeans as yesterday, I think – wish

I could go put on my yesterday's pair – and his black wool coat.

I love him.

I wish my mother did have her camera with her. I'd blow up the picture and hang it on my wall.

'Hi, Rachel,' he says. 'Hello, Mrs Weinstein.'

I almost laugh at the sound of *Mrs Weinstein*. No one calls her that.

'Please call me Carol,' Mom says. 'It's nice to meet you.'

'And this is my sister, Miri,' I say, motioning to her.

'Nice to meet you,' he says.

Super. We're all happy to meet each other. Now, with the boring pleasantries out of the way, maybe I can go on my quasi date. 'Be home twelve-ish,' I say, and before anyone else can speak, I wave goodbye and close the door behind me. I catch my mom winking at me, and I think Raf does too.

I'm trying telepathically to tell him to hold my hand, but it's not working. His A-list friends Ron, Justin (he's one of the sophomores in the band Illuminated) and Doree (what's she doing here?) are waiting for us outside Irving Plaza.

'Hey, Rachel!' Doree sings, linking her arm through mine. 'Isn't this awesome? Justin and I just started going out on Wednesday,' she whispers. 'I'm so happy Raf asked you. Now we can double.' I hope Doree doesn't raise her hand during the concert.

Raf takes out our tickets and hands them to the bouncer, who proceeds to brand us with green we're-underage-so-don't-sell-us-booze bracelets.

We push through the crowd and squeeze as close as possible to the front. Doree's influence, obviously. By the time the band members appear, we're only a few feet back from the stage.

The lights turn off and Robert Crowne's voice yells, 'Hello, New York!'

The lights flick on and there he is, Robert Crowne, only a few feet in front of me. Omigod. I can't believe I'm here. At a sold-out concert for Robert Crowne. There's no way I'm dreaming this time – it's way too loud.

The lights are low and a rainbow of primary colours washes over the room. Raf starts singing with the music. Justin plays his imaginary guitar and Doree, shocker, waves her hands in the air to the music.

I can't help myself. I start to dance. The music, the crowd, the company . . . the gorgeous dark-haired Robert Crowne on stage. He's wearing black leather pants and a long-sleeved silver shirt (I bet he's boiling) and is moving all over the stage. He looks just as sexy as he does on TV. Everything feels perfect. Who knew having rhythm could be so much fun? I spend the next two songs letting my body connect with the music. And then I remember Raf, and I look up, and he's watching me, and suddenly we're dancing together. No twirls or dips or anything like that, but just moving and flirting and having a blast.

'You're an amazing dancer!' he yells over the sound of the electric guitar.

'Thank you!' I yell back.

'Listen, I was thinking . . . Do you want to go to Spring Fling with me?'

171

Bullseye! 'I'd love to,' I say, and smile at him. He smiles back at me.

Now, that's a date. And not a quasi date. A 100 per cent pure-date date.

15

Getting 'Tude from Tammy

'**W**eren't you at your dad's last weekend?' Tammy asks.

'Uh-huh,' I say, pretending to be preoccupied with the contents of my locker.

'So what happened to you this weekend? I called you a gazillion times.' She looks genuinely confused. The fact that she doesn't even consider I blew her off makes me feel like a piece of gum on my shoe. (Can someone explain why there are so many pieces of gum on the ground? What reason could one possibly have for spitting his gum on to the sidewalk? Are people so lazy that they can't wait till they reach a garbage can?)

'Sorry. It was just one of those weekends,' I say, desperately racking my brain for something to distract her. Maybe I should pretend-slip? Or dump my pencil case on to the floor? Brainstorm! 'I have awesome news!'

She leans against her locker and gives me an OK sign. 'Yeah? What?'

Operation Distract Tammy successful! Hmm. Now, how do I tell her the good news without mentioning my weekend? I don't want to get into a discussion about

Friday since I probably should have invited her, so I'm going to dive right into the awesome part. I motion to her to follow me into the girls' bathroom. I don't want to hyperventilate in front of everyone. When the door swings closed behind us, I gush, 'Raf asked me to Spring Fling!'

Since Tammy is well aware of my Raf/Mick obsession, I expect her to jump up and down in delight. Or at least smile.

Instead she shakes her head and looks at me as if I've just told her my mother is a Martian (which truthfully wouldn't be so far off since she's a witch, but whatever). 'Are you crazy?' she asks. 'You can't go to Spring Fling.'

'Why?' What's her problem? I turn the water on, wet my fingers, then run them through my hair.

'Hello? Your dad's wedding is on the same night.'

Oops. I forgot about that tiny snag. But still, that doesn't mean Tammy has to thunderstorm all over my parade. Maybe she's jealous that I have a date and she doesn't.

I see her concerned face in the mirror, eyes wide, slight overbite piercing into lower lip, and I realize what an idiot I am. Tammy isn't jealous. She's just stating the obvious. She got an invitation to the wedding, after all.

She doesn't know about Miri's new talent or our secret plan, so of course she thinks I have to go to the wedding. 'I guess I was so excited that he asked me, I forgot it was on the same night,' I offer as explanation.

'I'm really sorry.' She pats me on the shoulder. 'Don't be disappointed. I'm sure he'll ask you to the next dance.' Her face brightens. 'I have an idea. Why don't you ask your dad if you can bring a date?'

174

Poor clueless Tammy. First of all, there is no way I would make Raf suffer through the wedding, aka the horror show. It's one thing for Tammy to be there as a friend, but a boy I'm trying to get to like me? No chance. And second, and more important, there is *no way whatsoever* that I would allow Raf to see me in that hideous pink-flamingo monstrosity. 'Yeah, that's a good idea,' I say. As if. The bell rings, and I add, 'We should get to homeroom.'

We're heading upstairs when I spot Raf charging through the hallway, his coat still on. He perks up when he sees me and motions for me to hold on. After shoving his stuff into his locker and taking out his books, he walks over to us. 'Hey, girls.'

'Hey.' Sometimes my lack of creativity kills me. Why do I sound like such a robot around boys like Raf?

'Hi, Raf,' Tammy says, grinning.

He smiles, and I notice he has a dimple in his left cheek. How adorable! How amazing that I notice something new and spectacular every time I see him. 'Hurrying off to win another maths competition?' he asks me.

He's teasing me! How adorable is that? 'I'm not giving up till I come in first,' I say.

He laughs and drums his pen against his notebook. 'You tell me who the loser who beat you is, and I'll take care of him.' The second bell rings. 'Got to get to class. See you later, Rachel.'

I exhale. I watch him disappear down the hall (what an adorable butt! It's barely even there!), and then Tammy and I hike the stairs two at a time.

'You two are so cute together,' Tammy gushes. 'So what's the story? Are you, like, a thing now?'

'I don't think so. We've only been out once.' Kind of. And he didn't even kiss me. After the concert, he walked me home (Because it was a date? Because he didn't want me getting kidnapped/followed? Because he was dying to spend those few more precious moments alone with me? Who can say?), and when we reached my front door, I thought, This is it, he's going to kiss me, he's just going to dive into it and why oh why did I not pop the piece of spearmint gum that was sitting in my pocket the whole night into my mouth? Is it supposed to do its job from inside my jacket? And he leaned in . . . and patted me on the shoulder. On the shoulder. Is there something wrong with my lips? I knew they were too small – he keeps missing them entirely. Maybe Spring Fling will be the big night. I'm definitely investing in new lip liner. Anyway, I think it's time to fill Tammy in on Saturday night, which is when he popped the question. I'll just have to leave out the details that led up to it. 'I have so much to fill you in on.'

'Seems like it. Do you want to do something after school today?'

What day is today? Oh yeah. Monday. Since my amazing quasi date with Raf, my mind's been in a haze. 'Can't. Sorry. I have rehearsal.'

'Oh. Right,' she says, and looks down at her shoes.

I feel like a jerk for continuously ditching her. She's never been anything but a good friend. 'Why don't we do something on Wednesday?'

She half smiles. 'Yeah? No rehearsal?'

'Nope. We have Wednesdays off. London has Pilates. It'll be great. You'll come over. We'll watch a movie. Maybe convince my mom to order Chinese.'

'Sounds great,' she says, and gives me the OK sign. We find two seats by the left wall in homeroom, and I tell her about my quasi date.

'Did you see what Janice Cooper was wearing today?' Stephy asks after school at practice.

Doree bursts out laughing. 'Yeah, stirrups. From, like, the eighties. How funny is that? She's in one of my classes. I swear, just seeing what she'll show up in every day keeps me from falling asleep.'

The rest of the girls in the cast laugh. We're sitting on benches in the cafeteria, taking a ten-minute break. We've been working on our all-girls dance for the last hour. My bum muscles are killing me from all the shaking. Jewel and I have an awesome duet where we strut down the catwalk together and then both do the body wave. I love the body wave. I become the body wave.

'Her hair is from the eighties too,' Melissa says. 'I think she might actually crimp it.'

I know they're sounding horrible, but I don't think they mean to. Gossiping is their way of letting off steam. In any case, I'm in too good a mood to let anything upset me. I'm going to Spring Fling! I'm going to Spring Fling!

Kind of. I still have to deal with the annoying little issue of my father's wedding, as Tammy so generously pointed out.

I dig inside my schoolbag to find the candy bar I bought at the supermarket. As my dance-mates continue cutting into every girl who isn't here, I tear open the wrapper. 'Anyone want some?' I ask, and take a bite.

They all stare at me, eyes wide, jaws dropped, apparently completely dumbfounded.

Should I have offered them some before I took a bite? It's not a big deal. I can break off a piece from the other end.

'You're going to eat that?' Melissa asks.

Oh, come on, not her too. 'Why? Because of the South American thing?'

They all continue to stare at me. 'In less than a month you have to dance in front of the entire school,' Melissa says. 'Do you know how many calories are in that?'

'Two hundred and seventy-two,' Doree pipes up. Suck-up.

'Eleven grams of fat,' Melissa adds.

Stephy scoots closer to us. 'Thirty grams of carbs.'

I'm about to wrap it up and hide it in my bag when Jewel says, 'Who cares? If she's hungry, let her eat it.'

Thank you, Jewel! I take a second (and a mite smaller) bite.

'Easy for you to say, Jewel,' Melissa argues. 'Not everyone is born with your body and your metabolism.' She eyes my thighs.

I think I've lost my appetite. I stuff the candy bar back into my bag.

London strides into the room and we all scurry off the benches and back to our assigned spots, five freshmen on the right, five sophomores on the left. Today she's wearing green. Why is she entitled to make a fashion statement, but Janice just gets laughed at? Personally, I think Janice looked cool in a retro sort of way, but London reminds me of an M&M. (Or maybe my brain is stuck on chocolate.)

'Ready to finish up, girls?' London asks, and we all nod. Not that we have a choice. London's questions are always orders incognito. 'Excellent,' she says. 'We're almost done. We'll wrap it up on Saturday. Then, on Sunday, I want to hold a full-cast rehearsal. So why don't we meet this Saturday afternoon at two? Just for an hour.'

Uh-oh. I raise my hand.

'You don't have to raise your hand, Rachel. This isn't class. I won't give you a detention.'

Melissa snickers, and my cheeks heat up. Is it possible they found out about my detention? Is it loserish to get a detention? I thought it would give me a rebel edge. Or maybe they don't even know and I'm making a crisis out of a spelling mistake.

I lower my hand and feel mildly ridiculous. 'I can't make practice this weekend. I'll be at my dad's on Long Island.'

'That's so cute,' London says. 'You still do the weekend at your dad's thing?'

Still? I didn't realize it was something you grew out of. 'I kind of have to go.'

London sighs. 'Rachel, the show is in three weeks. And you've only been with us for one. When we accepted you at this late date, I warned you that you would have to devote all your time to the cause, and now you're backing out of your end of the deal. Is that fair, Rachel?'

Why is she talking to me as if I'm seven? All eyes are on me. I have a sinking feeling that maybe Laura Jenkins didn't drop out of the show, that maybe she was booted out. Please tell me that London's not going to freak out. I think I might cry if she freaks out.

'I-I.' W-why am I st-st-stuttering? 'I have to be on Long Island.'

There's no way Miri will cast the truth spell on STB without me. If I miss this weekend at my dad's, we'll have to wait two more weeks. That'll leave just one week before the wedding. What if the spell doesn't work? Would we have time to concoct something else?

'What if, instead of meeting on Saturday, we meet on Sunday before the big rehearsal?' I offer. 'I'll take a morning train back into the city. That way we all have our Saturday free.'

Jewel and some of the sophomores nod.

'I'd prefer to meet on Saturday,' Melissa quips.

I'd prefer she shut up.

London considers my proposal. 'All right. Maybe I'll spend Saturday talking to the designers. Anyone want to tag along?'

Doree, of course, raises her hand.

Wednesday morning I'm running into school, late as usual, still in my coat, when an all-in-brown London blocks my path. 'Today,' she barks. 'After school. Emergency opening practice.'

I seem to remember having some sort of plan for after school. Pizza? Chinese? What was it? 'I might have plans today . . . Isn't it our day off?'

London wrinkles her nose, as if she's tasting something vile, such as mac and cheese with ketchup (Miri does this. Is that really necessary? Does ketchup need to go on everything?), then plants her hands on her hips. 'I will not have my opening be a mess. My opening is going to be perfect. Do you understand? Perfect. And Pilates is cancelled. You'd think the instructor could have waited until after the fashion show to give birth, wouldn't you?'

Tammy! I have plans with Tammy. 'But—'

'No buts, Rachel. If you're going to bail on every practice, then you're not going to be in my show.'

Bail on every practice? I'm leaving my dad's early so I can be at practice. Doesn't that count for something? 'OK. Fine.'

She nods. 'Three o'clock, sharp.'

As soon as she slinks away, I run to my locker. Tammy is closing hers. 'Hey, Tammy,' I say, out of breath, 'save me a seat in class, will ya? I'll be there in two secs.'

'Don't worry. I'll wait for you.' She leans against the locker. 'Guess what I rented yesterday? The widescreen edition DVD of *Star Wars*. Fun, huh? And I bought the microwave popcorn that you love. The kind with extra extra extra butter.'

My mouth waters. Then I think of that candy bar, and that makes me think of the show. 'Tammy, I'm so sorry but London is forcing me to go to rehearsal after school.'

Her smile withers like a plant that's been shoved into a closet. 'Again?'

I pile the books I need on to the floor and snap my lock closed. 'Yeah.'

'Can't you not go?'

'Trust me, I tried.'

'Whatever,' she says, and storms off.

What just happened? I can't believe she did that. This is so not my fault. What am I supposed to do? I can't not go to rehearsal. Why does Tammy have to be such a drama queen?

I pick up my books and hurry to homeroom.

Tammy is sitting by the door, next to Annie, with no saved seat for me.

Humph. I'm about to take a seat by my lonesome when Doree gestures to me from the front row. Well, thank you, Doree. I'd rather sit with her anyway. At least she won't lay on the guilt.

'Hey, sexy,' she says. She's tearing out pictures of hairstyles from a magazine. 'So is it true? Raf asked you to Spring Fling?'

This is more like it. Fun, girly conversation. 'Yup. How'd you know?'

'Justin told me last night on the phone! I can't believe you didn't tell me earlier. Do you guys want to go together? We could rent a limo. Did you buy an outfit yet? I'm trying to decide what to do with my hair. How are you doing your make-up?'

Definitely more like it. 'I don't know. You?'

I feel Tammy's eyes on me, but I don't turn around. She can share her extra-extra-extra-buttered popcorn with Annie instead.

16

STB Unwittingly Swears to Tell the Truth, the Whole Truth and Nothing but the Truth

'So you're leaving Sunday morning?' Miri asks. It's Friday night, and we're lying like two sardines in our shared room on Long Island. Miri wants to talk, but I'm exhausted after a hellish week of rehearsals. I had practice every day at lunch and after school. The only number I'm in that still needs work is the freshman dance. Even though Melissa is choreographing it, I'm looking forward to it, because I'll get to dance with Raf again.

I do feel a teensy bit guilty for leaving my dad's early on Sunday, but really, it's my only option. If I don't, I'll get kicked out of the show. I'm already annoyed that I'm missing a huge party at Sean Washington's apartment tonight. *Everyone* is going to be there. Everyone except me. At least this time my absence isn't because I wasn't invited. 'Why don't you leave early with me?' I offer.

'Nah,' she says, raising her recently Band-Aided fingers to the ceiling so she can stare at them with disgust. 'I want to monitor the spell and make sure this is it. I mean *really* it.'

Today's pickup from the train was identical to the last one. Once again, STB pulled a Jekyll and Hyde. When Dad jovially took us to the car, STB was syrupy sweet. I told them I had to leave early on Sunday, and she said it was nice that I was involved in school activities. But the second he shut the car door to pick up the Chinese food (after her show-offy 'Honey, don't forget my chopsticks!'), she whipped her head around and glared at me. 'Did you forget about our fitting appointment on Sunday?'

I withered into my seat.

'Now I'll have to reschedule. Oh well. And, Miri, how are your fingers? Any better?'

Miri crossed her arms and shoved her fists under her armpits. Not her most attractive position.

'The wedding is in three weeks,' STB reminded us, as if we needed reminding. 'Here comes your father. Bet he forgot my chopsticks.'

What I don't understand is why she doesn't just buy chopsticks. Then again, there's not much about her that I do understand. I mean, why does she even want to marry my father? She obviously doesn't like his kids.

Dad got into the car, deposited the food in STB's lap and started driving.

'Did you remember my chopsticks?' she asked.

He slammed his hand against his forehead. 'Oops. Should I turn around and go back?'

'Oh, don't worry, sweetie. It's not worth it.'

What is up with STB's two faces? She's like Frosted Mini-Wheats. Sweet on one side, crusty on the other. 'I can't wait to hit her with the truth spell,' I say to Miri, who is now making shadow puppets with her bandaged fingers in our shared bedroom that night. I close my eyes and flip on to my stomach. 'He'll soon see what a horrible woman she is, and that'll be the end of those fake *oh, sweetie*s! So when do we put our plan into action?'

'In about an hour.'

Ping. My eyes spring open. 'What? I'm asleep here.'

'You're not asleep. You're talking.'

'I'm almost asleep.'

'The spell needs to be done at midnight,' she says. Her eyes are glowing in the dark.

'That abraca-sucks.'

'That's what the book says. We have to do it then, or it won't work tomorrow when we give it to STB.'

I pull the covers over my head. 'Do you really need my help? Didn't you say this one has no complicated fractions?'

Something heavy hits my feet. I think she just threw her pillow at me. 'I still need you!' she says. 'You're the Cosmic Witness.'

Whatever. 'I'm taking an hour's nap,' I say in my most annoyed voice, and let my heavy eyelids close. 'Wake me when it's time.'

The next thing I feel is her shaking me. 'It's time.' Groan. 'There's no way that was an hour.' I watch her open the blinds and move the glass of water she poured earlier to the window sill.

She pulls the borrowed beaker, a handful of mint leaves and two almonds from her knapsack, then proceeds to crush the nuts on a paper towel with a spoon. That done, she puts all these ingredients into the beaker, then goes back to the window. 'At least it's not cloudy outside. The

185

spell won't work if we can't see the moon.' She clears her throat and whispers:

> *Honesty is clear at the midnight hour.*
> *Let STB—*

She slaps her hand against her forehead. 'I meant Jennifer. I don't know if I can use an acronym. I'll have to start over.'

Double groan.

She scratches her head as though in thought. 'But since we call her STB, maybe I should refer to her that way in the spell.' One of the Band-Aids comes off in her hair and dangles there, as if a spring has come loose from her brain. 'But what if the spell gets confused because we don't call her Jennifer? Why don't I say She Who Drinks the Spell instead?'

'Sounds good,' I mumble. Who cares? I want to go back to sleep.

Miri clears her throat again.

'It's clear already!'

She scrunches up her face and purses her lips in concentration.

> *Honesty is clear at the midnight hour.*
> *Let She Who Drinks the Spell show her true colours.*
> *This I command as I stand in the moonlight,*
> *Let her words ring right and true.*

Despite being under the covers, I feel the rush of cold. She shakes the beaker, plugs it with its stopper and lays it on the floor beside her bed.

Was that the spell? That couldn't have been the spell. 'That didn't even rhyme,' I say.

'Not all spells have to rhyme.'

'I kind of like them better when they do. And that would have been so easy to rhyme too. Whoever wrote it was just being lazy. All you had to do was switch *right* and *true*.' Raf's poetry skills must be rubbing off on me.

'Yeah, what about *hour* and *colours*?'

I rack my brains for a rhyme, but come up empty. 'Hey, I can't do all the thinking around here.'

She gets back into her bed and pushes her hair out of her face. 'Send your comments to the complaints department.'

'There's a complaints department? Where is it? In a cave somewhere?'

'I'm kidding,' she says.

'Well, duh,' I snap. It ticks me off that she gets to do the fun part while all I get to do is be the Cosmic Witness. Where's the cosmic justice in that?

'*Girls, wake up!*'

What is that noise? Why is there a screaming in my head?

I open my eyes slowly to see STB looming over me. 'I've scheduled an emergency fitting for your bridesmaid dresses at eight o'clock.'

Eight o'clock? That means it's – I lift my head only high enough to see the bright red numbers on the clock – 7:05. 7:05 on a Saturday?

She has got to go.

'It's too early' I hear from Miri's bed. She must be hiding, because all I can see of her is a mass of wavy brown hair.

STB's hair is perfectly straight and slinky, and her make-up is flawless. She probably goes to bed fully made up. 'It's the only time Judy could fit us in,' she explains. 'So be thankful. Now get up. The bus leaves at seven thirty.' By *bus* she means her Lexus purchased with my father's money. Maybe Miri should turn her into a real bus driver. As if working for her money would ever occur to her. I can just imagine her in a fluorescent yellow driver's vest.

'And I would appreciate it, Rachel, if you would tidy your side of the room before the departure,' she says as she storms out the door.

She wants us to get up, eat breakfast *and* clean? In twenty-five minutes? 'You need to take care of her now,' I hiss at Miri. 'Just rub it all over her.'

Miri sticks her bare feet into her slippers and shakes her head. 'She needs to drink it, remember? Don't you pay attention? The spell was for She Who Drinks the Spell.'

'Then we need to get it into her coffee,' I say.

'When we stop at Starbucks, you'll run in and dump the potion into her cup.'

'Why can't you do it?'

'Because I do everything else.'

True. 'Sounds fair. But why am I offering to get her coffee? She always gets it.'

She fingers the Band-Aid on her pinkie. 'Tell her you want a cup of coffee too. Tell her you've started drinking it.'

I take the fastest shower recorded – how many drops can fall in three seconds? And by the time I come out, both my and Miri's beds are perfectly made. I don't know if she did it manually or magically but, either way, I approve. Two pieces of toast and twenty minutes later, we're set to go. As soon as we pile into the car, STB says, 'We're making a quick stop at Starbucks.' When I tell her

I want some too, and offer to run in for her, she looks surprised. She shrugs and hands me a twenty. She's paying for her own downfall! I love it; it's so sneaky. 'I want an iced caramel macchiato with soy milk and half an artificial sweetener,' she says.

'Me too!' Prissy hollers from the backseat. 'Can I have one too?'

'No, dear,' STB says. 'Coffee stunts your growth.'

I look at my chest. All kinds of growth? I can't really afford to take chances.

I order two of the coffees that STB asked for from a super-short woman with a skunk-like white stripe in her black hair. Might as well go with what STB asked for, even though I have no idea what it is.

'What cup size?' Skunk Woman asks.

Tee hee. She said 'cup size'. 'Small.' Unfortunately.

'A tall?'

Maybe she didn't hear me. 'No,' I say. 'A smaaaaaaall.'

'A tall is a small.'

'That's the most ridiculous thing I've ever heard.' Besides, if she knows that small is tall, why even ask?

She sighs. 'Do you want coffee or not?'

'Yes, please.' The world of coffee is more complicated than I thought.

I pay her, and she tells me to wait at the end of the counter. After I watch a gazillion other people order – 'Skim caffè latte!' 'Cappuccino!' 'Frappuccino!' – mine are finally ready. I gingerly remove the beaker from my purse and pour a smidgen of the potion into STB's cup, then return the rest to my purse. Then I add artificial sweetener to both.

Back in the car, as I'm about to hand her a cup, I'm

paralysed by my own carelessness. Our two coffees look exactly alike. Which one did I put the potion in?

Miri watches my hesitation and drops her head into her hands in despair. Me blabbing the truth all over town could pose a problem. Must think. I try to remember which hand is holding which coffee . . .

Hers is the left one. Definitely. I hand her the left one. Uh-oh. I think I made a mistake.

She immediately takes a sip. 'They seem to have added mint.'

Score! I gave her the right one! When we pull into the dressmaker's parking lot, I mouth to Miri, 'How long does it take to work?'

She shrugs.

I continue mouthing. 'And how do we turn it off?'

She shrugs again. Then she smiles. 'I brought everything we could possibly need to make the antidote in case of a problem,' she whispers.

Problem? Us having problems? You don't say.

'Thanks for seeing us at such short notice,' STB says to Judy. 'Rachel apologizes. Miri, you go first. You're always the most difficult.'

I hate her. To keep my mouth too busy to tell her off, I take another sip of my yummy drink.

Miri sulks as she goes into the changing room. Maybe I should accidentally spill the coffee on our butt-ugly dresses so we won't have to wear them.

Prissy is on her knees, playing with slivers of past dresses on the floor with one hand and picking her nose with the other.

STB is staring weirdly at the ceiling. Soon Miri, clad in

her now completed pink doily, stomps back into the main room. 'Wow, Miri,' STB says. 'You look gorgeous. Like a princess.'

I almost drop my coffee. Miri looks up in shock.

'When I was your age,' STB says, blinking rapidly, 'I always wanted a dress like this. You guys are going to look terrific in the pictures.' She sighs. 'Rachel, I don't know how you could have forgotten about the fitting. Weren't you looking forward to it? I was. I enjoy the time we get to spend just us girls.'

What is she talking about?

Judy looks up. 'Are you all right, Ms Abramson?'

STB nods slowly. 'I'm just happy. I'm lucky, you know? To have found love a second time.'

'You're lucky, Mommy,' Prissy sings. 'And I'm going to be a princess!'

We must have given her the wrong spell. The sappy cheeseball spell.

Miri and I nervously eye each other in the mirror, waiting for her to speak again. She doesn't open her mouth until five minutes later, when I have my dress on.

'You look so beautiful too,' she says, and sighs.

She's lost it. I do not look beautiful. But I do look a bit like Glinda the Good Witch. I squeeze my eyes tight and silently chant, 'Let STB spill her coffee on this dress, let STB spill her coffee on this dress . . .'

Maybe looking like a witch will help me kick-start my powers. Maybe I'll trick the fates into thinking I should be a witch because I'm dressed like one!

STB tosses her now-empty cup into the garbage pail.

Guess that didn't work.

While STB helps Prissy change into her dress, I

191

whisper to Miri, 'I think you screwed up and made her hallucinate.'

Miri looks terrified. 'I know. Something's weird. What do we do?'

As they emerge from the dressing room, STB is playing with Prissy's hair. 'I love you so much, honey. Do you know how much? More than the stars in the sky. More than a trillion billion stars!'

Baby talk? There's definitely been a screw-up somewhere. 'Maybe we gave her a nice potion?' I mouth to Miri.

Yes, must have been a nice potion. At least that's what I believe until STB calls my dad from her cell when we're finished and back in the car. 'We're on our way home from the dressmaker . . . You're where? At the office? . . . No, I'm not happy with you being at the office. Your children are visiting you and they want to see you. Rachel has to go back early on Sunday, which is another reason why you should be home today. You can go to the office on Monday. And it would be great if you could start preparing brunch.' And then she hangs up.

What was that? Miri kicks the back of my seat. I can't believe STB just told my father off. I have never heard her tell my father off. Ever. I turn around and Miri and I share a look. Is it possible the spell just kicked in? My father is finally going to see what a horrible woman she is?

We arrive home to find my father in the kitchen, leaning over a frying pan on the stove. He's never made a meal in his life. I didn't even think he knew what a frying pan looked like, never mind where it was.

'How are my favourite girls?' he asks.

'Fine,' we all say simultaneously.

Prissy dances around the kitchen floor in her socks. 'I look like a princess in my dress, don't I, Mommy? For the wedding I'm going to wear lipstick and green eye shadow and—'

'What are you making?' I interrupt, putting my arm around my dad's waist.

He flips an egg. 'Eggs with smoked salmon.'

STB kisses him on the cheek. 'And for Miri?'

And for Miri? What? Miri and I both freeze in our tracks beside the kitchen table.

'She can eat this,' my father says. 'It's not meat.'

STB sighs. 'Honey, can you please be considerate of other people's needs? You know she doesn't eat fish. Sometimes you can be so selfish. You tend to focus only on what you want, not on what makes others happy. Like yesterday, when I asked you to get me chopsticks and you didn't even bother to remember. We would all be a lot happier if you considered other people's feelings. And dietary preferences.'

Um . . . have I been transported to an alternative universe? Has STB's body been poached by an alien soul?

I'm in shock. My dad, Miri and even Prissy are in shock. If our jaws had dropped any lower, they would have crashed against the perfectly polished floor. I don't think anyone has ever called my father selfish before. In the entire time he was married to my mother, I don't recall her ever telling him off.

His face contorts into a configuration I have never seen. His mouth gets all squiggly and crooked. He's going to blow a fuse. He's going to freak. There's going to be a screaming match louder than the most deafening rock concert of all time.

 193

He opens his mouth. He closes his mouth. He opens his mouth again. Time has stopped, like in those sci-fi movies with the cool special effects.

'Sorry,' he says. 'I didn't realize I was being selfish. I'll try harder to be more considerate.' He divvies up the eggs and slides them on to plates. 'Miri, what can I make you? How about some pancakes?'

Omigod.

Miri looks at me and then at my dad. 'Thanks,' she responds slowly.

Our spell must be kicking in. STB is saying what she really feels. Any second now, she's going to start ripping into us.

Except for my dad, who's still cooking, we're all sitting at the kitchen table.

This would be a good time, Monster Dearest. Go ahead, do your stuff. Start berating us.

She smiles at me.

Time to take this into our own hands. Literally. I kick Miri under the table, and I motion for her to bite her nails.

She nods. Then she picks off the Band-Aids one by one from her fingers and goes to town, as if she hasn't eaten in weeks. She's nibbling, she's chomping, she's picking, she's ripping. It's a virtual nail feast.

STB pats her on the head. 'Miri, I can see I'm fighting a losing battle with your fingers, so I'm going to stop bugging you. But I want you to know I'm only trying to get you to stop because I know how tough a habit it is to break. I used to bite too, and I seriously damaged my teeth and nail beds. I also got sick all the time, because the germs on my fingers ended up in my system. The

194

Band-Aids trick worked for me, and I was hoping it would for you. But I guess not.'

Miri stops picking and looks at me for help.

But I'm as confused as she is. Why isn't STB being mean? Why isn't she hurling insults across the salt and pepper like a volleyball over a net? We need to try something else. What else would she be mean about?

I peruse the room and settle on my dad's striped yellow shirt as he cooks the pancakes. He hasn't changed since returning from the office, and he's wearing one of his most hideous items of clothing.

'Great shirt, Dad,' I say. 'Don't you like it, Miri?'

'Oh, I love it,' she says.

Here it comes. I point to the yellow atrocity. 'Jennifer, what do you think?'

'I don't love it,' she admits.

Yes!

My dad looks down at his shirt in surprise.

She shrugs. 'It makes you look like a banana.'

Prissy giggles. 'A banana! You look like a banana!'

I try to wipe away a smile with the back of my hand. Too much. What's he going to say to that? He's not just going to stand there and be insulted, is he?

The room is so silent I can hear the sizzling of the pancakes. 'Really?' he says finally. 'But you've never said anything before. Speaking of bananas, Miri, do you want some in your pancakes?'

'Um . . . sure,' she says.

Prissy jiggles in her seat. 'Can. I have bananas in my eggs?'

'No, honey, bananas don't go with eggs,' STB says,

and then turns back to my dad. 'I know, and I should have. Sometimes you don't have the best taste in clothes.'

He's going to blow up. He's going to put down the banana he's cutting for Miri and explode. He shakes his head and . . . laughs. 'I thought you liked it. That's why I keep wearing it.'

Why is he laughing? She just insulted his wardrobe! He should be freaking out.

She adds some salt to her eggs. 'Well, I don't. Sorry.'

He turns off the stove. 'Are there other articles of clothing of mine you don't like?'

'Definitely.' She chews slowly, seemingly taking a mental inventory of his wardrobe. 'Your green fluorescent sweater? I wouldn't wear that in public if I were you.'

'I wish you would tell me these things. I rely on you to be my mirror to the outside world.'

'We'll go through your closet after brunch. Put together all the clothes I don't think suit you and give them to a shelter.'

'Thanks, Jen. I appreciate it.' And then he leans over the table and kisses her. Yes, kisses her. This is *not* the plan.

When he finally pulls away, STB says, 'Why don't we have a fashion show with your stuff, just like Rachel's fashion show? Rachel, you can show your dad how to do the walk!'

Abort plan! Abort plan! Why are they planning horrendously embarrassing family activities instead of yelling and screaming?

'When is the show, Rachel?' my dad asks. 'I'm sorry. I forgot the date.'

196

'The Friday night before Spring – before your wedding.' Oops. Caught myself just in time there.

'Honey,' STB says. 'You knew that. That's why we scheduled the rehearsal dinner for Thursday night. I'm very excited to see you in the show, Rachel,' she continues. Her eyes are blinking furiously and she fingers her earlobe, as if even she can't believe what she's hearing. 'And I'm really proud of you.'

Miri drops a forkful of banana pancake.

'And I'm proud of you too, Miri. Really. The fact that you've dedicated yourself to tae kwon do training shows excellent focus and drive. You're a wonderful role model for Priscilla. You both are. Except for Rachel's slobbiness. I know you girls think I'm tough on you two,' she continues, 'but it's only because I care about you and want you to learn to be the best people you can.'

My father's eyes start to tear, he's so happy.

I'm about to spit out my eggs. 'Er . . . thanks. Um, Miri, can I talk to you for a sec?'

She jumps from her chair. 'Yeah. I'm done anyway.'

I drag her up the stairs by her elbow and close our door. 'What did you do? This isn't an honesty spell; it's a nauseating spell!'

'I swear I followed the instructions properly,' she says, shaking her head in dismay. 'I don't know what's happening.'

'It must be the wrong spell. This isn't her being honest. She doesn't think we're role models. She hates us.' I narrow my eyes. 'And we hate her. It's making Dad like her even more! You have to make an antidote! You have to reverse the spell!'

'I can't reverse it if I don't know what kind of spell it is.'

Her face clouds over. 'There's only one way to find out. One of us has to take it,' she says slowly.

'Don't look at me. I'm not taking another potion. What if it counteracts the dancing spell? I have to be in a social situation tomorrow. You take it.'

She nods, bites her thumb in contemplation, then pulls it away. 'All right. I'll take it.' I pull the beaker out of my purse and she downs the rest of the potion. 'I think I'm going to puke,' she says. 'That tasted like garbage.'

I hear laughter coming from my father and STB's room. 'That sweater is so ugly!' STB shrieks. 'It's so ugly we couldn't even give it away. We'll have to burn it. Rachel, Miri, come and join us!' she calls. 'This would be more fun if you were here!'

What is wrong with her? 'In a minute!' I shout back. Apparently, the post-brunch fashion-show activity has begun. I lie on my bed, kick my heels up against the wall and focus on Miri. She's sitting in the centre of the room, blinking repeatedly. 'Is it working?' I ask.

'I don't know.'

'I should start asking you things. Like a lie-detector test. Is your name Miri?'

She rolls her eyes. 'Yes.'

'How are you feeling today?'

'I'm mad at you because you're leaving early tomorrow.' As soon as the words are through her lips, she clamps her hand over her mouth. 'Oops.'

What? 'You're mad at me?'

She nods. 'I can't believe I just said that.'

'You can't be mad at me.'

'Why not? You're deserting me to be with your friends. This is our time together. And I think you're being

198

selfish. Yesterday I had to play solitaire in bed so I could stay up until midnight.' Her face looks so sad. 'Why couldn't you have waited up with me? And then you made me feel guilty for waking you.'

My cheeks feel hot. 'Mir, I was exhausted. I'm sorry.'

'It's not just that. I know you're jealous about this whole witch thing, and I'm sorry about that. I don't know why I have it and you don't, but it's not my fault. And I'm scared. I'm really scared. I'm afraid I'm going to accidentally cause someone to get hit by a car, or maybe start a war. And I don't like doing spells by myself. I made up that thing about needing a Cosmic Witness.' She starts to blink repeatedly. 'I'm just really scared of this power.'

Miri – scared? I do a backwards somersault off the bed and lay my head in her lap, resting my ear against her knee. 'I'll try to be more supportive, OK? But I have to leave early tomorrow. I don't have a choice. If I'm not at practice, I'll get kicked off. You don't want that to happen, do you?'

She shakes her head and waves her hands in the air, as if she's trying to get someone's attention. 'The whole idea of the show is stupid. I know it's how the seniors raise money for prom, but I think it's just an excuse for obnoxious elitism.' She clamps her hand over her mouth again, stifling a gasp. 'Sorry!'

'I guess the spell is working, huh?'

She nods, mouth still held closed.

'Girls?' STB calls from the hallway. 'Are you going to join us?'

I cover the spell book with my feet, and Miri wipes her eyes.

STB opens the door without knocking. 'I wish you girls

would want to spend time with me. I know you think I'm mean, but I only get mad at you when I think you're doing something wrong. I wish you liked me. Because we're going to be a family. I'm going to be your mother and—'

'We already have a mother,' Miri interrupts.

Uh-oh. Two truth-tellers cannot possibly lead to anything good.

STB nods. 'I know. Your poor mother. I feel terrible for her.' She licks her lips, as though all this honesty is drying them out. 'Sometimes I worry that your father will stop loving me, and leave me. He's so wonderful. Smart and generous and loving and full of energy. I'm so crazy about him it terrifies me. Maybe I'm also tough on you two because I want to keep my emotional distance in case he does leave me—'

This is too much. I do not want to hear about STB's deepest fears and insecurities. Especially since I'm trying to make them come true.

Miri nods. 'We're hoping that's what's going to—'

'Never happen.' I tackle her before she gets us grounded for life.

STB backs out of the room. 'Well, come join us when you're finished.'

'Are you crazy?' I whisper to Miri.

'I couldn't stop myself. Next I was going to stand up and scream that I'm a witch.' She gives me a sheepish smile. 'I guess the spell really does work.'

'Well, you downed a huge amount.'

What does that mean, then? STB likes us? Does she really think we're role models? Did she realize she was acting out of character? Is she looking forward to us being a family? I don't buy it. And I don't care. She's still not good enough for my father.

But something she said is bugging me, like a tag left in the back of my underwear, scratching at my lower back. About being afraid that my dad will stop loving her. Is that why I never get mad at him? Or tell him when his clothes are ugly? Am I afraid that he'll stop loving me too? Like he did Mom? My head hurts from all this truth-telling.

'Antidote,' I say. 'For both of you. Now.'

She starts mixing.

17
Plan C

'Hi, Bee-Bee,' Jewel says, pinching my waist. 'How was your weekend?'

'Fine. Yours?' My weekend was not fine at all. What am I going to do? My father is never going to break it off with STB if our plans keep backfiring.

'Crazy. We went to Sean's on Friday.'

Groan. 'Was it fun?' Perhaps a pipe burst and the apartment had to be evacuated?

'It was the best,' Melissa interrupts. 'Too bad you couldn't make it. Hope coming today wasn't too much of an inconvenience.' She's lying on her back on a cafeteria table, her chin pointed up at the ceiling as though she's tanning.

Excuse me? What is with the attitude?

London shows up twenty minutes late, clad in cherry red. Red sweatpants, red tank top, red running shoes. She looks as if she's bleeding.

We spend the next two hours practising. And I have to say, I'm pretty good.

'I just can't get that move,' Jewel complains, hands on her hips.

'The spin at the end?' I ask, shuffling over to her. 'Let me show you.'

Melissa butts in between us. 'I can show her,' she says, grinding her teeth.

Why does she look as if she wants to bite my head off? Jewel was my friend first. Really, this chick has some nerve. 'What's your problem?'

She points a finger at my face. 'You're my problem.'

Uh-oh. This is getting a wee bit heavy for me. She's not going to want to fight me, is she? I have no idea how to fight; that's Miri's department. And she's way taller than I am, so I'm pretty sure I'd lose.

The other dancers are staring.

'Liss, you've got to chill,' Jewel warns.

Melissa looks as if she's about to yell at all of us, but instead she storms out of the cafeteria.

Jewel shrugs, as if this happens all the time. 'I'll go get her.' She chases out of the room after her.

What was that? 'Did I miss something?' I ask the other girls.

Doree shakes her head. 'She's such a prima donna. Just ignore her.'

'But what did I do?'

'She asked Raf to Spring Fling and was *not* pleased when she heard he'd already asked you.'

'Melissa likes Raf?' I ask. That's news to me.

'Yeah,' Stephy says. She's sitting on the floor, stretching. 'I didn't know until Friday. When she freaked out. She actually puked in the bathroom.'

'I heard she might be bulimic,' Doree says.

'She's so pathetic,' London adds, then waves us closer. 'When Laura dropped out, Melissa begged Mercedes to

203

let her be Raf's partner for the formal-wear number. She can't stand Gavin. She claims he's a goth freak who steps on her feet.' She lowers her voice. 'But Mercedes can't stand her and said no.' She looks around the room. 'Why don't we break for lunch? Everyone's coming in thirty minutes anyway.'

Stephy, Doree and I head back to our lockers. 'So that's why Melissa is so rude to me, huh?' I say. 'Because of Raf.'

'My hair must look like crap,' Stephy says, reparting her hair into new pigtails. 'What were you saying? Oh, right. Liss. I'm sure it doesn't help that Jewel's your new best friend. They used to be inseparable.'

My new best friend? Jewel and I were best buds for *ten years* before we even knew Melissa existed. But to these girls I didn't exist before the show. They probably think I transferred to JFK in February. Something occurs to me. 'If Mercedes and London don't like Melissa, why is she choreographing the freshman dance?'

'Because of her mom. London thought that if she was nice to her, she'd get to be in a video.'

'It ain't going to happen with those thighs,' Stephy comments.

'What thighs?' London has no thighs. Are these girls insane?

'They're massive,' Doree agrees. 'A junior who saw them in the flesh in the Hamptons last summer said they're all cottage cheesy.'

'Just because Melissa was the best dancer doesn't mean she knows how to string together a routine,' Stephy declares. She snaps an elastic on her pigtail. 'So, what do you girls want for lunch? Mixed or low-fat Caesar?'

I'd suggest burgers, but they'd probably faint if I so

much as mouthed the word. Calories! Carbs! Grams of fat! But before I can even think about lunch, I need to have something cleared up. 'What do you mean, "was the best dancer"? As in past tense. What happened?'

Stephy snorts. 'You did.'

I'm known as the best dancer in the cast? Imagine if that goes on my yearbook caption! Best dancer. Awesome. Much, much cooler than maths genius. Although together they make me look pretty well-rounded. Perfect for college applications.

I'm starting to feel sorry for Liss. After all, I've stolen her boyfriend, best friend, title and potential Ivy League position.

My sympathy subsides after lunch when I sense her sending virtual poisonous darts at my head. If Melissa was a witch, I'd be a cat for sure. Not even. Catnip.

The glowering gets worse when the rest of the cast, specifically Raf, shows up. 'Hey,' he says after giving me a quick kiss on the cheek. 'I missed you at Sean's.'

He kissed me! He missed me! 'I was at my dad's.'

He tosses his coat on to a table and unravels his grey wool scarf from around his neck. 'You go every second weekend?'

'Yeah.'

'Good thing the dance falls on an odd weekend, huh?'

'Yup,' I say quickly. Nothing else important happening on that weekend. Nope, nothing at all. Especially not my dad's wedding. Sigh.

I have got to take care of that.

When I finally arrive home at seven that night, I discover that the elevator is broken. Again. I trudge up the stairs and, even though I'm exhausted, I am far less out of breath than I was a few weeks ago.

I open the door to find my mother, hands on her hips, glaring at me. 'Freeze, young lady.'

Uh-oh. The apartment reeks of smoke, so I know I'm in trouble. We must have been found out. Outed from the broom closet. She must have been tidying Miri's room and come across Miri's lists of spells.

'I-I-I think b-before you say anything, you should know—'

'Rachel, I was expecting you hours ago. You have to let me know where you are.' Her cigarette ash falls on to the floor. Very classy. 'I pictured you lying on some subway platform, hurt. I even called Tammy, looking for you.'

Yes! We have not been outed. Shows how psychic I am. 'Sorry, Mom. I'll try to remember to call.' Tammy must have been surprised. We've barely spoken since I had to cancel our after-school get-together. We're not ignoring each other – we say hello and goodbye – but we've been sitting with other people in class.

Mom crouches down to wipe up the spilled ash, then wags her finger at me. 'No, you *will* call, or you won't be in the show.'

I swallow hard. Too much is riding on the show to not be allowed to be in it now. 'If you bought me a cellphone, then you'd be able to call me.'

'There is no reason for a fourteen-year-old to have a cellphone. But if you want one so badly, save up.'

'There is a reason, if you don't know where I am,' I say, and slip off my coat. 'I bet Dad would buy me one.'

She turns around and marches into the kitchen. 'So ask him. Let's talk about something else.'

'Maybe I will,' I say, following her.

She gives the bubbling pot on the stove a stir. 'Miri mentioned that you're taking her to the peace rally this Saturday. That's nice of you. Can you pass me the olive oil?'

Peace rally? Oh, right. I lift myself on to the white counter so I can reach into the cupboard. I hand my mom the bottle. Then I stay seated where I am and swing my feet. I forgot about my sister's bargain.

And to think Miri was giving me grief about ditching her today, when I already generously agreed to take her to this peace rally. Outside. In the cold. That's a pretty sisterly thing to do. Unless I happen to have fashion-show practice at that time. Uh-oh. 'What time am I going to this peace rally with Miri?' I ask, slightly panicked.

My mom shrugs. 'Sometime in the afternoon. I'm going to the office while you're there. We're swamped with summer honeymoon planning. I'm sorry I've been at work so late, but the good news is, we've done some great business. Did I tell you I was nominated as one of *New York Magazine*'s best travel agents?'

'That's cool, Mom,' I say, a little distracted. Saturday morning is rehearsal for the freshman dance, the one Melissa is choreographing. And Saturday evening is the all-girl rehearsal. Which means no problem for the peace rally, but no possible time for a date with Raf. I'm hoping he'll be at Mick's on Friday. Apparently Mick's parents are going out of town. Again. And I should see plenty of Raf in the next three weeks, since we have dance rehearsals scheduled every day after school and every lunch period. As well as Saturdays and Sundays. There's no way I'll be able to go to Long Island in two weeks. Miri's going to freak.

Next week we have our designer fittings! I am so excited for my Izzy Simpson dress! And to get my hair and make-up done at Bella Salon in Soho. I guess they're hoping all JFK's wannabe girls will book them for prom. The JFK administration lets us take a half day to prepare for the show. I've never had my make-up done. Maybe I won't wash my face before Spring Fling. Speaking of which, what am I wearing to Spring Fling? And how am I going to pay for it? I can't ask my mother to buy me something when she doesn't know I'm going. Maybe I can borrow the Izzy Simpson dress. I can't wait to wear it onstage in front of the entire school!

'Hello? Rachel?' my mother asks while stirring the pasta. 'I seemed to have lost you over there. Everything OK?'

'What?'

She reaches for the strainer and then carries the pot to the sink. 'Excited for the big day?'

Am I ever. My fifteen minutes of fame. 'I think it'll be a lot of fun. You're coming, right?' I forgot to ask her if she wants any extra tickets. Everyone in the show gets six reserved seats right up front. I promised three to my dad (although I'm hoping STB and Prissy will be history by then), and there will be one for my mom, one for Miri, and I guess one for Tammy if we ever make up.

My mom drops the strainer, and the pasta spills all over the sink. 'Am I coming? To your father's wedding? No, honey, I think I'll sit that one out.' She picks up the noodles. Her fingers are shaking.

My cheeks feel hot, and it's not from the stove. 'I thought you meant the fashion show.'

She presses her fists against her stomach and laughs. Her eyes squint into slivers. 'Oh, of course I'm coming to your show. How much are tickets?'

'Ten bucks apiece,' I say, staring at my hands. They're my dad's hands. Long fingers, barely-there cuticles, fat thumbs. 'All money goes to the senior prom. But you're guaranteed good seats.'

Weird how she won't be at the wedding. If there is a wedding, I mean. How do you live with a man for fifteen years, have his children and then not be invited to the most important day in his life? The second most important day, if you count the day he married you.

'We'll be there,' my mom says, shoulders relaxed now that we're no longer talking about the wedding. I'm not dying to discuss it with her either, but if my ex-husband was getting married, I would want to know all the gory details.

Unless the gory details hurt.

I remember when my dad broke the news. It was a Friday night in August. Jewel and I had spent the afternoon in Central Park, working on our tans for the fast-approaching first day of high school (the same tan that I later accidentally exfoliated off with the Dead Sea mud mask). Miri and I took the six o'clock train to Port Washington and, when they picked us up, we went straight to Al Dente, a fancy Italian restaurant.

I didn't notice the rock until halfway through my Caesar salad. STB (we christened her later that night) was wearing a glittering diamond the size of an apple. I nearly choked on an anchovy. I'm not a fan of them on a good day.

I stared in horror. 'Is that . . .?'

My dad squeezed STB's bare shoulder (she was wearing a white silk strapless top with her black pants) and announced, 'Jennifer and I have decided to get married.'

I almost barfed the croutons across the linen tablecloth.

Miri's eyes filled with tears. My father assumed they were tears of happiness and said, 'Look how excited the girls are!' And then his glass of red wine spilled all over STB's top, which thankfully killed the Hallmark moment for them.

Hmm. In retrospect, the wine mishap must have been Miri's subconscious at work, since no one touched his glass. My dad blamed the table's uneven legs. Way to go, Miri!

When we arrived home on Sunday, we found my mother washing her weekend dishes. As Miri opened her mouth, I tried telepathically to tell her, 'Don't say anything! Don't tell!' but it didn't work. She said, 'Daddy's getting married,' and the happy-to-see-us expression vanished from Mom's face. Her cheeks puffed up as if she was blowing a bubble, and she put down the plate she was holding and slowly crumpled on to the kitchen floor. The water in the sink continued running.

'I'm sorry,' Miri whispered, shocked at the effect of her words. Then my sister started to cry. I didn't know if it was because of the pain she felt or the pain she had just caused. And then I started to cry. I sat down next to my mom and buried my head in her lap.

I felt her fingers running through my hair. I didn't want to look up, didn't want to know if she was crying too. I couldn't bear it. How could he do that? How could he leave us and marry someone else? How could she let that happen?

Then my sister sat down on the floor and told me that everything would be OK. And the two of them braided my hair until I felt calm.

Except for mentioning a few mandatory details ('Sorry, Mom, I won't be spending that weekend with you. It's the you-know-what'), I wasn't planning on ever talking about the wedding.

'Can you get two plates down?' she asks now.

Another wedding conversation safely avoided. Now all we have to do is avoid the wedding.

I spend the entire next day at school trying to come up with Plan C. When I get home, after an exhausting day of classes and both lunch and after-school fashion-show rehearsals, my mom is reading a romance novel and Miri is grunting and counting in Korean behind her closed door. '*Hana!*' Grunt. '*Tul!*' Grunt. '*Set*—'

I burst in to find her barefoot and snap-kicking at her reflection in the mirror. 'We have less than three weeks left.' I'm panicked. Practically hyperventilating. 'Why are you wasting time with anything besides the plan?'

'I have other responsibilities, besides the wedding,' she says. 'Like tae kwon do? Schoolwork? *Net!*' She snap-kicks and grunts one last time before sitting down at her desk. 'Don't you?'

Who has time for responsibilities during a crisis like this? Although now that I think about it, I have a maths midterm on Wednesday. And I'm supposed to finish *Huckleberry Finn* for next Wednesday. Which shouldn't be a problem, because I can normally read a book in a week. I'll start with fifty pages tonight. And I have a French midterm next Thursday and . . . Stop! Must keep my priorities straight! 'What are we going to do?'

'We've run out of options,' Miri says. And that's when I notice what I never, ever thought I'd see in a billion years. 'What is that?' I shriek.

'What?'

'That!' I point to her fingers, which are wrapped in Band-Aids. Willingly. 'Have you lost your mind?'

She turns bright red and looks down at her notebook. 'I don't want to ruin my nail beds.'

I *know* that's not the only reason. Too bad she took the truth-spell antidote and is no longer being honest. 'Are you getting soft on me? On her? We have not run out of options. Magic is unlimited!'

'Well, I don't know what else to do,' she says, blinking her long eyelashes repeatedly.

That's because she's not even trying. Where is A^2? I spot it beside her bed, on the floor underneath a sleeping Tigger. On the floor! Is this how you treat an authentic spell book? I tilt it sideways so that the fur ball slides off, and I heave it on to her desk. 'Look at the book. It's right in front of you.' Must think. Wait a sec . . . right in front of you. My heart rate speeds up. 'We're missing the obvious.'

She flips open the book. 'What's the obvious?'

'We need him to stop loving her.'

'We already tried that,' she says slowly, as if I'm in preschool and she's teaching me the alphabet. 'Everything we do makes him like her more.'

'Not everything,' I say, suddenly giddy and lightheaded, as if I'm floating in a sea of helium. 'What if he falls in love with someone else?'

Miri flicks through the pages. 'With whom? He doesn't know anyone else.'

'Yes, he does.' I raise my eyebrows, and give her my best *hello?* look.

'Our mother?' Miri says, finally understanding.

'Yes, our mother. We make him fall in love with Mom.' We're both silent, savouring the sweetness of the possibility like melting chocolate ice cream in our mouths.

After a few moments, she looks up at me, excitement creeping into her cheeks. 'I . . . but . . . emotion spells aren't permanent,' she says, her voice creaking. 'Especially love spells.'

'It doesn't matter,' I whisper. 'By then, the wedding will be cancelled.'

Miri shakes her head slowly. 'What about Mom? She'll be hurt all over again.'

'Don't you see? It won't wear off. If he fell in love with her once, he can do it again. He just needs a shove in the right direction. A push to help him realize that he made the biggest mistake in his life by leaving. This is perfect! Not only will we be saving Dad from marrying STB, we'll be getting him back with Mom. We'll be killing two birds with one stone.'

'Dad and Mom back together,' Miri says wistfully.

'She's still in love with him,' I say. My heart is thumping fast and hard, as if I just ran up a hundred flights of stairs.

Miri nods. 'I know. She still has that sweatshirt. You know the ratty grey one? The one he—'

 213

'The sweatshirt,' I say. 'Perfect! We can use that for the spell! Let's go get it.'

'She's reading,' Miri says, jumping from her chair and pacing the room. 'Here's what we're going to do. I'll distract her when she's making dinner. I'll ask her about the witch trials. She loves talking about that. Do you know that we can trace our roots to Salem? Isn't that cool? Mom says we still have relatives there, and I can't wait to meet them. I didn't even know we had family in Massachusetts. I asked her if that's where Aunt Sasha lives, but she still wouldn't talk about—'

I tap the side of my head. 'Focus, Miri, focus. We can take a road trip next year. Right now let's work on Operation Steal Back Dad's Sweatshirt.'

She jumps from foot to foot. 'Sorry. OK. You sneak into her room and find the sweatshirt. Then, after dinner, I'll put together the spell – let's hope we have the ingredients in the house – and then we'll slip it under Mom's pillow before she goes to sleep.'

'She's going to sleep on the entire sweatshirt? Don't you think she'll notice?'

'Maybe we'll cut off the arm and just use that.' She flips through the book until she finds the appropriate love spell. 'Let me get a head start on the other ingredients.'

At eight, my mom finally gets off her bed and heads to the kitchen, deciding it's time to make us dinner. Maybe I should put on appropriate spy clothes. Just what do spies wear these days, anyway? Maybe I should stop worrying about my clothes and go find the stupid sweatshirt before she's finished in the kitchen.

Her bedroom door is open, and I slither in. Hmm. Now, if I were a sweatshirt that was being hidden by an

214

ex-wife, where would I be? Under the bed? I drop to my knees and lift the bed skirt. No, but she could certainly sweep under there.

Maybe she keeps it with her other sweatshirts. Camouflage. So we won't notice. I open her dresser and search through the drawers. One shelf. Nope. Two. Nope. Three. Nope.

Where is it?

I check in the closet. No Dad's sweatshirt, but plenty of purses, shoes and old concert T-shirts. Would it kill her to buy some new clothes?

The microwave dings. Uh-oh. Time's running out. Where is it? I rifle through her bra and underwear drawer. She could use an update here. All her lingerie is beige. No wonder she doesn't have a boyfriend. She'll need to invest in some new stuff now that Dad has been exposed to STB's unmentionables, because I've seen them drying around the house, and they're all pink and frilly. At least now I know what to get Mom for her birthday. Is it creepy to get your mother lingerie?

I've checked everywhere and it's gone. Impossible. I search the dresser again. And then the closet. It must be under one of these purses. Why does she have so many purses? And wedge sandals. Does anyone even wear wedges any more? Where is the stupid sweatshirt?

'Rachel?'

Busted. Mom. Standing at her door. Wondering why I'm in her closet. Why am I in her closet? I try to appear nonchalant by twisting my ponytail around my wrist. 'Yes, Mom?'

'What are you doing?'

'I-I-I . . .' Must think fast. Why can I never think fast

when I tell myself to think fast? 'Looking for shoes. Yeah. I need a lot of shoes for the fashion show. You know, a different pair for every number. So I thought you might have something I could borrow.' I hope I didn't already tell her the designers are lending us heels.

She looks confused. 'But you wear a six and I'm a seven.'

Right-e-o. 'I know, but some of these shoes are so old I thought you might have bought them when you were a smaller size.'

She shrugs. 'All right. But dinner's ready.'

That was close. Close, but no cigar. Or sweatshirt.

A few minutes into our plates of revolting peanut tofu, my mom throws down her fork. 'What's wrong with you?' she demands. 'Stop making faces; it's not that bad. It's a new recipe and it's healthy.'

First of all, it is that bad. The lumps of tofu are jiggling on my plate like Jell-O, but that isn't why I'm making faces. I'm attempting to illustrate to Miri that we're having serious sweatshirt-locating issues.

'I wasn't making faces about the food. I was thinking that I *couldn't find* the shoes I wanted. I don't know *where* they are. I'm thinking you must have *thrown it out*.' Oops. 'I mean, thrown them out,' I correct.

'What shoes?' my mom asks.

'Um . . . you know. The silver ones.'

'What silver ones?'

Distraction needed! 'Mom, um . . . this recipe is delicious.'

She beams with pleasure. 'See? You have to give new tastes a chance. I'll definitely make it again.'

Fantastic-e-o.

When we're finally finished, Miri and I clear together

(it's technically her turn again, *finally*, but she set the table for me while I was rummaging in the closet) and my mom goes to her room.

'I can't find it anywhere,' I whisper. 'I even checked the wash, despite my scepticism that she ever cleans it.'

Miri's head wobbles from side to side. 'That's so sad.'

'I know. But that's why we're doing this. He's going to fall madly in love with her again, and she'll be happy.' I dump the leftover tofu into the garbage. Good riddance.

'Right. Except what do we do if the spell wears off?'

'I told you, once he's out of STB's grasp, he'll stay in love with Mom.' Miri's brown eyes widen with doubt, so I decide to tell her what I've always suspected but never wanted to admit. Even to myself. 'The Step-Monster was probably responsible for them breaking up.'

'What are you talking about?' Miri asks, rinsing off a dish.

'Corne on, think about it. He claims to have met her six months after he left Mom. Isn't it possible he met her . . . um . . . before?'

Miri pales. 'You mean he cheated on Mom?' We both stand still, listening to the sound of the water. And then Miri rips off each of her Band-Aids. 'She has got to go. If we can't find the sweatshirt, we have to find something else that belongs to him. It can't be a gift he gave. It has to be something that was his personally. Do you have anything?'

'His maths trophy?'

'I think she'd notice a metal statue under her pillow,' Miri says.

If she didn't look so forlorn – probably because of what I told her about Dad's quasi or otherwise affair – I might

 217

laugh. 'So what do we do?' I ask, filling the baking tray with soap to let it soak. 'Wait until next weekend?'

She sighs. 'I guess so. Although that only leaves one week for him to call off the wedding. What do you think?'

I blow a soap bubble over her head. 'We have no choice.'

So much for unlimited options.

18

Why Gambling Does Not Pay

'**O**ne more time!' London screams at us.

It's Tuesday and I'm sweating through an all-cast after-school practice for the opening. Since the freshman girls are up first, London has already made us repeat our part twenty times.

The music starts again and we go through the motions. It's really not that hard. All five of us will be spread across the stage and, when the *Chicago* medley starts, five spotlights will shine on us as if we're nightclub singers. Then we do a twenty-second choreographed dance, and the rest of the cast rushes on.

'You're not in sync!' London shrieks. She starts the music again. I feel as if I'm a scratched CD that keeps playing the same line.

After we finally get it right, Jewel and I go to Soho to scout for my Spring Fling outfit, and I find the perfect dark green dress.

'You look hot,' Jewel says, circling me in the changing room. 'You should wear your hair up.'

Jewel has always liked my hair up. For our middle school Valentine's dance she helped me put it into a

French twist. And one Halloween she spent an hour making me two perfect Princess Leia buns, or cinnamon buns, as Prissy called them.

'Let me see what it would look like,' she says, untangling the chopsticks from her hair. Her curls spring over her shoulders and, without even thinking, I pull one so it uncoils and then bounces back, and she laughs.

She twirls my hair until it perfectly tops my head, and strategically places two long strands on to my forehead. 'We'll style those with my curling iron.'

We smile at each other in the full-length mirror. 'Thanks, Jewel.'

I'm going to look perfect. Thank God Miri lent me her last eighty dollars to buy a dress, which I promised, promised, promised to pay back out of my allowance. Eventually.

After shopping, Jewel and I go back to her place to study for maths. 'Rachel, honey, what a surprise!' Mrs Sanchez says when Jewel asks her if I can stay for dinner. 'We missed you,' she adds, and I almost hug her. I missed her too.

It's lunchtime on Wednesday, and I rush to the drama room, where the freshman dancers are meeting. I open the door to find Raf by his sexy self, lying across the carpet, a textbook under his head.

'Hi,' I say, and sprawl down beside him. Yes! Alone time with Raf! Maybe he'll take this opportunity to kiss me! Or to ask me out for Saturday night. Our quasi date was *two weeks* ago. Doesn't he want to go out again before Spring Fling? Does he like me or not? Did he just ask me to Spring Fling because I'm a good dancer? This whole dating/quasi-dating thing is turning me into a chronic question-asker.

Omigod, I'm turning into Prissy!

'Hi,' he says. 'What's up?' He runs his fingers through his dark hair and I wonder what it feels like. Smooth? Soft? Silky? Maybe like cashmere? Not that I've ever worn cashmere. Or know what it feels like. Would I even be able to feel the difference between it and cotton in a Pepsi/Coke-style test? I imagine myself blindfolded, hands out, palms caressing the different materials.

'My parents want me to go to New Orleans with them during spring break,' Raf announces, shattering my daydream.

Oh, no. He's backing out of Spring Fling! He's going to leave early, and then my dad's wedding will be cancelled and, after all the scheming, I'll be at home on 3 April watching *Star Wars*. Again. 'Oh?'

'My brothers don't want to go, but I told my parents I'm game as long as they fly down on Sunday after the dance.'

How sweet is he? Not only does he still want to go to the Fling with me, but he's a good son. He's like chocolate mixed with candyfloss mixed with Kool-Aid. If I wasn't so in love, I would get a cavity.

Jewel walks into the room, smiling when she sees us together. 'Hey, lovebirds. Bee-Bee, how'd you do on the maths test?'

'OK,' I say, trying to sound nonchalant. I definitely aced it. I finished in twenty minutes and spent the rest of class studying for next week's French test and writing in my notebook, *Je m'ennuie*. 'You?'

221

'Pretty good,' she says, still smiling. 'Thanks for helping me study.'

I figured she had done OK. During the test, she was scribbling furiously, wrapping her curls around her thumb like she always does when she's thinking hard. She wasn't eating the back of her eraser, which is what she does when she's upset.

I wonder how Tammy did. I'd ask her. If we were talking.

The rest of the freshmen trickle in. Finally Melissa storms into the room, carrying two plastic chairs. 'Everyone up. The moronic JFK administration wouldn't approve my stripper choreography, but they said I could do a gambling theme. So we'll be using chairs in the dance to give the number an edge.'

Chairs? What is she talking about? I don't want to dance with furniture.

'Eight of us,' she continues, dropping our plastic dancing partners into the centre of the room, 'Jewel, Sean, Raf, Doree, Stephy, Jon, Nick and I will be the main dancers. We'll be gamblers at a poker table on the catwalk. Rachel and Gavin, you two will be dressed as casino dealers and will remain at the sides of the stage and *off* the catwalk.'

Quelle surprise. At least she didn't relegate us to behind the curtain.

Free lunch! Free lunch!

It's Friday and this is the first time all week that I don't have dance practice during lunch! It's my first real chance to sit at the A-list table. I search for Jewel in the caf. Where is she? I don't see Doree, either. Or Stephy.

Where are they? I don't see Raf, but he normally leaves for lunch. Come to think of it, I haven't seen him all day.

Did everyone go out for lunch without me? I feel sick to my stomach, and I haven't even eaten yet, so I know it's not food poisoning. Maybe they don't like me after all. I buy a grilled cheese and fries from the lunch ladies and then look for someone, anyone, to sit with. I spot Tammy at my old table, fourth from the back, eating with Janice, Annie and Sherry. Oh, well.

I carry my tray to their table and sit next to Tammy. 'Hi, girls.' I take a bite of my sandwich to make sitting here feel less weird.

Tammy squints at me. 'Excuse me? Do I know you?'

'Do you want me to sit somewhere else?' I spit out, along with small crust remnants.

She stares at me for a long second and then pushes her hands down, her scuba way of telling me to relax. 'I'm kidding. It's just that I never see you any more. Of course you can sit with us.'

Oops. I kind of overreacted there.

Sherry is giving me a strange wide-eyed smile from across the table. She pulls a sopping wet strand of hair from her mouth. 'Hi, Rachel. Love-ee your sweater.'

My sweater? I'm wearing the green one I bought at Macy's and have worn a million times. Is she kidding?

Annie is also smiling at me weirdly, and I squirm in my seat. What's wrong with everyone?

Janice stares at me, her face all serious. 'How is the fashion show?' she asks. She's wearing faded jean overalls. 'We're looking forward to cheering for you.'

Ah. The fashion show. I'm a celebrity returning to her

hometown. I give the group my most benevolent smile. 'Hard work,' I say.

'What's London Zeal like?' Annie asks, leaning towards me, squishing her supersized breasts together and giving the boys at the next table an eyeful.

'She's a riot,' I say with a wave of my hand.

'Is it true you're going to Spring Fling with Raf?' Sherry asks.

'Yup,' I say, then notice the confusion on Tammy's face. 'I think so. I had another event that night, but it's off now.'

Tammy's eyes bulge. 'What? The wedding is off?'

I give her my best *this-is-hard-for-me-can-we-talk-about-it-later?* look. She nods, eyes still bulging. When the bell rings and my groupies disperse, Tammy pats me on the back. 'What happened?'

'I'm not supposed to discuss it,' I say softly, lifting my legs on to the bench and hugging them into my chest. Probably bad luck to talk about the cancelled wedding before it's actually cancelled, huh? Kind of like letting the groom see the wedding dress before the ceremony. In a twisted sort of way.

'I honestly understand. Nobody knows family politics better than I do. But if you need to talk, I'm a hundred per cent here for you. I remember how screwed up I felt when my mother married my stepmother.'

My heart melts. Tammy is so nice. I've treated her horribly since I got into the fashion show. I should have Miri whip her up a happiness potion.

She smiles shyly. 'So does that mean I can tell Aaron I can go to the dance with him? I told him I couldn't because of the wedding.'

Omigod! 'What? He asked you to Spring Fling?'

She pulls the elastic from her hair, fluffs the light brown strands and lets them sit on her shoulders. I like when she wears her hair down. It makes her face look softer. 'Yup, he finally asked me.'

'Why didn't you tell me?'

'He asked me last week and we weren't exactly talking.' Her dark eyes cloud over. 'Look, I'm sorry for not being more understanding about your work schedule. I know it's tough, and I should be more supportive about something that's so important to you.'

She is so cool. If there was an award for the world's greatest friend, she would so win. She's apologizing for my not making enough time for her. And she said no to Aaron even though she's dying to go to the dance as much as I am. She would rather hang out with me at my dad's lame-o wedding. She honestly deserves a medal. Maybe I'll have Miri whip up one of those too.

'Thanks, Tammy,' I say, overflowing with gratitude. Then I add, 'And I should make more time for my friends.' With that, we link arms and head to our lockers.

On the stairs we run smack into an all-in-white London. She shakes her fist at me and screams, 'Where were you?' at the top of her lungs.

Whoa. I slide backwards in fear. 'Where was I when?'

'Hello? At lunch? We had a meeting today. I took off class so I could meet with all the freshmen and sophomores to see the formal.'

What is she talking about? 'I thought we were supposed to practice the formal dance on Sunday.'

'I changed my mind last night. I phoned Melissa and

225

she said she would call the rest of you. She told me she spoke to you.'

What a witch. And I mean that in a positively negative way. Melissa purposefully didn't tell me about the rehearsal so I'd look bad. Or maybe she didn't want me dancing with Raf. She makes me want to puke. Maybe her bulimia is contagious. 'I'm sorry,' I say. 'But Melissa never told me.'

'Whatever. It's too late now. But you'd better not miss any more rehearsals or you're out of the show. I don't care how good you are,' she growls before stomping off.

I lean against the wall, shell-shocked.

'Don't worry about it,' Tammy says, patting me on the back. 'They can't kick you out now. The show's in two weeks. And you're too good.' She tries to make me feel better all the way to our lockers, but I'm too busy steaming to pay attention. I hate Melissa. If only I was the witch instead of Miri. I'd put a hex on her for sure. Turn her into a mouse. No, too cute. A rat. Or a frog. Or a tuna fish that I could mash up and feed to Tigger.

'What are you doing tonight?' Tammy asks as she spins her lock combination.

Should I invite Tammy to come with me to Mick's? He's having another party. I probably should. But then I'll have to hang out with her, and I would rather spend the evening flirting with Raf than, sorry, babysitting Tammy. I open my locker and pull out my books. 'I don't know. I'm usually really tired after rehearsal. I'll probably just crash.'

'I understand. Call me if you want to hang out. I could just come by. We don't have to do anything crazy.'

'Why don't we see how the day goes? Oh, hey, wait a sec.' I hand her one of the fashion-show tickets. 'I don't know if you want to sit with my family, but I got six awesome seats.'

'Thank you!' she says, and gives me the OK sign.

I charged my family for the tickets, I had to – London was very clear that we were responsible for the cost. I'm not made of money. But I owe Tammy.

After school, I head to the cafeteria for the all-girl dance rehearsal and make a beeline for Melissa. She's in her pretend tanning position. But this time she's wearing sunglasses.

We're inside. There's no sun.

I loom over her, so that if there *was* sun, I'd be blocking it. 'Thanks a lot for telling me about the lunch practice.'

She lifts her shades and bats her eyelashes. 'Didn't I?'

Of course her eyes are blue. Why aren't my eyes blue? It's so unfair. She gets red hair and blue eyes. 'No, you didn't. I missed it and got told off by London.'

'That's too bad.' She flicks her sunglasses back down.

Loathing overwhelms me like nausea. Maybe this intense emotion is enough to spark my long-overdue powers. I close my eyes, purse my lips and focus.

> *Next time this chick*
> *Is on her way back from class,*
> *Give her a push . . . no . . . a kick, yeah, a kick,*
> *And make her fall on her—*

Jewel pinches my waist before I can finish the thought. Hey, that was pretty good. If this witch thing doesn't work out, I can always become a poet.

*

I'm sitting with Jewel, Melissa, Doree and Stephy on the living-room couch at Mick's, and Melissa is making fun of all the people who were not lucky enough to be invited.

'Oh, shut up,' Jewel says, and rolls her eyes. 'Not everyone can be as fabulous as you, Melissa.'

'As fabulous as us,' Stephy says, giggling.

That's me. Fabulous. Part of the fabulous group. Fabulous and miserable. Miserable because Raf isn't here. I'm wearing my good jeans and a great silver V-neck top I borrowed from Jewel. And I spent twenty minutes doing my eyeliner.

And then I got here and ran straight into Will, who told me that Raf is sick at home with a fever.

I should bring him chicken soup. Does it count if it's instant?

Melissa kicks the marble coffee table. 'Did you guys see what Janice Cooper was wearing today?'

Stephy cracks up. 'Yes! Overalls. What is she, a farmer?'

And that's when the worst thing in the world happens.

Before I left the apartment, I gave Miri two instructions. One, if Raf calls, tell him I'll be at Mick's and I'll see him there. Two, if Tammy calls, tell her I was really tired and went to sleep.

So here I am, cross-legged next to Jewel on the couch, when Jeffrey Stars walks into the living room. Followed by Aaron Jacobs. Followed by . . . Tammy.

What is she doing here?

Her mouth drops open when she sees me. And then she just stares.

'Hi,' I choke out. I want to sink into the couch pillows. I want to disappear. I really wish I had that invisibility cloak. Maybe she didn't call my house. Maybe I can tell her I called her, and her moms told me she was here.

'I just spoke to your sister,' she says. Her top teeth grind into her bottom teeth. 'I guess you woke up.'

'Yeah,' I say, and slump deeper into the couch. I played Russian roulette and lost.

She turns to Aaron. 'I want to go home.' Aaron puts his arm around her and, without looking back, the two of them leave.

I should chase her. But what would I say? I didn't want to babysit you? I wanted to hang out with Raf? With Jewel?

The girls beside me immediately crack up. 'What was that?' Melissa shrieks.

'Are they a couple?' Doree asks.

'Shnoz and Acne?' Melissa says, then laughs.

My mouth drops open. 'Why do you call them that?' I ask.

Doree giggles. 'Because yesterday he had the biggest zit ever. And she has the biggest shnoz. But I shouldn't say that,' she tells the others. 'Rachel used to be friends with her.'

Doree, Melissa and Stephy laugh even louder.

I stare at the carpet. *Used to be friends with her*. But now I've traded her in. For the *fabulous* company beside me.

Jewel pats me on the back and gives me a quarter-smile.

I wonder if just a few months ago Doree said something demeaning about me and then added, 'But I shouldn't say that. Jewel used to be friends with her.'

And Jewel just sat there, staring at the carpet.

I'm eating a quick breakfast before Saturday's rehearsal when Miri runs into the kitchen, wearing a T-shirt and underpants. 'You'll be back at one, right?'

'Yes, Mir, I'll be back at one. For the rally. I haven't forgotten.'

Her smile lights up her face. 'Awesome! I'm so excited. I'm going to spend the rest of the day training with mom and then practising my high roundhouse kick.' She squats and lifts her fists to her hips, in the ready position. 'I can't seem to nail it. It's much weaker than my snap kick. It's probably because—'

'Do you have everything you need for Dad's love spell next weekend?' If I wanted a tae kwon do lesson, I'd sign up. And I'm beginning to wonder what exactly takes place during these mysterious training sessions. If I didn't have, oh, ten million things occupying my thoughts, I'd ask.

'Almost,' she says, and whips out a list from her shirt pocket. 'I need to pick up some yogurt. The one we bought last time is past its expiry date. Oh, did I tell you that Tammy called last night? I told her you were sleeping, like you said. She left you a message.'

I swallow my cereal along with the lump in my throat. 'What did she say?'

'That Jeffrey invited Aaron to a party, and Aaron invited her. They wanted you to go with them. And if you woke up, to call her cellphone.'

Tammy definitely gets the greatest-friend award. And I get a kick in the butt.

The day gets worse. Melissa is in charge at rehearsal, which makes it particularly painful, and Raf is home sick.

At least I have Jewel.

'Melissa, how much longer are we going to be?' I ask.

She stops the music and positions her hands on her hips. 'Why? Do you have something else to do that's

230

more important? I'm sure London would love to know what it is.'

I can't believe she's threatening me. We were only supposed to be here until noon, and it's already half past. 'Whatever.' I'm out of here in ten minutes, no matter what.

'You sure? I don't mind if you go. London told me to tell her if you gave me any attitude.'

Why does she even need me here? I don't have to do anything but stand and look interested. I'm about to tell her where to get off when Raf hunches through the doorway.

Melissa gestures to all of us to stay put. 'How are you feeling?' she gushes.

'OK,' he says. 'I'm still tired, so I'm just going to watch instead of dance.' He looks pale, as if someone rubbed chalk on his cheeks.

An *aw!* goes through the room. Melissa massages his back. No way am I leaving now, when she's trying to fondle my quasi boyfriend.

'I'll be right back,' I mutter. Not that anyone can hear me from my exile in the corner of the room. I call my sister from the payphone by the bathroom.

'Where are you? I want to go already,' she squeals into the phone. 'I am so excited. I'm wearing tights under my jeans so I can stay warm.'

I take a deep breath. 'Mir, I'm really sorry, but there's no way I'm getting out of here anytime soon.'

'Oh.' Silence. 'But you promised.'

'I know I promised, but I can't leave. Melissa is being horrible and the show's in two weeks.'

'But the peace rally is today.'

231

'Miri, I can't. Ask Mom to take you.'

The next thing I hear is a dial tone. Did she . . . Did my little sister hang up on me? I don't believe it. She's never hung up on me. She's never hung up on anyone.

I slip back into my spot in Siberia.

'So nice of you to join us again,' Melissa yells over the music, then returns her hand to Raf's forehead. 'You don't feel too warm,' she coos.

What a miserable week. My sister and Tammy hate me, and my rival is flirting with my quasi boyfriend. Can't something good happen?

My body starts to tingle. I look up. Raf is watching me. I give him my best aren't-I-cute smile, and he winks. My skin feels warm, as if I'm being kissed by the sun.

This will all pay off in two weeks. When I'm at Spring Fling with Raf. When I won't need the sun to feel like I'm being kissed.

It's all worth it.

Isn't it?

19
The Enchanted Parent Trap

The next week passes in a blur of rehearsals, mid-terms and assignments.

Monday: rehearse at lunch, rehearse after school. Go to Soho and get fitted for Izzy Simpson dress. Woohoo! Come home, still getting silent treatment from Miri about missing peace rally. Trail her around apartment, tail between my legs, until she finally breaks down and forgives me. Realize I've forgotten all about Huck Finn. Plan on reading a hundred pages. Fall asleep after five.

Tuesday: rehearse at lunch, rehearse after class. Go back to Soho for second designer fitting. On way home from practice, realize impossibility of reading an entire book in one night. Do something always promised self would never, ever do. Stop at bookstore and buy CliffsNotes.

Wednesday: rehearse at lunch. English class. Oddly, instead of getting nailed by Ms Martel for reading CliffsNotes instead of real book, know all answers and come across as Huck Finn genius. Apparently, Ms Martel gets questions from teaching guide at back of CliffsNotes. Would call her lazy, but that would be like pot calling kettle black. (No idea what that means. Why would a pot call a kettle black? Who has a black kettle? Have never seen black kettle.) Rehearse again after school. Return to Soho for third designer fitting. Feet begin to ache.

Thursday: mortified by Hayward when she holds up perfect score in front of whole class. Jewel gets A-, which she's pretty excited about. No idea what Tammy gets, since we're no longer friends. Rehearse at lunch. Write French midterm. Rehearse after school. Back to Soho. Feet begin to swell.

Friday: rehearse at lunch. Rehearse after school. Back to Soho for final fitting. Feet now feel as if they've been set on fire whenever pressure is applied. Get home in time to argue with sister about reasons for not accompanying her to Long Island. Reminded by sister that STB will be mental case with wedding so close, and that twenty-nine wedding updates have been sent to guests in past week. (In-boxes have twice been clogged with massive JPEGs.) More begging follows. Notice sister's pursed lips and sudden waft of cold air, and warn sibling that if she jinxes the show in any way, she will find herself in serious hot water! Lips unpurse and room warms up. Review plan to steal father's belongings, and send sibling on way. Will miss father this weekend, but happy ending is in store.

Saturday: all-day rehearsal. Feet in severe pain. Might have to amputate.

By the time I stumble home from *another* all-day rehearsal on Sunday, I feel like a cavewoman, barely able to stand upright.

'Did you get something of Dad's?' I ask, poking my head into Miri's room. She'd better have. The wedding is in six days.

Six days!

She's writing at her desk and doesn't look up. 'Yup.'

'What did you take?'

'A sock,' she says, still not looking up. I know she's mad at me because I deserted her this weekend, but there was nothing I could do. It's now eight thirty Sunday night, and she arrived home even earlier than I did.

Why is she being so annoying? Hello, Miri, look up! I plop myself on to her bed and lean my feet against the wall. 'A dirty sock or a clean sock?'

'Clean.'

'Good. Because I've smelt Dad's dirty socks, and I doubt Mom would be able to sleep on one.' At least that's one trait from my parents I didn't inherit. Smelly feet. I think. I bend my leg towards my nose. Smells fine. 'What other ingredients do you need?'

She keeps writing. 'Don't worry, I took care of it.'

'You took care of all the ingredients?'

'Yeah. All done. And the spell. And the fractions. The sock is already under Mom's pillow.'

Oh. Well. 'All righty then. You're very efficient.'

She continues writing, fully ignoring me. How long can a person hold a grudge?

Monday night we're in the middle of yet another revolting vegetarian dinner (sloppy joes made with spinach, mushrooms, cabbage and some unidentifiable beige vegetable) when someone buzzes from downstairs.

235

'Are you expecting anyone?' Mom asks, putting down her fork.

We both shake our heads. Raf coming to proclaim his love? I skip over to the intercom. 'Who is it?'

'It's Dad!' Dad? Omigod. Dad! It worked! He's here! 'Come on up!' I scream into the intercom. I know screaming is annoying for the person listening, but I'm too excited to think clearly.

My mom takes a long sip of her water. 'Is that your father?'

'Why, yes,' I say, trying to act all cool and casual, which is mighty difficult. Miri jumps up from the table and starts tidying the kitchen.

'Why is he here?' my mom asks, then flattens down her hair. Bet now she wishes she'd paid more attention to those roots, huh? 'Did you girls get into any kind of trouble? Something happen I should know about?'

'No,' Miri and I say simultaneously.

Knock, knock. I leap towards the door. 'Hi, Dad!' I sing, and then try not to gasp at the sight of him.

His shirt isn't tucked in, the few hairs he has left on his head are standing up and pointing in different directions, and he has thick bags under his eyes. 'Hi, Rachel. I . . . uh . . . found a book Miri left at the house. I thought she might need it.' He thrusts the book at me. 'Can I come in?'

'Sure.' I step aside to let him pass.

My mom, still fidgeting with her hair, joins us in the hallway. 'Hi, Daniel. Nice to see you. Everything all right?'

His eyes light up like two headlights when he sees her. 'Hi,' he says softly. I don't believe it. He's looking at her as if he's Romeo and she's Juliet. He's in love with her again! Hallelujah! Cupid's arrow has landed!

'Miri forgot a book and I thought she might need it,' he rushes to explain.

'Yes, she did. Look!' I hold up the hardcover like a trophy. It's my science textbook from last year, but who's counting? 'So, Dad, would you like some tea? Mom was just going to make a pot.'

My mother stares at me as if I've lost it. 'I was?'

She'd better not blow this. 'Why don't you two sit down and catch up, and I'll boil the water,' I say. I fill up and plug in our *white* kettle.

My father accepts the invite and sits down next to Miri at his old chair at the table. My mom has that baffled, I-just-woke-up look on her face, but sits across from him anyway. I wipe off the glob of sloppy joe that's smeared across the Formica counter and clear the dinner plates.

'Look how helpful they are,' Dad says to Mom. 'What's gotten into them?'

She twirls her hair between her fingers. 'Miri has always been helpful, but Rachel is a whole new girl these days. She's even in great shape. That fashion show is doing wonders for her. She actually took the stairs yesterday without complaining.'

That's not true. I complained, just not out loud.

My father snorts. 'This is the same girl I had to carry on my shoulders in the Diabetes Walkathon?'

They both laugh. Normally, I would get mad at him for bringing it up (I got tired and bored ten minutes into the walk and forced him to carry me the rest of the way), but not this time. The kettle whistles and I place their teas in

237

front of them, saying, 'I have a lot of homework to do, so I'll be in my room if needed.'

'Me too,' Miri adds, and we both burst out of the kitchen, high-fiving all the way to our rooms.

By eleven, I'm in bed, and I can still hear their voices. Hers, girlish and giggling; his, happy and relaxed. Miri opens my door and tiptoes inside. 'He's still here,' she whispers, beaming. The laughter from the kitchen wafts through the walls.

'I know. I just said goodnight.' Seeing them together, sitting at the kitchen table like they used to do in the old days, gave me a surge of warm happiness. Like it's cold outside, but I'm sitting on a cosy couch, wrapped in a woolly blanket, facing a roaring fire.

The next morning, my mom is sipping her coffee, a half-smile on her face.

'What time did Dad leave?' Miri asks, chomping her oatmeal as if she's been fasting for weeks. I pour myself some Cheerios.

'Around one,' she says. 'It was nice. And weird. We haven't talked – you know, *talked* – in a long time. But I don't understand what's going on with him. Has he been fighting with Jennifer?'

Miri and I get very interested in our cereals.

My mom goes back to sipping her coffee.

STB must have freaked if he came home at two in the morning. Maybe he didn't go home. Maybe the wedding's already been called off. 'What did he say?' I ask. That he's in love with you? That he has dumped/is about to dump STB and is moving back home?

238

'We just talked. About you two. About life. And how it . . . creeps up on you.'

Yes! Awesome! Woo-hoo to the power of a billion! Abracadabra fantastica! Welcome back, Dad! And Spring Fling, here I come!

Good things happen in threes.

First, with the help of my new best friend, A^2, I've managed to reach the Holy Grail of divorced kids and get my parents back together.

Second, Raf has been a sweetheart all day. He dropped by my locker to say hello not once but *twice* and sat next to me during lunch rehearsal.

'Justin wants to know if we want to split a limo so we can all go to the dance together on Saturday,' he says.

Is showing up to the dance in a chariot with my prince charming OK? Duh, yeah.

Third, after school we picked up our designer outfits. At the Izzy Simpson boutique, I was handed a gorgeous red embroidered silk tea-length dress and adorable wooden three-inch heels with red bows, which I seem to have no problem dancing in. Jewel's outfit is similar, but her dress is green and flows all the way to the floor. It's a little long for my taste (I like my calves), but she's happy.

I'm going to look so glam! I wonder who will bring me flowers. After the closing number, we all stay onstage and the MC (Will Kosravi) calls all our names in alphabetical order, and we walk down the catwalk to accept our bouquets. I'll have to remind my mom to make sure to buy me one.

The only damper on my great day was Tammy. She

fully ignored me. She didn't acknowledge me when I walked late into class, or even when I passed by her locker.

I tried to apologize. 'Tammy,' I said, blocking her in the hallway. 'Can we talk?'

'No,' she muttered, and walked away. And the hand gesture she gave me is just too rude to even discuss. Unbelievable. She'd better not be planning on using that fashion-show ticket. With attitude like that, she can cough up the ten bucks and sit in the back.

I get home from rehearsal, expecting to hear news of the cancelled wedding.

'No news,' Miri says. She's lying on her bed, legs up, reading.

But Spring Fling is in four days! I plop down beside her. 'Maybe I should call him.'

'Don't, Rachel,' Miri warns, shaking her head. 'He's probably confused right now, but he'll do the right thing. He won't marry one woman when he's in love with another, especially when the object of his affection is the mother of his children. He'll call us by tomorrow for sure.'

'He'd better. It must take at least a few days to cancel a wedding properly. They have a hundred guests. Someone has to call them and tell them not to come.'

'Maybe she'll email them. It'll be the perfect closure for the annoying wedding updates. Or maybe they'll make the announcement at the wedding rehearsal dinner and then call everyone else.'

Groan. I do not want to trek all the way to Long Island on Thursday for a soon-to-be-defunct-wedding re-

 240

hearsal. The final fashion-show dress practice is after class until six, which means I'll have to run from school to the train to make it to Long Island by seven thirty.

No. My dad would not do that to us. Tomorrow he'll call us with the cancellation news. It's the right thing to do.

By the time I get home at eight at night on Wednesday, I'm soaking wet from rain and extremely nervous.

The entire cast has been outfitted for all our numbers, the dances are perfect, the stage crew has finished the sets and the limo for Spring Fling has been reserved. The entire kick-off weekend for spring break has been perfectly arranged except for one slight issue: the stupid wedding hasn't been called off yet.

I ignore Miri's advice and dial my dad's number.

STB answers on the first ring, her voice wobbling. 'Hello?'

'Hi, ST— Jennifer, is my dad there?'

'Rachel? No, he isn't. He went for a walk.'

'In the pouring rain?'

She laughs, but it sounds strained. 'He took an umbrella. I don't know why he went, honestly. He's been acting strange all week.'

Yes! Strange! An I-have-to-re-evaluate-my-life walk!

'All righty. I just wanted to say hi.'

'So you'll be here by seven thirty tomorrow?'

'Yup.'

'And everything's ready for the show on Friday?'

'Yup.'

'After the show, do you and Miri want to come back here? That way we can get ready for the big day together.'

 241

'Uh, why don't we wait and see on that one?'

'Whatever you want. I'll tell your dad to call when he gets back.' She hesitates. 'If it's not too late.'

He calls. But not until twelve thirty. (Must have been a marathon of a walk – yes!) I'm already halfway into Spring Fling dreamworld when I hear the phone ring.

My mom picks up. 'Daniel, hi,' I hear her say. 'Are you OK? You don't sound OK. Are you on your cell?' Her voice drops to an infuriatingly low pitch, so I'm forced to climb out of bed, sneak into the hallway and shove my ear against her door.

'I can't help make that decision for you . . . You made your bed and now you have to lie in it . . . It's been so long . . . My feelings have changed . . .'

Oh no oh no oh no!

And then: 'Of course I still care about you . . .'

Oh yes oh yes oh yes!

I fall asleep, with the door as my pillow, a satisfied smile on my face.

I can't believe I still have to go to the sham of a rehearsal dinner. Between the fashion show and the wedding, I'm all rehearsed out.

The fashion-show dress rehearsal goes perfectly. The sets are gorgeous. The designers managed to put the Eiffel Tower back together for the formal, they've imported real sand for the all-girls 'Miami' number, and they've painted massive slot machines for the Vegas freshman dance. Their most impressive accomplishment is their virtual Manhattan skyline for the closing, which features a mini Empire State Building that changes colour every thirty seconds. The auditorium is lined with rows and rows of chairs, and the twenty-foot-long catwalk has been resurrected from storage.

The rehearsal begins with us, the five freshman girls, onstage. We run straight through the ten numbers, right to the final bows. I'm pretending to receive my flowers when London Zeal's name is called. After she does her fake wave to the audience, the entire cast cheers and applauds. Clad all in black (OK, I'll be fair here: we're all in black for the New York number), she's smiling from ear to ear. 'In my four years of being in JFK fashion shows,' she says, 'this one is by far the best show. Ever.'

We cheer even louder. I have to admit, despite all the hard work, this was definitely an amazing experience. I'd probably be enjoying the pay-off more thoroughly if the whole wedding fiasco hadn't turned me into a wreck.

'Now get some beauty sleep,' she concludes, 'and I'll see the girls at one tomorrow at Bella Salon!'

We head to the gym locker rooms, which are squashed between the auditorium and the cafeteria, and are where we'll be changing our outfits between numbers tomorrow. I'm about to dash to the train when Raf waves me over. 'Hi,' I say, too nervous to look him in the eye.

'Where are you off to?' he asks, buttoning up his jacket.

'Oh, um . . . I have to talk to my dad about something.'

'Cool. See you tomorrow. It'll be chaos, so if we don't have a chance to talk, I'll pick you up at eight thirty on Saturday.'

I feel queasy. What am I going to do if my dad's a big wuss and doesn't call off the wedding? It's in two days! What am I going to tell Raf? Oh, sorry, my dad's getting married tonight, did I forget to mention it? Can the limo

243

make a pit stop in Port Washington so I can run down the aisle and then jump back into the car?

What to do, what to do, what to do? Skip my dad's wedding and be grounded for the rest of my life? Can a parent who's not living with you do that? Tell Raf I'm sick and I'm stuck in bed and miss the best night of my life?

'We're going to party on that dance floor,' he says, then salutes me as he strolls off.

Is that all I am to him? A dancing partner? Or will he finally kiss me? How will I ever graduate from quasi girl-friend to girlfriend if I have to be on Long Island?

Here I am. At the private room at Al Dente. I'm having the same Caesar salad I almost vomited when STB and my dad first announced they were getting married, and I'm about to puke again. This time I should have asked them to hold the anchovies.

And this isn't even the end of it. After we all finish stuffing our faces, we have to head to the hotel banquet hall, the Garden, and practise walking down the aisle. Come on. Don't they think we can figure it out? We all know how to walk.

Miri has gnawed away most of the skin on her fingers and is trailing blood on the white tablecloth. Ew. If I weren't so nervous myself, I would let her know how vile she's being.

It's over. No, not the wedding. My life.

There are twenty people here, including my father's law partners; my uncle Tommy and his second wife, Rebecca; my cousins; Jennifer's sister and brother and their spouses and kids (thankfully Prissy is off chatting gibberish with them); Jennifer's parents; and my bubbe.

She's the only person who seems even more pissed off than me and Miri about being here. She's sitting in the corner, scowling, constantly asking the maître d' if the heat is still on. She's not the best-tempered of women.

Except for my grandmother, everyone of age is highly tipsy. Especially my father. Everyone else has been polishing off bottles of Chardonnay, but my dad has opted for vodka on the rocks. Many, many of them. This is the first time I've ever seen him drink anything besides wine with dinner.

'I guess we lost,' Miri whispers. 'He's not going to break it off. Maybe he doesn't want to hurt her feelings. Maybe he'll turn himself into an alcoholic for the next month, trying to drown his pain, and then the spell will wear off and he'll love STB again and that'll be that. She's horrible and now she'll be related to us and we'll have to get used to it.'

I sigh and take another bite of my salad. I can't believe it. What's the point in having a sister who's a witch if you can't even get rid of one lousy step-monster? 'Maybe we should put a spell on Mom and have her interrupt the wedding. You know, when they ask if anyone cares to object, she'll jump up.'

Miri snorts. 'Why don't I cast spells on everyone at the wedding? Have all the guests simultaneously object for various reasons.'

I giggle. 'Now that's funny.'

'So that's it? We give up?' she asks.

My heart sinks like the *Titanic*. It's over? My potential happiness was so close, and now it's swamped at the bottom of the sea. Is there no way to hoist it back to the

245

surface? There has to be a rock left unturned . . . something I haven't thought of . . .

Nothing. I've got nada. Do you know what two positives multiplied by zero is?

[Brilliant plan + brilliant plan] x zilch = a big, fat zero.

'I give up. I'll have to tell Raf I'm sick.' I practise coughing. Maybe I'll tell him that I have meningitis. Or that I'm dying of a broken heart. That one certainly feels true. Or maybe I'll tell him I caught whatever he was sick with last week so he feels guilty, too guilty to ask Melissa to replace me in the limo – or in his arms. Sigh.

STB taps her glass to get everyone's attention.

'Thank you all for coming,' she says, standing up. 'I want to take this opportunity to say how much I love you all. How blessed I am to have met Daniel and to have fallen in love with him. He's kind and generous and loving and sweet and brilliant, and I'm honoured that he has chosen me to be his wife.'

The guests politely applaud. My father rises. 'I love you too, Carol.'

Everyone freezes.

Carol?

Did he just say Carol? Not Jennifer, but Carol?

Yes! Yes! Yes! Yes to the power of a trillion!

STB's face drains of colour. Like an orange shirt washed in the laundry with bleach.

The awareness of what he has just said pops into my dad's eyes. 'I mean . . . I meant . . . I think . . .' He sits down. Omigod. Are those tears in his eyes? 'I'm sorry, Jen,' he whimpers. 'I'm still in love with Carol. I can't marry you.'

Total chaos ensues. My dad is crying, Prissy is crying,

246

Mrs Abramson is crying, and even my grandmother is crying (which is strange, considering she never liked STB either). And STB looks as if she just swallowed a lobster – whole. Mr Abramson jumps up and tries to punch my father in the nose, but hits a waiter instead when my dad ducks. A plate of someone's penne arrabbiata splatters on to Mrs Abramson's yellow suit.

Miri and I stay perfectly still, squeezing each other's hands under the table. The wedding is off. I should be screaming for joy, but I'm too afraid to move.

And I can't help watching as a fat tear spills from STB's eye and splashes on to the tablecloth.

If this is what I want, why do I feel so nauseous? I push away my plate.

Must be those anchovies.

20

This Is No April Fool's Joke

It's baaaaaack!

It's only six thirty in the morning, but I'm wide awake, rehashing the disaster of last night. The silent train ride home with Miri. The queasiness in my stomach. My mother asking us how the dinner went, our evasive shrugs indicating that it went well. (Yeah, right.)

'No more spells,' Miri said before we disappeared into our separate rooms.

I tossed and turned all night, wondering why my dad hadn't come straight over, if he had called his guests to tell them the wedding was off, if STB had blown a cork – while worrying that all this wondering would make my eyes puffy from lack of sleep.

If only puffy eyes were my one facial issue. The pimple I feel expanding on my nose is much, much worse than any under-eye circles. Circles can be concealed with make-up. A second nose cannot be masked. I fly (well, not fly exactly; I'm not the one with powers) out of bed to the mirror. My nose is one big red zit. Santa's Gift has returned! Too bad none of the numbers tonight is set in the North Pole. I can't believe that today, of all days, my nose is the colour of a fire hydrant. The one day I'm going to be onstage in front of the entire school, in front of a thousand people. What am I going to do? I can't have this pimple on my face during the fashion show! No one will be able to pay attention to the routine – they'll be too distracted by my huge pimple. No, I take that back. No one will be able to see the routines because my pimple will block their view.

Eureka! An idea!

I knock twice on Miri's door and then open it and tiptoe to her bed. Her mouth is open and her hair is fanned out over her pillow and she looks really young and sweet. I almost can't bring myself to disturb her. Almost.

I tap her on the shoulder. Repeatedly.

She opens her right eye. 'What?'

'Look,' I say, full of desperation.

She opens the other eye and grimaces. 'How could you wake me with that horrific thing?'

'Don't joke. I need you to make the clear-skin spell.'

She flips on to her stomach. 'I don't want to do any more magic.'

'I know you said that yesterday, but please? Puh-lease?' Don't tell me she's going to draw the line now. With this red light bulb on my nose.

'It's too early,' she whines.

'Don't make me rub it on you.'

She shrieks and pulls the covers over her head.

'My face is loaded and I'm not afraid to use it,' I threaten.

'OK, just don't touch me. Step away from the bed.'

I take five steps back, and she pulls the covers down to

249

her shoulders, revealing a grin. Then she glances at the clock radio and moans, 'It's only six thirty!'

'I know. But it's a big day.'

She rubs her eyes. 'Let me find my notebook. Good thing we bought lemon juice and those salts for Mom.'

It's two thirty and I'm gorgeous. Pimpleless and gorgeous.

Maybe gorgeous is a slight exaggeration, but I look good. Really good. Better than I've ever looked in my entire life.

Sophie (a very tall, broad-shouldered hairdresser with bright fake-red hair and a face full of make-up, who might have been a man before he/she became a stylist) spent thirty minutes putting my hair in curlers. Then I sat under a heating lamp for another twenty minutes, giggling with Doree, who's having her hair put into a tight bun. Melissa's having her long red hair braided. Jewel is straightening hers. Stephy chopped her locks and now has a short bob to her chin and looks a bit like Tinker Bell.

And just when I began to worry that my earlobes were melting, Sophie let me out and used a dozen curling irons and other unnamed contraptions to turn each strand of my hair into a perfect curled tendril. I am no longer an ocean head. I am more of a . . . mermaid enchantress.

Then Natalie (who looks as if she could be Sophie's twin sister/brother) tweezed my eyebrows, then spent forty minutes applying my make-up. I have cheekbones (who knew?)! My skin is flawlessly smooth, my brown eyes look huge and Bambi-esque (he/she used so much mascara that my lashes are almost touching my nose), and my lips look luscious, red and kissable. Like a delicious plum. Raf may not be able to wait for Spring Fling – he may spring and fling himself on my mouth during the *Moulin Rouge* formal for a taste.

I can't stop staring at myself in the many mirrors. Of course, when I stand too close to my reflection, I can see the four inches of foundation, which is a bit clownish. But from far? Gorgeous.

'You girls look so hot,' London says, parading through the room in a white cotton bathrobe and white cardboard flip-flops. She and Mercedes are getting full-body treatments, including manicures, pedicures and massages, courtesy of the salon.

We're done by six, two hours before the fashion-show doors open, and the five of us hail a cab. The driver doesn't want to squeeze us all in, but we beg and plead and try to look our cutest, and he tells us to hurry. Jewel climbs in first, then me, then Doree, and Stephy squishes on to our laps. Pouting, and bearing a striking resemblance to Pippi Longstocking, Melissa mopes as she gets into the front seat. 'JFK High School,' she orders. 'And drive carefully because we just had our hair done.'

'It's going to be awesome,' Doree says. '*We're* going to be awesome.'

'I can't believe the show is today!' Stephy squeals. I expect her to start tossing pixie dust around.

I can't believe I'm here. In the cab with these four A-list girls, looking the best I have ever looked.

'I'm so nervous,' Jewel shrieks. 'I think I'm going to vomit.' The cabbie slams on his brakes to avoid hitting a pedestrian, and Jewel groans. 'And this drive isn't helping.'

'Come on, everyone,' Doree screams. 'Get excited. It's

going to be the best night of the year. Rachel, you gotta smile. They sold one thousand tickets. One thousand people are going to be watching us!'

I give her a half-smile. I should be feeling euphoric. This is everything I ever wanted. Isn't it?

The cabbie slams on his brakes and my knees slam into the divider. This time it's not to avoid an accident. My stomach cartwheels into my throat. The moment has arrived.

'We're here! This is it!' Doree shouts, and we pile out. We enter the school through the auditorium door and find the rest of the cast lounging around the caf.

Raf is sitting with Sean Washington and Will, eating pizza. He whistles when he sees me. That should cheer me up. He should cheer me up. He's cool and smart and sexy and sweet, and he likes me. Maybe.

I feel a nagging in the pit of my stomach. What's wrong with me? This is supposed to be one of the best days of my life. Why am I being so gloomy and cynical?

'Hey, Raf,' Will says, tousling his brother's hair as I approach them. 'Your Spring Fling date is smoking hot.'

'Get your greasy pepperoni hands out of my hair,' Raf says, swatting him away. 'Or I'm going to get Mom to throw tomatoes at you while you're MC-ing. She's in the front row, thanks to you.'

Who'll be in my reserved seats? My guess is that STB isn't coming tonight. Or Prissy. After the rehearsal from hell, my dad might not make it either. I don't even know where he is. Or where he spent last night. Maybe he moved back into Putter's Place. I'm assuming Tammy isn't going to use the seat I gave her either. Super. I'll have four empty seats in my section. At least Mom and Miri will be here to cheer me on.

I follow the other girls into the locker room to change. I can already hear the rustling of people in the auditorium, parents arriving early, chatty friends excited to see their classmates. One of London's friends is standing guard at the auditorium's back door, making sure that no one sneaks out into the hallway and to the locker rooms to see us before the show.

Despite the designer clothes and freshly washed and sprayed hair, the locker room still smells like feet.

'This is it,' Jewel says, stepping into her metallic pink strapless dress. I'm wearing an identical dress, but in metallic red. I zip up the back of her dress and tell her how awesome she looks. The dresses make us look more like we're at a rave than singing at a 1920s jazz club, but whatever. The fact that the five of us are opening the entire show is cool.

I pull up my skin-coloured tights, then step into matching red metallic shoes and ask Jewel to zip me up. 'Thanks,' I say, and spin around. 'How do I look?'

She starts at my feet and slowly looks up. 'Amazing.' But then her gaze rests on my face, and she grimaces. 'Uh-oh,' she says.

'Uh-oh? What's uh-oh?'

'I think you need some more concealer. Or you might be having an allergic reaction to the make-up.'

'Are you kidding?'

'I have some concealer,' Doree offers, already in her metallic yellow outfit.

I run into the connected bathroom to look in the mirror at what they're all yammering about.

Oh, no. It's baaaaaaack.

How is it possible that Santa's Gift is making a comeback when I just used the clear spell on it this morning?

'Excuse me,' I hear from outside. 'You can't go in there. You're not one of the dancers.'

'I have to talk to my sister,' pleads a voice. Miri? What is she doing back here? She's not supposed to come backstage.

The next thing I know, she's inside the bathroom, gaping beside me in the mirror. Her face is pale, her lower lip trembling. 'I have to talk to you,' she says. 'I have to talk to you *now*.'

'Apparently so.' I point to the hideousness on my nose. 'What's going on?'

She looks around furtively and, despite us being alone by the sink, she gestures for me to follow her into a stall.

I lock the door behind us. 'What's going on?' I ask over the toilet bowl. She's starting to freak me out. 'Did you hear from Dad?'

She gnaws on her thumb. 'Don't get mad at me. It's not my fault.'

The roof of my mouth gets desert dry and I feel dizzy, but I have no desire to sit on the toilet seat while wearing my metallic red gown. 'What are you talking about?'

She chomps her thumb. After spitting a crumb of nail into the toilet bowl, she pours out the whole story. 'Dad showed up when we were getting ready to come to the show. He said he wanted to go as a *family*. And then he started begging Mom to get back together with him. Claiming that he was so in love with her that he couldn't see straight. Saying that he called off the wedding and that he wants to move back in. I was in my room getting changed and I heard the whole thing. And then Mom said she needed to think and she had a headache, and she went into the bathroom to get an aspirin. And here's the thing. I think I kind of made a mess under the bathroom cupboard this morning with the sea salts, and I think she must have figured out that something was up.' Miri winces. 'Um, I don't think it helped that I left my spell observation notebook on the floor.'

'Miri!' I scream. 'I'm going to kill you!'

'I know, I know, but I was tired and in a rush.' Tears spill down her cheeks. 'First she saw the clear-skin spell. And then she must have seen the love spell, because she barged into my room. She motioned to the kitchen and demanded, "Did you do this?" I had to tell her the truth, don't you see? And not because of any truth spell, because I just had to! She ripped a piece of paper out of the notebook, licked it and ripped it into a million shreds, then opened the window and tossed them outside, reciting some spell. Afterwards she turned to me and said, "I've overruled every spell you have ever done." And then she yelled at me and told me I was irresponsible and asked me if you had been in on this too. I had to tell her. Then we went back to the kitchen. Dad was all pale and confused-looking and was pacing back and forth. And now we're all here. In our seats. And Mom is all pissed off and Dad looks miserable and it's really uncomfortable out there.'

I feel sick. 'So does this mean what I think it means?'

She points to my nose. 'None of the spells I cast work any more. Not the clear-skin spell, not the Dad-in-love-with-Mom spell, not the high-roundhouse-kick spell, and not the—'

'What high roundhouse kick?'

'Oh, never mind that. But I'm really sorry. What are you going to do?'

Wait one sec. Did she say *none of the spells*? 'What about the dancing spell?' I yell.

'Gone,' she says sadly.

Omigod. I can't breathe. Did this stall just shrink? I think I'm hyperventilating. I look at my watch. Ten to eight. 'I have to find London,' I mumble. I unlock the door and run back to the locker room. 'Has anyone seen London?' I squeak.

No one pays any attention to me. They're all too busy squealing and practising last-minute moves. I can't go on. London will have to understand. I hurry into the hallway.

She's standing at the door to the auditorium, reviewing her clipboard. 'Ready?' she asks when she sees me.

'I'm sorry, London, but I can't do it. I'm sick. So very sorry. You'll have to work around me.'

Her eyes narrow, and she shakes her fist at me. 'I don't care if you're *dying*, Rachel. Dying! You're going up there.' She looks at her watch. 'Now.'

No way. 'I can't.'

'You have to.' She digs her nails into my arm and drags me back to the locker room. 'All freshman girls, on the stage, let's go, the curtain opens with you.'

'But, but—'

'Shut up, Rachel. You are not going to screw this up for me, do you understand? You have stage fright. I had it my first year too. You'll get over it as soon as the lights go on. You'll be fine. You know the moves.'

I take a deep breath. It's true. I *do* know the moves. I've learned how to dance. I can remember how to do it. I look down at my red shoes. Maybe it's like *The Wizard of Oz*. Maybe the magic has been in me all along. I just had to realize it for myself. Yes! I can do this! The magic is in me!

Heart hammering, I follow London and the other girls backstage. The five of us get into our positions on the pitch-black *Chicago* set. I hear the roar of the crowd, a thousand people in their seats.

I can do this.

'Good luck, guys!' Doree whispers.

And then the medley starts. The crowd screams again, the curtain pulls up, the spotlight shines.

Showtime.

21

I'm So Going to Need to Be Home-schooled

The music begins.

'Go, girls!'

'Looking good!'

'Yeeeaaaaaaaaaaaaaaaaaaaaaaaaaaah!'

The spotlight is beaming into my eyes, and I can't see further than the end of the stage.

I can do this. I can so do this. I remember the moves. I lift my arm the way I'm supposed to, the way all the girls are doing, and I'm fine. Yes! I'm fine.

Sort of. They're about a half-second ahead of me. Oh, no. I'm off a beat. Why can't I catch up? It's like I'm the girl in the choir who's singing just a little louder and squeakier than everyone else.

But as soon as I'm about to start panicking, our five-second segment is over, and the rest of the cast comes in and it doesn't matter any more.

Phew. No one seems to have noticed my off-beat rhythm. At least, I don't think so, since no one comments.

So far so good.

The next dance I'm in is the freshman Vegas number, the one Melissa choreographed. After I change into my

'Take a Pepto and get over it! Now go change for the formal!'

I avoid the other girls' gazes as I put on my gorgeous Izzy dress. It can't get much worse. Anyway, the formal is slow, and slow dancing is all about the sway. Anyone can sway, right?

Uh-oh. I realize there is another problem as soon as I step into the hallway. These wooden heels are high. Now that my rhythm isn't quite perfect, I shudder when I think about what these stilettos will do to my balance.

I'm just about to fall flat on my face when I feel a strong arm around my waist. Raf. 'You look amazing,' he says, beaming. Obviously, he *wasn't* watching the all-girl dance. He was probably backstage changing and has yet to hear about my disastrous performance.

Oh, no. I forgot about the pimple. *He's looking right at the pimple*. I am a hideous, catastrophic freak.

'Ready to knock their socks off?' he says.

I'm more concerned about knocking him off the cat-walk. 'Yup,' I say, shielding my nose with my hand.

I wobble backstage. I can do this. It's slow. Slow and romantic. I can do this. As long as I don't trip over my own feet, I can do this.

When the *Moulin Rouge* song starts, the twenty of us are in proper position. Then the ten boys strut down the catwalk, and we follow. I wobble, but make it to my spot in front of Raf. Woo-hoo! I made it! He twirls me, and then we do our sexy moves. Well, he does the sexy moves, and I try to look sexy, but I guarantee I am coming across as wooden and therefore unsexy. This is confirmed when Raf whispers, 'Relax,' during our dip. His lips are only an inch from my face. And then he asks, 'Are you OK?'

This is not the romantic moment I've been waiting for my entire life.

I nod and try very hard to remain focused. Once that part of the dance is done, I breathe a huge sigh of relief. Yes! Now all I have to do is make it off the catwalk and back to the stage.

Couple by couple, we walk to the stage in two lines. We're the last ones in line, Jewel and Sean right in front of us.

And that's when it happens.

I step on the back of Jewel's dress. I told her the dress was too long.

She goes down fast. And then, like dominoes, so do Melissa, Doree, Stephy and the entire line of girls in front. One of the sophomores lands in the Eiffel Tower and beheads it.

The set designers scream from offstage.

The entire audience gasps.

Dazed, Stephy looks around, rubbing her elbow. Doree's bun is undone and a mess. Melissa rubs the back of her head.

Omigod. Omigod. Omigod.

I send Miri a desperate look, silently begging her to make the stage swallow me up, but her head is in her hands.

Omigod. Omigod. Omigod.

The music continues playing, but no one moves. They're all glaring at me. Eventually, the music stops and we shuffle silently offstage. Raf won't even look at me. He'll obviously never talk to me again. I destroyed the entire show.

As soon as we're offstage, Melissa, Jewel, Doree and

Stephy circle me like sharks. I can hear Will making MC cracks about bringing France to its knees.

'What the hell were you doing out there?' Melissa yells. 'You ruined everything.'

There's a golf ball in my throat. 'I'm sorry.'

Jewel just shakes her head.

'I'll skip the closing,' I say. 'So I won't do any more damage.'

'No way,' Doree says, waving both her hands. 'We need you in the closing. The freshman segment is only twenty seconds, and it'll look stupid without all of us. But wear your sneakers instead of the stilettos so you don't ruin that number too.'

'Idiot,' Melissa snorts. 'Loser.'

Unfortunately, along with my talent, my designer sneakers have disappeared. So against my better judgment, I change into my all-black outfit and beaten-up black boots.

I'm sitting on the toilet seat, silently bawling my eyes out in the same bathroom stall Miri and I visited earlier. I am never coming out. Ever. Well, at least not until everyone has left the building.

Melissa was right when she called me an idiot. How much worse can it get? I thought. How could anything beat decapitating the tower and everyone laughing at me?

It got worse.

After I changed into my black pants and tank top, I got into position. But when the entire cast was supposed to be in sync, I sashayed the wrong way. I swerved at the wrong time. I turned at the wrong time. I was a total mess. But wait. That part wasn't the horrible part.

Since the bows were right after the closing number, I had to wait onstage (while all the freshmen and sophomores gave me poisonous looks) as Will called each person's name in alphabetical order. He called out the entire cast and, of course, the audience cheered and screamed and rushed the stage to give their loved ones bouquets. And then he announced, 'Rachel Weinstein!'

No one cheered. Or maybe someone did, but I couldn't hear because of all the laughter. I walked to the front of the catwalk like I was supposed to, only to find that no one was waiting to hand me flowers. Not even my parents, although I could hardly blame them. They likely had other issues on their minds.

And then, before I could run off the stage in humiliation, Will called, 'London Zeal!', the final name in the show, and she strutted down the catwalk, waving at the audience like a queen and grabbing her bouquets.

That's when I tripped on my own two feet, fell into London, and knocked myself, her and all her flowers off the stage.

And heard the sickening *crack*.

'My leg! You walking *disaster*!'

That was her screaming, not me.

She shrieked again and then hit me on the head with a rose. I apologized profusely before bailing out of there like a convict on the lam.

I've been in this bathroom stall for forty minutes and through the door have had to endure the worst kind of berating, since no one knew I was here and they ripped into me freely. Not that I expected any mercy, after what I did. Melissa called me a loser, Doree said she would never talk to me again, and when I heard Stephy say that

London was carted off in an ambulance, I fully lost it. I had to flush repeatedly so no one would hear me crying. No one's come into the bathroom in the past ten minutes, but I'm still not ready to come out.

I'm going to have to transfer to another high school immediately. Unless the news of this disaster has spread to every school in the tri-state area, in which case I might have to be home-schooled or convince my mother to move with me to Iowa. Although now she probably hates me too, so she'll most likely ship me off to boarding school.

Needless to say, I am not looking forward to going home. If only there was somewhere else I could go. I can't even escape to my dad's, since I've just ruined his life. STB's life, too. Prissy will have to be in therapy for the rest of hers. Tammy hates me. There is no way Raf will ever talk to me again, never mind take me to Spring Fling.

I will never again be A-list. I've been permanently demoted to the L-list. As in *Loser*.

Someone enters the bathroom and takes the stall next to mine. I try to stop crying. I recognize the pointy-toe shoes under the stall. Jewel's shoes.

'Jewel,' I murmur. Jewel was my best friend for so long. She'll know what I should do. She won't dump me now in my time of need.

'Rachel?' She flushes and opens her door.

'Is anyone else out there?' I whisper.

'Just me.'

I venture out and, again, burst into tears. I'm like a broken water fountain.

She's fingering her still-straight hair, which is starting

to frizz at the tips. 'Um . . . don't cry. Everything will be OK.' I want her to pat me on the back or something, but she keeps fidgeting with her hair.

Then I get an idea. I don't have to go home. When I used to get into fights with my mom, I would just go sleep at Jewel's. 'Do you think I could sleep over tonight? This has been, like, the worst day ever.'

She takes a step back. 'Tonight? Actually, I'm going to Mercedes' tonight. For a cast party? Maybe another time.'

I look her in the eye. 'But I need you now.'

She backs out of the bathroom. 'I can't,' she says, a little sadly. The door swings closed behind her.

And just like that, she dumps me. Again. I don't know what to do with myself, so I walk to the mirror and stare at my reflection. A cast party. Nice.

I've stopped crying, but my make-up is a mess, my pimple is screaming and my hair is all over the place. The ocean has been through a nasty storm. I've gone from superstar to social leper in less than four hours. I've lost my best friend, again, as well as my almost-boyfriend.

I take a deep breath and leave my refuge. My mother and sister are waiting for me, leaning against the wall in the hallway. I try to read the expression on my mom's face. It ain't looking happy. Super. Just what I need. To get yelled at.

She puts her arm around my shoulder and hugs me.

I start crying all over again.

When we get home, all I want to do is crawl under my covers and never come out, but my mom says, somewhat ominously, 'Come to the kitchen. I want to talk to both of you.'

Miri and I sit and stay silent while my mom makes and then pours herself a cup of tea. She sits at the table and shakes her head. 'What you two did was cruel. Cruel to your father, cruel to Jennifer—'

'But she isn't good enough for him,' I interrupt.

She silences me with her hand. 'I know you two don't like her, but who your father marries is not for you to decide. But not only were you cruel to them, you were cruel to me. Do you have any idea of the hurt you caused?'

'We were trying to help you,' Miri says, sniffing.

'Help me? You thought making me think that your father was in love with me again would help me?' She shakes her head and takes a sip of tea from her I♥NY mug. 'It took me two years to get over him. When he left, I was a mess. I cried myself to sleep every single night.'

'I didn't know that,' Miri says softly, her eyes filling with tears. Mine do the same.

'I was trying to be strong for you girls. I was so crazy about him, and then suddenly he announced that he didn't feel the same. I didn't even try to get him to change his mind. I figured what was the point? You can't make someone feel something he doesn't want to feel. So I did my best to make a life for myself. To care about my career and to raise you two without him. And soon I found that I was able to fall asleep at night without crying. Slowly, I got over him. Gave away the hope I'd been clinging to.'

Gave away the sweatshirt, I realize.

She smiles sadly. 'I began to see what the marriage had really been like. The way he used to work late every night

267

and not be there for me – or for you. The way he always put himself first. My unhappiness led to anger, but in time that faded too. I realized that he wasn't solely to blame. When we were married, I never told him how I felt. I used to be so quiet and meek. Maybe if I'd been stronger . . . if I'd spoken up . . .' She shakes her head. 'Would have, could have, should have,' she intones, as if casting a spell. 'I've moved on, and so has he. I've grown stronger, become more confident. And he's changed too. He's not so self-absorbed.'

Miri rolls her eyes, and my mom laughs. 'OK, so maybe he has further to go than I do, but you have to admit, he's trying.' Her face turns solemn. 'Part of me will always love him – but not in that way. That's gone.' She points an accusatory finger at us. 'But you two! Just as I was starting to feel happy again, really happy, he reappears in my life, claiming to love me again. And then I find out that it's all fake . . . All the pain came back, and it hurt.'

'We thought you wanted him to love you,' I say through a constricted throat.

'If I valued a relationship based on love that was fake, love that was an illusion, don't you think I would have cast a love spell myself?'

Oh. Miri and I both slump in our chairs.

'I'm a witch, remember?' she continues. 'When your father left me, I could have cast a spell to make him stay. But I didn't. Because that's not the kind of love I want.' And then she stands up and puts her mug in the sink.

My cheeks burn with shame. After the way I made a fool of myself onstage, you'd think I'd be used to the feeling by now, but I'm not. *Self-absorbed*. That's me, all right.

Miri got Mom's witchcraft, and I got Dad's self-absorption. If there's an S-list, sign me up.

Stupid list.

Shame list.

I've used everyone – Mom, Dad, Miri and even STB – to get what I thought I wanted. Only, what I thought I wanted is worthless. Fake friends. Fake love. Because love that's not voluntary isn't love at all.

For the first time ever, even though her nails are gross and her roots are a mess, and even though she doesn't date, I wish I could be more like my mother. Wise. Powerful.

'I'm sorry, Mom. I'm sorry, Miri.' My eyes fill with tears. Again. 'How am I going to fix this?'

Miri shrugs. 'Dad went home to apologize to STB, but I doubt she'll take him back. I don't know how to fix it either.'

I put my head in my hands, and my mother runs her fingers through my dishevelled hair. 'I don't know if this is something you *can* fix,' she says.

And I know she's not talking about my hair.

22

Shake That Booty

Instead of sleeping, I plan. And drink instant coffee. Lots of instant coffee. It's no iced caramel macchiato, but it does the trick.

I wake Miri up at seven. 'Here's what we're doing. I am going on the 8:22 train to Port Washington to convince STB to take Dad back. Until then I'm calling the one hundred and eight friends and family members on that email list to tell them that the wedding is back on. Assuming that they're mostly couples, that's fifty-four phone calls at forty seconds each. Should take me thirty-six minutes. Meanwhile, you'll shower and call the hired help beginning at nine. I've allotted you three minutes a call to speak to and plead with the sixteen essential service people. Altogether it should take you forty-eight minutes. Tell them that the wedding is still on. If any of them gives you a hard time, call me at Dad's at ten and I'll start banging on doors. Got it?'

She jumps out of bed, looking relieved and amazed. 'Wow. Your brain is like a magical calculator. So you'll fix it?'

'I'll try,' I say, even though I have no idea how. Hmm.

Maybe maths is my superpower. Maybe I'll quiz STB on various equations until she breaks down and forgives him. Nah. I'd be better off threatening to start biting my fingernails. Of course, I still have to find my dad, and no one seems to have a clue where he is. Maybe this isn't such a good idea.

'Rachel,' my mom says, poking her head through the doorway. She's wearing her usual charm of an outfit that's sure to pick up the men: T-shirt, green-striped sleep shorts and white sweat socks. 'Can I talk to you girls for a second?'

We nod, and she sits on Miri's desk. 'You know I don't believe we should use magic to play with people's emotions. I believe that everyone should be allowed to feel real emotions.'

Yes, Mom, we know, we know. I glance at my watch.

'But I think that ST—' She clears her throat. 'I mean, Jennifer, is probably suffering from some emotional trauma right now, and I feel partly to blame. After all, the powers did come from me. And, Miri, I should have realized that, despite your maturity, you're just a child, and that of course you would want to explore and play with your powers.' She hands me a spray bottle. 'That said, I want you to use this on your future stepmother.'

Huh? 'You want me to clean her?'

She shakes her head. 'Last night I made a spell for you . . . and worked a little magic on the wedding band, caterer and all the non-guest cancellations that took place.'

Miri claps. 'My job just got loads easier!'

'Yes, but this doesn't mean I condone the use of magic for any future problems,' my mom goes on, wagging her finger at Miri. 'In fact I hope this experience has taught you that every spell has a consequence.' She closes her eyes for a second, looking pained. I wonder what she's thinking about. 'In this case,' she continues, opening her eyes, 'we can make an exception. After all, magic got us into this mess.'

'And this will get us out?' I ask, pointing at the bottle.

'It's not complicated,' my mom explains. 'All you have to do is spray it at Jennifer's chest. It's a heart-reversal potion.'

Yes! Miri and I throw our arms around her frail shoulders. 'You're the best!' I tell her.

'I know,' she says, smiling.

Fifty-four phone calls, lots of hasty explaining and one train ride later, I arrive at the house on Long Island. I ring the doorbell and get into firing position. It's freezing. Why is it so cold today? It's already April!

I hear footsteps, the door opens, I'm ready to spray . . .

My father and STB are holding hands.

Oh. Well. 'Hi,' I say, for lack of anything better.

'Hi, honey,' my dad says. 'We made up.'

So I see. STB, still in her low-cut bathrobe, is smiling broadly. I follow them into the living room and close the door behind me. 'When did you get here?' I ask my dad.

'After the show. I spent all night pleading and begging Jennifer to forgive me for my cold feet.'

I spot what appear to be at least ten dozen long-stem red roses in vases on the dining-room table. I'm sure those didn't hurt my father's cause either.

STB pats my dad's bald spot. 'The ranting at the rehearsal dinner was a case of temporary insanity.'

'I should have had a bachelor party to get the craziness out of my system,' he jokes.

She casts a warning glance at my father. 'Don't get any ideas, Daniel. Your bachelor days are over. You'd better be on your best behaviour for the rest of your life, because you're on permanent probation.' He kisses her on the cheek and she blushes. Then she turns back to me. 'Rachel, don't tell me you've dragged slush in from out-side. Has no one ever taught you to take off your shoes before entering someone's house?'

Hmm. If I spray this potion all over her exposed cleav-age, will her heart get reversed again?

Be good, I remind myself, resisting the urge to shoot.

STB sighs. 'We'll have to reschedule the wedding. On Thursday night, I called everyone to cancel.'

'No!' I say, banging the spray bottle against the table. 'You don't. Miri is calling everyone as we speak to tell them it's still on. I um . . . I knew you two would get back together . . . yeah. I just knew . . . and um . . . I think I'll go . . . um . . .' I hold up my spray bottle. '. . . dust.'

STB looks at my dad and beams. I'm hoping it's because of the wedding, and not the cleaning.

The next thing I know, the two of them are making out. It's kind of gross, actually. I can see tongue. So I back out of the kitchen and call home to make sure everything is working out as planned. Miri assures me that everyone is back on schedule for tonight.

Of course they are. My mom is an awesome spell-maker.

To be nice, I start running a bath for Prissy (we've got to get a move on, here!), and while the tub is filling, I take a deep breath and make a phone call.

Tammy's answering machine picks up on the first ring.

'Hi, it's me,' I say. 'I know you probably hate me for everything I did. And you have every reason to. I've been a crappy friend, and I want to say that I'm sorry. Sorry for what happened at Mick's, for blowing you off for Jewel, for everything. You've been a terrific friend from day one, a real friend, and I didn't properly appreciate you until now. Anyway, the wedding is back on, and I'm at my dad's. You don't have to call me back or anything. I know you're busy getting ready for the dance tonight. I hope you and Aaron have a blast.' I hang up and hope that one day she'll forgive me.

Time to get Prissy ready. ('I love baths because they're warm and soft and I have a bath pillow and it smells good and do you like baths, Rachel?')

It's the least I can do.

Miri gets to my dad's two hours later ('You were right! The phone calls took me exactly sixteen minutes! Why can't I have a cool superpower like maths?'), and then we change into the putrid pink outfits, which are unfortunately ready and waiting for us in our closets.

'Can you girls help me?' STB calls from their room. Prissy and Miri jump on to her bed. My dad's in the bathroom, shaving.

STB is facing the mirror, her back to us. The zipper on the back of her elegant A-line strapless beaded beige dress is undone. Her blonde hair sits in a perfect bun at the nape of her neck. 'I'm sorry I didn't make it to your show yesterday, Rachel,' she says. 'I was really looking forward to it. But I couldn't . . .' Her voice trails off. In the mirror, her cheeks glow and her lips shimmer.

 274

'I understand,' I say, and zip up her dress. And I realize I'm finally ready. Ready to let STB become Jennifer.

The ceremony is simple and beautiful. Except for Prissy picking her nose, Miri going to town on her fingers, and me still looking like Rudolph, the entire service is picture-perfect.

After marching back up the aisle, I bolt to the bathroom. Too much instant coffee. When I swing open the doors, I see familiar hair and a familiar nose.

Tammy, in a long blue satin dress, is washing her hands.

My throat tightens and I can't speak. I run to the sink and throw my arms around her. 'I . . . can't believe you're here,' I whisper.

She hugs me back. 'Of course I'm here. It's your dad's wedding.'

'But I was so horrible.'

'Yeah, I know. But I remember when my mom was getting married. It's hard. I acted like a nut-job too. I cut all my hair off and hid in the closet.' She shrugs. 'Anyway, I remember how it feels.'

'You're awesome.' I will never blow off Tammy again. She's a true friend. Wait a sec. 'What about Spring Fling? You were so excited that Aaron asked you.' I can't believe she'd miss the dance for me!

'Actually,' she says, blushing, 'he's here. I figured that maybe Jewel wouldn't be here, and I know you were allowed to invite two friends, so I asked him.' She grimaces. 'Uh-oh. Should I not have done that? Did you ask Raf instead?'

I laugh, even though hearing his name pinches my heart. 'No, after last night's disaster, trust me, Raf doesn't want anything to do with me. Especially be seen dancing with me.' Or take me to a dance.

At least I'm not at home watching *Star Wars* again.

'You're sure it's all right that Aaron's here?'

I give her the scuba OK and, arms linked, we walk back into the reception hall, where the band is playing some cheeseball wedding-celebration song.

Miri and Prissy are dancing in the middle of the room, along with most of the guests. 'Come here!' they both shout when they see me.

Are they crazy? I'm never dancing again.

'Let's boogie,' Tammy says, and waves Aaron over. He looks really cute in his grey suit.

'I don't think that's a good idea,' I mumble.

And then my dad and Jennifer join the crowd, and suddenly everyone's shaking and grooving and I don't really have a choice, do I?

So without even a trace of rhythm, and looking as if I'm undergoing shock treatment, I join my friends and family on the dance floor. And have a blast.

23

Not a Glass Slipper but Close Enough

'Hello?' we call into the apartment.

It's Sunday morning, and we're back home. My dad and Jennifer dropped us off at the train and then caught a plane to Hawaii for their honeymoon. Prissy went home with her grandparents. I hope they can take it . . . All that chattering can be a bit much for old people.

'Hi, girls,' my mom says from the kitchen. 'I'm in here making that peanut-butter tofu you love so much.'

She arranges the grossness in a casserole dish as we slide into our chairs. 'So?' she asks, raising an eyebrow. 'How was it?'

'Nice,' Miri says.

'Yeah,' I add. 'Really nice.'

She smiles. 'Good.' Then she scratches the back of her neck and grimaces. 'Rachel, you had a very unhappy visitor last night.'

What? 'I did? Who?'

'Raf. He was wearing a suit and claimed he was here to pick you up for a dance. When I said I didn't know what he was talking about, Tigger tried to attack him. I told him you were at your father's wedding.'

I don't believe it. Not for a single millisecond did I expect him to show up. To want to be seen with me in public. 'What . . . happened?' I croak.

'What do you think happened? He left. I wasn't going to the dance with him.'

I leap from my seat and run to the phone in my room. I dial his number (which I know by heart, even though I've never had the nerve to call him). It rings once, twice. Three times. Answer the phone, Raf!

'Hello?' a deep voice says.

'Raf? I am so sorry. I feel like such an idiot.'

There's nothing but heavy silence on the other end.

Oh, no. Oh, no. 'I didn't think you'd want to go with me to the dance after—'

'Rachel? Is that you? It's not Raf. It's Will.'

The humiliations just keep on coming. 'Sorry,' I mumble. Stupid, stupid, stupid. 'Um . . . is Raf there?'

'No,' Will says. 'He's in New Orleans with my parents.'

'Oh yeah.' I forgot. I stretch the phone cord out and wonder if it will fit around my neck.

'Why did you tell my brother you'd go out with him when you knew your father's wedding was the same night? Not cool. He was looking forward to going to the dance with you. He really liked you.'

His choice of tense is not lost on me. 'I am so sorry,' I repeat.

Again, silence. Guess there's not much else for us to chat about. 'Bye,' I say.

'Later.'

I can't believe how badly I blew it. Even after I made a

complete fool of myself, he still liked me, and I ruined everything. Stuck a pin directly into the balloon of my potential happiness. Not a pin – I attacked the poor balloon with a chain saw. I flop on to my bed and groan into my pillow.

My mom knocks against the open door. 'Yes?' I say through the pillow. I am never coming up for air. I don't care if I suffocate.

'Did you two make up?' she asks. La, la, la. How simple she thinks my life is.

'Not yet.'

'OK. When you do, give him back his glove. It must have fallen out of his pocket when Tigger attacked him. Dinner will be ready in ten minutes.' Humming to herself, she returns to the kitchen.

Glove?

I pop into a sitting position.

A grey wool glove is resting on my comforter. A grey wool glove that belongs to Raf.

I stare at the glove. The glove stares back at me.

OK, I know we agreed that love spells are off-limits. But come on! This glove isn't just a normal glove. It's a sign.

Why else would Tigger have attacked him and made him drop it?

One little spell can't really hurt anyone.

What was it Mom said? When magic gets us into a mess, we can make exceptions? Right?

'Hey, Miri . . .'

The magic continues in
***Frogs & French Kisses*, coming in 2006!**